BAD BOYS
WITH
RED ROSES

BAD BOYS
WITH
RED ROSES

JANELLE DENISON
TINA DONAHUE
SHARON CULLARS

KENSINGTON PUBLISHING CORP.
http://www.kensingtonbooks.com

CONTENTS

Still Mr. & Mrs.

Janelle Denison

One

Luke Kincaid strolled into the high-tech security offices of the Mystic Casino, where his surveillance team was busy watching the gaming area and keeping a lookout for any potential trouble. From any of the dozens of color monitors mounted on the wall they could observe the casino from every angle. All at once, if need be.

A quick sweeping glance at the images flickering on the monitors told Luke that it was a slow and unexciting Thursday evening. However, he knew by this same time tomorrow the casino and hotel would be filled with gamblers and guests descending upon Las Vegas for the weekend, and that's when the real fun began for his surveillance team.

"Hey, Kincaid, check out the hot babe on camera seventeen," Mike Barrett, one of his top security agents and Luke's good friend, said from behind him, his voice infused with amusement. "She's one of the many reasons why I love my job."

Luke smirked as he watched a money transfer take place at a craps table. He knew without looking at the monitor exactly what had caught his friend's attention. "I take it she's got a great ass, huh?"

"Oh, yeah," Mike replied appreciatively. "This one's world class. And she's got long legs that go on forever. Check her out for yourself."

Luke cast a cursory glance at the screen Mike had indicated. Sure enough, one of the security cameras was focused on a woman's backside as she strolled through the gaming area toward the blackjack tables. Because there wasn't a whole lot going on at the moment, he went ahead and took in the low-riding jeans hugging her hips, along with the endlessly long legs and super-fine ass tucked inside them, and was definitely impressed by her curves. She was wearing a pink camisole-type top that showed off the smooth skin along her back and shoulders and made him curious to see if the front view lived up to her sexy, head-turning backside.

To keep cool in the one hundred and ten degree summer heat, she'd piled her thick, curly golden blond hair on top of her head, but a few wispy strands had escaped and fluttered along her neck as she walked. He wondered how long her hair was, and how it would look cascading over her shoulders and down her back . . .

"There's no ring on her left hand from what I can see," Mike said, interrupting Luke's thoughts as the woman slid into a vacant chair at one of the blackjack tables. "I'm off in less than an hour, and if she's still around I'm going to find out if she's free for dinner."

Luke shook his head and laughed, used to Mike's playboy tendencies. "Looks like you just found your flavor of the week."

Mike flaunted a cocky grin. "You're just jealous that I have a very active social life."

Hardly, Luke thought. "I do just fine socially, thank you very much."

While there was no denying that Luke enjoyed female companionship, he preferred to keep his personal life private, and his affairs short-term, physically satisfying, and emotionally uncomplicated. After giving himself so completely to one woman, only to be betrayed and devastated, he wasn't about to allow any female to have that much power over his heart and emotions ever again.

"Oh, man," Mike breathed in awe. "She might have the body of a temptress, but she's got the face of an angel. Take a look."

Luke lifted his gaze back to the monitor and realized that Mike had switched to a different camera, one that enabled them to view the customers straight on. At first glance, the woman looked vaguely familiar, prompting a jolt of adrenaline to kick up the beat of his heart. He immediately shook off the odd, unexpected reaction.

Then he looked longer. Harder. And felt a strong sense of unease sweep through him. One he was hard-pressed to ignore.

There was no way it was *her*. He told himself he was just imagining things, but the resemblance was so similar that he couldn't disregard the possibility.

"Give me a close-up of her face," he said to Mike.

His friend chuckled, and with a push of a few buttons on his keyboard, the camera panned in on the woman. "Nice to know you're not immune after all, Kincaid."

Luke ignored the lighthearted gibe, because as soon as the woman's features came into sharp focus he felt as if he'd been sucker punched right in his solar plexus. Disbelief constricted his chest as he stared at her lovely face, recognizing with too much clarity those light green eyes that were flecked with gold and deepened to a dark shade of jade in the throes of passion. And then there were those sensual lips that had the ability to curve into the sweetest of smiles one moment, and in the next make him weak with lust with the hottest, softest, most seductive kisses a man could ever hope for.

Her complexion was still peaches-and-cream smooth. As for that unruly, curly hair she'd pinned up, he knew exactly what it looked like down. He also had intimate knowledge of what the silky strands felt like wrapping around his fingers and trailing over his naked body . . .

Even though his insides were already twisted into a huge knot, he couldn't stop his gaze from drifting lower, to the Vee of her lace-edged camisole top and the impressive cleavage he found there. Last he remembered, her small breasts had been a perfect handful. Judging by the plump flesh filling out her top now, it was apparent that she'd been a late bloomer and had grown into her curvaceous body with grace and style.

The past eight years had matured her from a young guileless eighteen-year-old girl who'd professed to love him forever to a stunningly beautiful woman that men fantasized about having on their arm . . . or in their beds. The proof of that was in the effortless way she'd captured the attention of not only Mike, but the two men sitting at the table with her, and the dealer and pit boss as well.

"What the hell is Rachel Hudson doing here?" he muttered, speaking his thoughts out loud before he realized he'd done so in front of his good friend. He stiffened defensively, and waited for the inquisition to come.

Mike cut a surprised glance Luke's way, his brows raised high. "You know her?"

Shit, Luke thought, knowing just how persistent Mike could be when his curiosity was piqued. Except his past with this woman was something he had no desire to talk about. To anyone.

Luke released a harsh breath before reluctantly replying, "Yeah, I know her."

Mike waited for an explanation, but when Luke kept quiet, his friend didn't hesitate to prompt him. "How about a few details, Kincaid? Like *how* do you know her?"

Looking back at the monitor and the blond woman who'd walked out of his life without any attempt to contact him, Luke felt the past collide with the present. "I was married to her," he said, and the initial shock that transformed Mike's expression was almost worth the pain of confessing the truth.

Mike's mouth opened, snapped shut, and then he shook his head and laughed. "Yeah, in your dreams," he said, still chuckling. When Luke didn't join in or admit to the elaborate tale, Mike grew serious, and uncertain. "You are joking, aren't you?"

Luke shoved his hands deep into the pockets of his khaki pants, wishing like hell he *was* kidding, because after eight years of silence this was a scenario he never would have imagined or predicted. "Do I look like I'm joking?"

Realization finally dawned for Mike. "Jesus, Luke. I've known you for what, six, seven years now? I never knew you were married."

"It was a long time ago," he said with a shrug that was more stiff than the I-don't-give-a-damn attitude he'd been striving for. "And it's not something I like to talk about."

"Obviously," Mike replied drolly. "How long has it been since you've seen her?"

"Eight years. Ever since she and her family moved from Las Vegas to New York." Luke redirected his gaze to a different monitor, one that focused on the poker tables, instead of the woman who'd caused him so much heartbreak.

"Wow. She's a long way from home." Mike's tone was infused with open speculation. "I wonder what she's doing here in Las Vegas?"

It was a question Luke didn't have an answer for. He supposed she could be here for a vacation. It was probably pure coincidence that she'd walked into the casino where he worked. But after so many years of being away, he couldn't help but wonder what had brought her back to Las Vegas . . . and why now?

Needing to sort through his thoughts without his friend

distracting him with a barrage of questions, and wanting to keep the other man busy so he didn't continue to ogle Rachel, Luke gave Mike something else to concentrate on.

"Keep an eye on that guy loitering around the poker tables," Luke said, pointing out a younger man trying to remain inconspicuous, but not quite managing the feat. "I'll be in my office if you need me for anything."

Luke left the main security offices, and once he was enclosed in his own private, personal space, he sat down at his desk and turned on the three monitors mounted on the wall in front of him. He keyed in a few codes, and the screens flickered then displayed three different angles of Rachel sitting at the gaming table—providing him with a front, side, and back view.

Of its own accord, his mind tumbled back to the first day of their senior year in high school, when he'd literally bumped into Rachel in the hallway as they were rushing to their second period classes before the tardy bell rang. He'd knocked the schoolbooks from her arms, and as they both bent down to pick them up off the floor they'd glanced up at the same moment.

He'd meant to apologize, but the instant their gazes met his mouth went completely dry. She had the most fascinating green/gold eyes, and her pretty face had been framed by soft, loose curls. Then she slowly, shyly smiled, and that's all it took for him to want her as his own.

Despite the fact that he came from the wrong side of the strip, so to speak, and that Rachel's father made no attempt to hide his displeasure over their relationship, they were inseparable and dated exclusively their entire senior year. Falling in love came naturally, and by the time they graduated high school they both knew somehow, someway they wanted a future together—even though Rachel had a scholarship to attend New York University in the fall. And wasn't it convenient that Randall Hudson had accepted a job transfer to New York so that the entire family could remain close to Rachel?

But that summer none of those issues had mattered, because Luke planned to surprise Rachel by moving to New York as well. He didn't have the money or means to attend a prestigious college, but he had drive and ambition and was determined to prove to Randall and Carol Hudson that he could support their daughter and give her everything she needed.

One Saturday evening in early August, just a week before Rachel was due to leave for New York with her family, the two of them were driving down the main strip, taking in the hotel marquees' bright, flashing advertisements and the lively outdoor entertainment. Once they reached the end of Las Vegas Boulevard, Luke glanced over to where Rachel was sitting in the passenger seat of his old, used Ford truck. Her window was down, and she had her arm propped on the frame as she enjoyed the warm summer breeze caressing her face and sifting through her unbound hair.

"So, what would you like to do tonight?" he asked as he continued driving toward downtown Las Vegas, where there was more action to be seen. "Anything special?"

On the right-hand side of the street, they passed the infamous Little White Wedding Chapel where many celebrities had gotten hitched at a moment's notice. Rachel glanced over at him, a breathtaking smile on her lips and a daring twinkle in her eyes. "Let's get married."

He never considered saying no. He was deeply, irrevocably in love with Rachel and wanted nothing more than to make her his wife and spend the rest of his life with her. It didn't matter that he currently couldn't support Rachel in the way her parents had provided for years, or that Rachel's father was going to be livid when he found out that they'd gotten married when he had much bigger plans for his daughter. No, nothing mattered except that Rachel wanted to marry him. He was certain that they'd figure out a way to make their marriage work. With or without her parents' blessing.

Less than an hour later they'd spoken their vows to one another in a modest ceremony, with the two of them wearing casual jeans and sneakers instead of a tuxedo and a wedding dress. Other than the single long-stemmed rose he'd bought for her, there were no flowers or frills or even a wedding band to slip on her ring finger. All they had, all they needed, was their love and an unequivocal desire to be husband and wife.

Or so he believed.

He had only enough money for a night's stay in a motel and that's where they consummated their marriage. Unfortunately, the blissful honeymoon lasted less than twenty-four hours. As soon as Rachel's mother and father learned what they'd done, all hell broke loose, and the next thing Luke knew he was banned from the Hudson household and forbidden to see Rachel. A few days later, when Luke was presented with a monetary bribe from Randall that he flat-out refused, he was then served with the formal documents necessary for an annulment proceeding.

Since he was unable to get in touch with Rachel, he waited for her to contact him. But once the entire Hudson family moved to New York and a month passed without any word from her, Luke went ahead and signed the annulment papers.

That had been the end of his short-lived marriage, as well as a painful lesson learned: That a guy from the wrong side of the tracks wasn't good enough for an uptown girl like Rachel Hudson.

Shaking off the memories of the past, he pressed a button that enabled him to hear the conversations at the table, then he leaned back in his chair and watched Rachel play a few hands of blackjack, and win each one. The guy sitting next to Rachel on her right openly flirted with her, even going so far as to ask her to rub his chips for luck. With a light, musical laugh, she obliged him. While her own good fortune held out, the other man's did not. Before long, she was the only remaining player at the table, with a nice pile of chips in front of her to show for her blackjack skills.

The dealer, Pete, grinned at her. "Looks like you're Lady Luck this evening."

"Which is amazing." She glanced down at her winnings in awe, a light flush on her cheeks. "I haven't been this lucky in I can't remember when. It's nice for a change."

The young man began reshuffling the deck of cards for the next round of hands. "Do you gamble often?"

"Actually, no," she replied with a shake of her head, and took a drink from the bottle of water the casino waitress had delivered for her earlier. "I live in New York, which isn't exactly a gambling mecca."

"I'd have to agree with you there," Pete said as the cards arched easily between his hands. "So, are you here in Vegas for business or pleasure?"

The dealer's questions were idle chitchat to fill up the few minutes it took him to shuffle the deck, but Luke couldn't have asked for a better inquisition because he was just as curious to hear her answers.

"Actually, I'm here for both. A bit of business mixed in with some much needed R & R." She placed her bet on the green felt table, then bit her glossy bottom lip in a way Luke remembered well—a dead giveaway that she was feeling uncertain about something. "Say, maybe you could help me with the business part of my trip."

Pete raised a brow, his expression wary. Especially since he knew that security could easily hear their conversation. "Well, that all depends on what kind of business you're re-ferring to."

"It's legitimate. I promise," she said, and laughed. "I'm an old friend of Luke Kincaid's. Last I heard, he was working here. Do you know how I can get ahold of him?"

Her request shocked the hell out of Luke—that she knew where he worked and that she was actually here to see him. *For business*, she'd claimed. He couldn't imagine what kind of business the two of them had to discuss after being apart for eight long, silent years.

He was completely confused. Undeniably baffled. And definitely intrigued.

"I'm not authorized to give out personal information," Pete told Rachel as he deftly and skillfully dealt the first hand to her. "But I can probably pass along a message to Mr. Kincaid for you."

"Great. I'd appreciate that." Rachel picked up her two cards and gave them a quick glance. A triumphant smile pulled up the corners of her mouth as she set her cards back down on the table, faceup, for the dealer to see: An ace and a queen of hearts. "Blackjack!"

Pete shook his head in amusement. "The lady wins again." He paid out her winnings and collected the cards.

"I'm not one to push my luck, so I think I'm going to call it quits while I'm ahead." She gave the dealer a ten-dollar chip, dropped the rest of her winnings into her purse, then withdrew a small pad of paper.

She proceeded to jot down a quick message. "If you can make sure that Luke Kincaid gets this, I'd be really grateful." Finished writing, she folded the paper in half and handed it to Pete. "I really need to hear from him. I'm staying here at The Mystic until Sunday afternoon. The note includes my room number, so he can give me a call."

Pete nodded. "Consider it done."

"Thank you," she said, looking visibly relieved that her note would eventually make its way to Luke.

She slid off the chair and Luke watched her stroll down

the carpeted pathway toward the elevator to the hotel tower. The sensual sway of her hips and her natural beauty had male heads turning in appreciation as she walked through the gaming area, but she seemed oblivious to the stares, and her allure. It was hard for him to believe that Rachel was still so guileless and unaffected after all these years. Not when he knew that she was capable of turning her back on the man she'd married—destroying his heart in the process.

Within five minutes the note she'd written for him was delivered to his office. He read her message, and knew if he picked up the phone and dialed her room number she'd answer. He'd hear her sweet voice. And finally find out what she wanted from him.

But instead of making the call he crumpled the piece of paper in his fist and tossed it into the trash.

Oh, he intended to contact Rachel, eventually. When it was convenient for him, and on his terms.

Two

While Rachel might have kicked-ass at blackjack the evening before, this morning she royally sucked at solitaire. It appeared her luck had vanished completely, along with her hope and optimism that Luke would call her hotel room.

With a frustrated sigh, she set the deck of cards on the small table, then stood and walked to the large window in the standard-size room. She'd opened the drapes earlier when she'd woken up, and now she gazed out at the unobstructed view of the Las Vegas strip below, taking in the extravagant architecture of the casinos and hotels that had been built during her absence.

She'd spent all of last night waiting for the phone to ring, and again this morning, but so far she hadn't received any calls. Considering it was nearly ten in the morning, she was beginning to think that Luke either hadn't received her message, or he'd chosen to ignore her note, along with her presence in his life after eight long years apart.

The latter was the most likely possibility, considering how she'd forsaken their marriage vows, and him, less than twenty-four hours after they'd promised to love and cherish one another, until death did they part.

Oh, she'd loved Luke, with all the passion and emotion a young girl was capable of feeling. But she hadn't cherished him . . . not in the way a wife should have stood by her husband's side when they'd been confronted with their first marital issue: Her father.

Old, painful memories surfaced, along with the recollection of her father's fury when he'd discovered that she'd married Luke. An impulse that had the ability to change the entire course of her future. A future Randall Hudson had no intention of letting her throw away on a boy he felt wouldn't amount to much, considering where he came from, and the kind of parents who'd raised him—a bar waitress and a drunk for a father.

Despite her begging and pleading, her father had immediately set an annulment in motion. He'd also threatened to disown her if she dared to contact Luke again. Her father had always been a strict disciplinarian, not to mention very controlling, and she and her younger brother and sister had learned early on that any kind of disobedience was met with a harsh punishment.

It didn't matter that she'd just turned eighteen and had every right to marry who she wanted. She'd been young and impressionable and much too influenced by her father's intimidation tactics to dare to defy him. She'd also been so certain that Luke would arrive in New York and fight for her and their marriage . . . until her father informed her that he'd paid Luke off in exchange for him stepping completely out of her life.

At the time, she refused to believe that Luke could be bought. But the more time that passed without a word from him, Rachel's confidence had begun to waver. When the annulment papers arrived with his signature agreeing to dissolve their marriage, she had no choice but to face the fact that their relationship was over. For good.

Completely heartbroken, she went ahead and started law

school in the fall. Then, at the end of their first year in New York, both of her parents had been killed when their car was struck head-on by a driver who'd fallen asleep at the wheel. At the age of nineteen, Rachel found herself the sole guardian of her fifteen-year-old brother Casey and her eleven-year-old sister Lynn.

She'd spent the past seven years raising her siblings, giving up law school for full-time employment as a secretary in a law firm instead. She'd also sacrificed any kind of social life to be there for Casey and Lynn in the evenings, to help with homework and to keep them from getting into trouble. Her efforts had paid off, because her brother and sister had turned into mature, responsible adults that she was incredibly proud of.

Through it all, she'd never stopped thinking of Luke or how their lives would have turned out if she'd had the courage and confidence to stand up to her father. It was those frivolous daydreams of being with Luke, and the more erotic fantasies of him that filled her nights, that had gotten her through the difficult task of playing single parent to Casey and Lynn.

She shook her head and laughed at herself for being such a hopeless romantic. For clinging to the memories of a man who'd no doubt moved on with his life. He probably hadn't given her much thought at all over the years, and now she was about to deliver some unexpected news that was bound to shock the hell out of him.

If he ever decided to contact her.

Turning away from the window, she glanced at the silent phone, then the digital clock next to it: 9:50 A.M. She was tired of pacing the floor and waiting for him to call, not to mention feeling cooped up and stifled in the small room.

So, she decided that she'd order a light continental breakfast from room service, then take a shower and get dressed for the day before the meal arrived. If she didn't hear from

Luke by the time she was finished eating, she'd leave the hotel for awhile, which would give her the chance to breathe in some fresh air to clear her head.

With that plan in mind, she placed the call for her fruit, croissant, and hot tea, then took a fast shower. Just as she stepped from the shower enclosure and was drying off, a brisk knock sounded at her door.

"Geez, talk about speedy room service," she muttered as she reached for her terry robe and hastily slipped it on. "I'll be right there," she called out.

Quickly wrapping her wet hair in a towel, she tightened the sash on her robe and opened the door to let the server inside. Except the tall, dark, and incredibly sexy man standing on the other side of the threshold wasn't a waiter. Or a stranger. No, it was none other than Luke Kincaid.

She sucked in a startled breath as she stared at the familiar, dark brown eyes and masculine features that had matured from a tempting bad boy to a devastatingly gorgeous man. Instead of the longer, shaggier look he'd favored as a teenager, his sable hair was now clipped into a shorter, clean-cut style that defined the strong, chiseled lines of his face. His once tall and lanky frame had filled into an athletically honed body complete with broad shoulders, flat belly, and lean hips. Faded T-shirts, torn jeans, and old sneakers had been traded in for a collared knit shirt, pressed trousers, and shiny, polished loafers.

His transformation had been extreme, leaving little physical resemblance to the boy she'd fallen in love with and married. But what hadn't changed was his ability to make her heart beat wildly in her chest and her knees go weak at the mere sight of him. Amazingly, the alluring attraction and desire were still there, and so was the deep, aching longing she thought she'd suppressed years ago.

Apparently, there was no getting over this man.

"Luke." His name escaped her lips on a soft, wistful note, and with more emotion than she'd ever intended to reveal. Reminding herself of why she was there in Las Vegas, she quickly recovered and found her true voice. "I was expecting you to call." *Not to just show up unannounced.*

He shrugged those wide shoulders of his. "Considering how far you traveled to see me after all these years, I figured a personal visit was the least I could do." His sensual mouth had curved into a sexy smile, but his gaze was undeniably guarded, even as those bedroom eyes scrutinized her with just as much interest as she had him.

By the time he finished his lazy perusal, her skin felt warm and flushed, as if he'd physically reached out and touched her, from her bared throat all the way down to her calves. For the first time in what seemed like forever, her body felt alive. Sexual. And utterly feminine. Her tummy fluttered in awareness, her breasts tingled, and her nipples hardened into taut, aching peaks. All for him.

She shifted self-consciously, the damp slide of her bare thighs reminding her that she was completely naked beneath her robe. "I was expecting room service and thought you were them," she said, and stepped back to open the door wider. "Since you're here, why don't you come inside and we can talk."

He strolled into her room, his arm brushing against hers as he passed. A casual touch that elicited a tantalizing shiver from her. Closing the door and berating her body for being so easy, she followed him inside.

He glanced from her unmade bed and rumpled covers back to her. His disarming gaze held hers for several long heartbeats, and she wondered if he was thinking the same thing she was: That the last time they'd been together had been in a room much like this one. On their wedding night.

Images of tangled sheets and their entwined bodies straining and arching in the throes of wedded bliss filled her mind, and she had to swallow back the soft moan that that sweet memory evoked.

Oh, God, there was no way she could have this conversation with him while she was wearing nothing but a robe. Not when she wanted him as much as she had eight years ago.

She swallowed hard. "Give me a few minutes to get dressed." Grabbing underwear and the outfit she'd planned to wear for the day, she disappeared into the bathroom.

Within five minutes she'd changed into a light blue gauze skirt and matching tank top, and applied just enough makeup to give her a natural look and her complexion some color. Since she didn't want to take the time to blow-dry her hair, she used a towel to rub the excess moisture from the strands, then ran her fingers through the long, curly tresses.

Feeling better and more in control now that she was dressed, Rachel stepped back into the room. She found Luke sitting in one of the chairs at the table in the corner, his long legs stretched in front of him and his hands clasped over his stomach. The way he studied her from across the room was unsettling. Then again, he was probably trying to figure out why she was in Las Vegas and what she wanted from him.

He'd discover the answer to that soon enough.

Glancing away from his intense stare, she noticed that her breakfast had arrived, but the waiter was nowhere to be seen. She looked for a room-service bill, but couldn't find one. "Don't I need to sign something?"

"I took care of it," he said in a low, rich voice that did crazy, intimate things to her insides.

So much for control, she thought wryly. "Thank you." Unwrapping a tea bag, she dropped the pouch into a cup, then added steaming hot water. "You really didn't have to do that."

"Don't worry about it." He brushed off the matter as insignificant. "Being able to comp a guest is one of the perks of working for the hotel."

She smiled and placed fruit and a croissant on a plate. "Must be nice."

The corner of his mouth lifted in a slow grin of his own. "I'll admit it comes in handy sometimes."

He absently fingered the deck of cards she'd been playing solitaire with earlier. Those large hands of his mesmerized her, made her remember the heat of his palms as he caressed her skin and the erotic stroke of his long, skillful fingers in sensitive places.

Shaking off the arousal settling low and deep, she placed her breakfast on the table and sat down across from him. "Would you like something to eat? I wasn't expecting company, but I'm willing to share."

He shook his head. "I'm fine. How did you know where I worked?" he asked, his gaze now as direct as his question.

He was obviously done with polite chitchat and wanted answers. "I hired a private investigator to find you." She cut open her croissant and spread strawberry jam on both sides. "From what I've been told, you've worked your way up to one of the top security positions here at the Mystic Casino. You've come a long way, with a great career."

His mouth twisted into a bitter smile that took her off guard, as did his vehement words. "What you mean is that I'm no longer a poor kid with a drunk as a father and no future ahead of him. At least not one that was good enough for you."

The resentment in his voice was unmistakable, making it abundantly clear that the past was still a sore spot with him, despite his own personal success. It appeared that she wasn't the only one whose heart and emotions had been battered and bruised.

"That was my father's opinion, not mine," she said quietly, then took a soothing drink of her tea.

He looked away, as if he regretted his outburst. After a moment, he exhaled a long, harsh breath and met her gaze again, his composure back in place. "Why are you here, Rachel?" he asked, point-blank. "And what do you want with me?"

Biting on her lower lip, she set her fork on her plate. No more beating around the bush. The sooner she revealed her reasons for her presence in his life after so long, the sooner they could deal with the problem. Since there was no easy way to break the news to him, she laid it out straight.

"Our annulment was never filed with the courts." She offered up a smile to soften the blow of her announcement.

He frowned at her. "What?"

The confusion creasing his features would have been comical if this had been some kind of elaborate hoax. Unfortunately, it wasn't a joke, but their reality. And just in case he wasn't able to comprehend the repercussions of those papers never being filed, she made it very clear.

"We're still married."

Three

Luke's mind reeled with disbelief as he tried to process Rachel's shocking announcement. Out of all the scenarios he'd imagined for her return to Las Vegas, nothing had prepared him for the stunning news that they were still husband and wife.

"Pretty bizarre, huh?" Rachel said softly, and with a wealth of understanding lacing her voice. While she'd had time to digest this news, he was still grappling to come to terms with it all.

A dry laugh escaped him. "Yeah, you could say that." Still dazed, he stood and walked over to the room's window. Hands on hips, he stared out at the city of Las Vegas below, trying to make sense of it all, but couldn't.

He turned back around, shaking his head in confusion. "I signed those papers and sent them back to your father's lawyer so you could sign them, and they could be filed. Did *you* not sign them?" It was the only logical explanation he could come up with.

A hint of sadness colored her eyes, surprising Luke. "As soon as I saw your signature on the documents, I signed them, too." Finished eating, she pushed her plate aside.

They were still married. He couldn't get that staggering realization out of his head. "Then how did this happen?"

Standing, she came up beside him, close enough for him to touch if he dared. "Even though we both signed the annulment papers, they were never filed in court."

"Jeezus." Come to think of it, he couldn't remember ever receiving a copy of the finalized annulment. At the time, it hadn't been something that had concerned him. He figured Randall Hudson had everything under his control and wouldn't let something as significant as the dissolution of his daughter's short-lived marriage escape his notice.

Luke scrubbed a hand along his jaw, then smirked at her. "I'll bet your father is beside himself that someone dropped the ball on something as important as this, huh?"

She winced at that, a pained look passing over her beautiful, classical features. "Luke . . . both of my parents were killed in a car accident seven years ago."

He swore beneath his breath for being so callous with his remark. "I'm sorry, Rachel," he said, softening his tone with genuine remorse. He never would have said something so insensitive if he'd known about her parents' demise. "I had no idea."

"Of course you didn't." She sighed, the sound tired and weary. "Needless to say, it's been a very long seven years. Then to find out that we're still married . . . well, it's been overwhelming, to say the least."

He could only imagine what Rachel and her younger brother and sister had gone through with their parents' sudden death and the ensuing years. Despite what he'd believed all these years, Rachel's life couldn't have been as easy as he'd always thought.

Much to his surprise, Luke felt the resentment he'd harbored for so many years begin to thaw, and in its place was a surge of empathy for her situation. He also experienced the urge to reach out, take her in his arms, and offer her comfort and support.

His hands curled into tight fists at his side as he resisted the impulse. Then again, maybe she didn't need his comfort and support any longer. He might still be her husband in name only, but there was always the possibility that there was a significant other in her life, which would make an official annulment all the more urgent.

The thought caused a bolt of unexpected jealousy to streak through him, giving too much credence to the feelings he still harbored for her, despite his attempts to deny every last one of them. There was still an irresistible attraction and awareness between them, but as he stared into her warm, soulful eyes, his chest seemed to constrict with pure, legitimate emotion. The kind that had eluded him for the eight long years that had separated them.

And that's when he knew he was in big trouble where this woman was concerned, because he still wanted her. Possibly still loved her. And, as he'd learned long ago, that was a dangerous place to be. The desire and lust he could handle, but he refused to allow his heart or emotions into the mix.

After a moment, she cleared her throat and glanced away, breaking the connection. "Back to our annulment, or rather our lack of one," she said with humor, putting their conversation back on the right track. "About a month ago I sold the house my parents had bought when we moved to New York, and while I was going through their things and deciding what to toss and what to keep, I came across a locked wooden box that belonged to my mother. I broke the lock and found our signed annulment papers inside, along with a journal that my mother kept."

A ripple of shock coursed through him. "Your *mother* kept the annulment papers?" he asked, unable to comprehend her reasons for doing so. "Why?"

Rachel folded her arms over her chest and gave him a halfhearted smile. "According to what she wrote in her journal, she didn't share my father's feelings about you and me not being together. She knew how in love we were, which apparently was not the case in her own turbulent marriage to my father. She married him because she'd gotten pregnant with me, but as you know my father was very controlling, manipulative, and he wasn't one to show much emotion. He was that way with my mother, as well."

All fascinating stuff, Luke thought. "But that doesn't explain why she'd intercept the annulment papers and deceive your father about it."

"My mother wanted us to have the happily-ever-after that she never had," Rachel explained, and brushed away the damp, curly strands of hair that had fallen along her soft, smooth cheek. "And she honestly believed it was possible for us, despite how young we were. She didn't file the annulment papers in hopes that you'd change your mind and come to New York to be with me."

He clenched his jaw, fighting the strong urge to tell Rachel that it was a two-way street—that she could have just as easily contacted him. And what made Carol Hudson think that Randall wouldn't interfere in their lives once again?

"Sounds like your mother was a dreamer," he said, unable to keep the sarcastic edge from his voice.

Rachel stepped up to the window and flattened her slender hand on the cool glass, then glanced back at him. "Maybe dreams were all she had, because her reality wasn't so charming." Her voice was as soft as the look in her dreamy eyes.

Luke didn't doubt that for a second. "Do you know if your mother ever planned on telling you that she never filed the annulment papers?"

"She wrote in her journal that she meant to give the two

of us a year to find our way back to one another. Her words, not mine," Rachel said with a light laugh. "She was obviously a hopeless romantic, as well. At least now I know where I get it from."

Luke silently agreed. That had been one of the things he'd adored about Rachel. Her whimsical, sentimental side, so opposite of his own hardened, jaded one. Those starry-eyed traits had not only softened some of his rougher edges during their year together in high school, it had also led to their spontaneous marriage that warm summer night.

He lifted a dark, inquiring brow. "All things considered, I guess it's a good thing that neither one of us remarried."

She shook her head, sending those spiral curls cascading like threads of silk down her back. "Getting married again wasn't even a blip on my radar the past eight years." A wry, almost tired smile touched her lips. "Between raising my brother and sister, working, and school, there wasn't a whole lot of time left over for dating, much less a social life."

He found himself perversely satisfied that there was no other man in her life, and that he hadn't been the only one who hadn't been able to sustain a long-term relationship. "Me either," he said, shocking himself by admitting something so personal, when this meeting should have been anything but.

Her guileless eyes widened in surprise, but before she could ask the curious questions glimmering in her gaze—questions that would lead to revealing answers he had no wish to share with her—he turned away and sat back down at the table. Leaning forward, he braced his hands on his knees.

"So, what do we do now?" he asked. Being a lawyer, she no doubt knew exactly what had to be done. She wouldn't have traveled all the way to Las Vegas without some kind of plan in mind.

She didn't disappoint him. "Well, the original annulment documents have obviously expired when they weren't filed, so I had a divorce attorney in the law firm where I work draw up new ones before I came."

She walked across the room to the leather attaché on the dresser and withdrew a sheaf of papers. Then she returned to where he was sitting and set the documents on the table in front of him. He didn't bother looking at them; instead he kept his gaze locked on hers.

She drew a breath that made her full breasts rise and fall too enticingly beneath the tank top she was wearing. "I just need you to sign the papers where indicated, and I'll take them back to New York with me," she said, sounding professional and efficient. "I'll also make sure they get filed with the courts this time. After that, the dissolution of our marriage will be official, and I'll be sure to send you a copy for your records."

Jesus. The whole process sounded no less cold and final than it had eight years ago, when Randall Hudson had issued the same ultimatum. Except this time he wasn't being bribed by her unfeeling, calculating father, or being served with a restraining order to stay away from this woman who was, ironically, still his wife. Instead, she was the one soliciting his assent and cooperation.

As he continued to stare at her, saying nothing, he caught the faintest hint of vulnerability flickering in her gaze. It was a quick, unguarded moment that told him that maybe this wasn't so easy for her after all. Possibly this direct, businesslike façade of hers was all for show, to keep her true feelings about him and the situation out of the equation.

Then she dampened her bottom lip with her tongue, and he knew without a doubt that he'd pegged her behavior accurately. Pure male instinct prompted his gaze to drop to her mouth, so soft and pink and glistening, tempting him like nothing had in a very long time. He thought about kissing her, tasting her again, and his groin tightened in reaction.

In that moment, he realized he wasn't ready to sign those damn papers and let her walk out on him twice. Not without taking something for himself in exchange for his John Hancock on those documents. Like that kiss he'd just imagined. Or something far more pleasurable. And if he was extremely lucky, once he had Rachel Hudson again, there would be absolutely nothing left between them and he could finally get on with his life and have a normal relationship with a woman again.

That was his grand plan, anyway, because nothing else in the past eight years had worked to banish her from his mind. "If you want that annulment, I have a deal to offer you," he said.

His unexpected reply took her aback. "Excuse me?"

Smiling, he reclined casually in his chair, knowing that he was going to shock her even more before they were through. "I noticed last night that you were very lucky at the blackjack table."

Her shoulders lifted in a slight shrug. "I did okay."

He inclined his head and tapped his finger on the deck of cards. "Are you feeling lucky now, Rachel?"

She glanced from the cards, to him, her expression cautious and uncertain. "Why does it matter?"

"Because I'm proposing one hand of blackjack between the two of us," he said, knowing the exasperation etching her features was about to be replaced with one of two things—either indignation or interest. He was hoping for the latter. "If you win, I'll sign the documents, right here and now. But if you lose . . . you give me a kiss."

Nervous laughter bubbled up from her throat, but she

didn't appear completely adverse to his suggestion. "You've got to be kidding."

He arched a brow in challenge, while fully enjoying the fluster of pink tingeing her cheeks. "What's the matter, sweetheart? Afraid you'll lose?" he taunted softly.

She could have easily told him she wasn't interested in playing games with him—that her only concern was having him sign the documents so she could be on her way, and that would have been the end to Luke's attempt to seduce her. Instead, he watched in fascination as Rachel's posture straightened, and that cute chin of hers lifted in a show of rebellion so unlike the girl he once knew.

"Of course I'm not afraid I'll lose." She promptly sat across from him at the table and reached for the deck of cards, all outward confidence and bravado. "But *I'll* shuffle and deal."

Luke laughed, deciding he liked this bold and feisty side to her personality. And her daring. "Fair enough."

A few minutes later, after she'd made sure the cards had been sufficiently mixed up, she dealt them each the first card, facedown, then the second card faceup. She'd served him a five, and herself a king of spades. As a general rule, he had to assume there was another ten card beneath her king, which sucked for him because his facedown card, a nine, gave him a total score of fourteen.

He cursed silently. The odds certainly weren't in his favor. Chances were he was going to bust if he drew another card, and he'd probably lose to her possible twenty points if he didn't. A goddamn catch-22 situation that didn't bode well for him.

"Hit me again," he said, and felt his heart literally jump in his chest when she presented him with a seven, bringing his total to a cool twenty-one. Now *that* was luck at its finest.

Calmly, and without giving anything away, he said, "I'll stay."

"All right." She exhaled a low stream of breath and flipped over her facedown card, revealing a two, not the ten Luke had anticipated. "Twelve," she said on a groan, while he grinned.

She was the recipient of one of the worst hands a black-jack player could possess. She also knew, judging by his faceup cards, that he had more than twelve, which forced her to take another card. She dealt herself a queen, and went bust. He revealed his own cards, and the twenty-one he'd scored.

He couldn't help but revel in his victory, and what he'd ultimately won. "C'mere, Rachel," he murmured, and crooked his finger at her. "I want you on my lap."

Standing, she rounded the table to where he was sitting, ready and willing to pay her debt. Except as she tentatively perched her soft bottom on his thighs and he rested one hand on her knee and the other at her waist, he realized she was way too stiff and tense for his liking.

Leaning forward, he gently nuzzled her neck and inhaled the intoxicating floral fragrance clinging to her damp hair and satiny skin, striving to put her at ease before he kissed her the way he was aching to. He felt a shiver course through her, heard her breath catch oh-so-sweetly, but she remained rigid and unyielding.

He pulled back and met her too bright gaze. "Relax, Rachel. I'm going to kiss you, not bite you." He stroked his flattened palm down her back in a slow, soothing caress meant to chase away her anxiety. "Or has it been that long since you've kissed a man?" he teased.

"Don't analyze the situation or me, Luke," she said, a bit too indignantly. "Just do it and get it over with."

He held back his amusement, guessing that he'd hit too close to the truth, considering she'd admitted that she hadn't had much time for dating. And yes, she was nervous, but not in a bad, negative way. She was uncertain, maybe a little fearful of unleashing the desire still simmering between them and where it all might lead.

They were both about to find out.

Sliding his hand beneath the damp fall of her hair, he cupped the back of her head in his palm and brought her mouth down to his. Her lashes fluttered closed, and the first touch of her soft, warm lips against his was a sweet, sensual awakening that took him back to the very first time he'd kissed her.

That same rush of lust and tenderness assaulted him, heating his blood and firing his need to deepen the contact and claim her completely. He wanted to devour her, possess her. He bit her bottom lip gently, and tugged on the flesh seductively with his teeth. When her mouth parted on a soft surrendering moan, he accepted the invitation and slid his tongue inside and touched hers, igniting a carnal hunger that made him burn for her.

The eight long years that had separated them melted away, and as he gave into the familiar heat and desire that only this woman had ever elicited from him, it was as if they'd never been apart. When he skimmed his thumb along her jaw and deepened the kiss even more, she turned toward him more fully, causing her hip to nestle against the stiff erection straining along the zipper of his slacks, and one of her soft, plump breasts to graze his chest. The sensation, even fully clothed, was electric and exciting.

She must have felt it too, because she shifted restlessly on his lap and pressed her cool palm to his cheek. The touch was intimate, as was the way she made those sexy little sounds in the back of her throat that told him just how aroused she was. He remembered her body language well, and how eloquently she could speak without saying a word at all when it came to her sexual yearnings. He knew what she wanted, and he didn't hesitate to give it to her.

With his mouth still hot on hers, he lifted his hand from her knee, slipped it beneath the hem of her top, and grazed his fingers along the soft, warm skin of her abdomen, then higher, until he reached the voluptuous curve of her breast. Then he cradled all that glorious fullness in his palm, and his mind spun with the sheer pleasure of having her in his hand. Her bra was silky and sheer, without padding, enabling him to feel her hard nipple, as well as strum that tightly puckered tip with his thumb. He took his time relearning her size, her shape, and how beautifully her figure had changed since her teenage years.

She was all sensual, responsive woman now, and not nearly as demure and modest as she'd once been about her body's reaction to his caresses. Neither was she hesitant about the way he kneaded and stroked her breast, and how his tongue mated with hers in a deep, erotic French kiss.

The attraction and passion was still there between them, so tangible and real: The smoldering heat; the undeniable chemistry; and a physical need that burned brighter and hotter than before.

He groaned against her mouth, low and rough. God, he wanted her naked, so he could see her bared breasts and taste her pert, velvet-tipped nipples. He wanted to look his fill of her feminine curves and trace every dip and swell with his hands and mouth. And then, when he finally had them both on the razor-sharp edge of need, he'd lay her on the bed so he could feel her slender thighs wrap around his hips, her body open and accepting as he pushed deep, deep inside of her soft heat for a nice, long, slow ride. And maybe then he'd finally be able to get her out of his mind. His blood. His heart.

A kiss had only whet his appetite for more, and he knew that letting her walk out of his life again wasn't an option.

At least not yet. Because it was very apparent to him that he needed to shake Rachel Hudson from his system, and he could think of only one way to do it.

Reluctantly releasing her breast, he slid his hand out from under her top and ended the kiss. They were both breathing hard, and she looked stunned by the intensity of their encounter. Her lips were wet and swollen, her lashes heavy-lidded, and her eyes dark with unsated passion.

"How about best two out of three?" he asked huskily.

Still caught up in the seductive spell of their embrace, vibrant desire sparked in her gaze. "For another kiss?"

Her interest was palpable, which definitely worked in his favor. "No, to spend the weekend with me." He paused for a moment, and just in case she had any doubts about what he was proposing, he made his intentions clear. "Intimately, Rachel. Two more days of anything-goes pleasure, and in return my signature on those annulment papers is all yours."

The dreamy haze cleared, replaced by panic. "I don't think that's such a good idea," she said quickly.

She moved off his lap, and he let her go, suspecting she needed a bit of breathing room after the shocking proposition he'd just issued. He gave her the physical distance, but didn't let up on his attempt to sway her.

"If your response to that kiss we just shared is any indication, then I'm thinking it's a really good idea," he said lightly, knowing his fierce erection and the nipples still pressing insistently against her top spoke volumes about how much they wanted one another. "Besides, the way I figure things, you owe me a real honeymoon, complete with conjugal rights."

She gaped at him, though there was no real indignation in her stare. "You can't be serious."

He shrugged and leaned back casually in his chair. "Legally, you're still my wife, and I'm still your husband."

"In name only."

He let a slow, challenging grin ease up the corners of his mouth. "One more hand of cards could change all that," he said, tempting her with his voice, then his words. "That is, if you dare."

Four

A challenge. A dare. One that Rachel was hard-pressed to resist, despite her reservations about spending the weekend with this man who still held too much power over her body and emotions. Her heart told her to cut her losses and get the heck out of there, but the part of her that was all woman urged her to go for it.

Absently, she gnawed on her bottom lip, her gaze on Luke, who was waiting very patiently for her answer. In him, at that moment, she saw the bad boy she'd been wildly, recklessly drawn to as a young girl, then had eventually fallen in love with. Every inch of him exuded male confidence, and those positively wicked eyes of his stared back at her, beckoning her to indulge in the thrilling pleasure so evident in that steamy kiss they'd just shared.

Even from across the room she could feel the irresistible pull of sexual tension swirling between them, and her pulse quickened in reaction. It was ridiculous to deny what she wanted so badly, and Rachel decided that she wasn't going to let anything keep her from stealing this time with him.

It was just pure lust and curiosity, she told herself. Nothing more. She knew she was playing with fire and risking the possibility of getting burned, considering all he wanted from her was two days of hot sex. But after seven years of being practical and responsible, not to mention a parent to her siblings with no time for a man in her life, she wanted to feel sexy and desired again. And Luke Kincaid, even after all these years, accomplished that and more.

A weekend affair was all she wanted. A provocative, erotic fling—not with a stranger, but a man from her past. A man who'd filled her dreams and fantasies for the longest eight years of her existence. Then she'd head back to New York without regrets, her past finally behind her, and get on with her life.

She smiled at him, embracing the impetuous woman making herself, and her desires, known. "If a weekend is what you want, it's yours. No card game necessary." Because now that she'd made up her mind, she wasn't about to risk losing two days with Luke on a single hand of blackjack. "The way I see things, we're two consenting adults, so there's no reason to play hard to get for something I want just as much as you do."

The stunned look on his face was comical. He clearly didn't expect her to give in so easily—and so candidly. Then he laughed, the sound deep, a little rough, and too damn arousing.

Standing, he slowly, lazily approached her, a gorgeous, compelling, self-assured male who captivated her on every level. "You're a helluva lot more assertive than you were at eighteen," he murmured once he stopped less than a foot away from her, an amused smile quirking the corners of his sensual mouth. "I like that. Makes me wonder if you're just as bold and brazen in the bedroom."

The intimate insinuation in his voice and the shameless heat in his eyes made her weak in the knees. "I guess you'll find out now, won't you?"

He reached out and stroked a finger along the edge of

her scoop-necked tank top, the warmth of his touch making her nipples hard and tight all over again—which he clearly noticed and seemed to enjoy. "Oh, I'm definitely looking forward to seeing just how adventurous you've become."

Considering she was seconds away from ripping off Luke's clothes and taking advantage of him right then and there, she didn't think being forward was going to be a problem. "Then we have an agreement?" she asked, wanting him to know she understood that their time together was temporary. "We'll have our weekend affair, you'll sign the annulment papers, and on Sunday afternoon we can go our separate ways. No strings or expectations of anything more."

His lips pursed for a brief moment, and a quick flash of annoyance passed over his features. "Sure, we have an agreement," he said, his tone suddenly cool. "But we're going to do it *my* way, so pack up your things. I'll send a bellman up to help you take your bags to my suite for the weekend."

"Your suite?" she asked, surprised that he had his own personal living quarters here at the hotel. And even more startled that he wanted her to move in with him for the next two days.

He nodded. "Since I work a lot of late, long hours, I have a suite here that I use on occasion."

While she was impressed that he'd achieved so much—an exclusive suite at The Mystic to use at his disposal on top of the house she had learned he owned on the outskirts of Vegas—she hadn't expected such an intimate arrangement between the two of them. While she was all for enjoying a fling with him, she preferred at least to have her own place to retreat to in the evening, and staying in his bed, all night long, just didn't bode well for her heart and emotions.

"I'd rather stay and sleep here, in my own room," she told him.

"I'm not giving you a choice, Rachel," he said in a tone of voice that left no room for argument. "I agreed to your terms, now here are a few conditions of my own. You're mine for the weekend. Whenever I want you. However I want you. And having you in my suite makes that very convenient."

She arched a brow, but found herself too intrigued by his erotic proposition to put up any kind of real fight. "That sounds very depraved."

"Oh, it is." He grinned and wound a long, curly strand of her hair around his finger, ensnaring her in more ways than one. "They don't call Las Vegas 'Sin City' for nothing, sweetheart."

A shiver coursed through her. Rachel had the distinct impression that there was going to be a whole lot of sinning going on between them before the weekend was through. And, Lord help her, she was looking forward to every sensual minute of it.

"Go ahead and put your things in the master suite when you get there and make yourself comfortable for the afternoon." He turned and headed for the door, clearly leaving her. "If you need to reach me, just call the hotel operator and ask for me and she'll put you through to my office."

"When will I see you again?" she asked.

With the door open, he glanced back at her. "Be ready for dinner tonight at six-thirty," he said, then he was gone.

In the wake of his departure, she sat down on the bed to regroup before packing up her things. So, she had the afternoon to herself, which she hadn't expected once they'd agreed to their deal. But now that she was free, a few hours at the spa getting pampered sounded divine and luxurious. Especially since it had been so long since she'd done anything frivolous just for herself. Then, once she was exfoliated, massaged, with toes and nails manicured, she'd check out the boutiques to see if she could find something sexy to wear for dinner tonight.

Something guaranteed to seduce the husband she hadn't been with in eight long years.

Luke walked into the marbled foyer of his suite and set his key card on the small entryway table near the door. The place was quiet, but he knew Rachel was there. He'd seen her come up to the room about forty minutes ago via the private elevator after spending the afternoon at the hotel's spa and salon, then perusing the boutiques. He knew this because he'd spent the day watching her on the security monitors in his office.

God, he was so pathetic, he thought as he headed toward the master bedroom. One day and he was addicted to her all over again. Couldn't get enough of seeing her, being with her, which is what had prompted him to arrive at the suite an hour earlier than he'd told her that morning.

After a quick search, he found her in the huge Jacuzzi tub in the master bathroom. He stopped at the door, braced his shoulder against the frame, and drank in the sensual sight before him. Her eyes were closed, and judging by the way her body was completely relaxed and her chest rose and fell in deep, even breaths, he was fairly certain she'd fallen asleep. The Jacuzzi jets were on low, making the heated water bubble just above the upper swells of her breasts, teasing him with brief glimpses of her rosy nipples and the silhouette of her curves beneath the surface.

Quietly, he made his way to the tub and sat down on one of the granite steps leading into the bath. Her hair was up, her pink lips parted, and her skin was smooth and flushed from the heat of the water, making him itch to reach out and caress all that sleek, damp, bare flesh.

His gut clenched. She was so damn beautiful. So "everything-that-had-been-missing-from-his-life" for so long. And no matter how much he resented how they'd parted ways in the past, he found himself grateful for the time he had with her now. He knew it had little to do with the physical attraction between them, but rather the sentimental connection tugging at all those places within him that he'd shut down the day he'd signed the first set of annulment papers, and sent them back to New York to end their marriage.

And now, to find out that they were still husband and wife—the notion blew his mind and wreaked havoc with his emotions. He'd spent the entire day thinking about the past and their time apart, and now all he wanted to focus on was the present, and his time with Rachel.

He gently touched her bare, wet shoulder, taking care not to startle her with his unannounced presence. "Hey, sleeping beauty."

Slowly, her lashes fluttered open and a sweet smile curved her lips when she saw him. "Hey, yourself," she murmured huskily. "This Jacuzzi tub of yours is absolutely decadent."

"I'm glad you're enjoying yourself." He traced his fingers along the line of water frothing just above her breasts, and felt a slight but telling shiver ripple along her skin. "So, do you plan on being lazy all day?"

"Lazy?" She arched a newly plucked and shaped brow at him. "This girl has had a very busy day."

"You're no longer a *girl*, Rachel," he said, infusing his voice with male appreciation. "From my viewpoint, what I see is all woman." A tempting, provocative woman he ached to make his again.

She tipped her head and gave him a sultry look that caused his blood to heat in his veins. "And do you like what you see?"

There was that bravado again, that bold daring that amused and intrigued him, and this time he decided to give her something just as irresistible and seductive. For her pleasure as much as his own.

"Ummm, I like what I see very much." He dipped his hand beneath the surface, trailed his fingertips to the hardened crest of one breast, then cupped the fullest part of her in his large palm. "You've developed beautiful breasts. I can't wait to take them in my mouth and suck on your nipples," he said, and plucked the delicate tip with his fingers.

She gasped softly, not in protest, but with desire. "Luke . . ."

"Shhh." He smiled, loving her uninhibited response to him, which made him curious to find out if she was still just as sensitive elsewhere. "You asked. Now be quiet, listen, and let me feel all the different ways your body has changed."

Beneath the eddying water, he skimmed those same fingers across her flat, quivering belly, then along the feminine dip and swell of her waist and hips—all the while arousing her with sensually charged words and explicit descriptions. Her skin was sleek and soft, the length of her slender thigh just as silky smooth. When he reached her knees, her legs parted for him—a wanton invitation he wasn't about to refuse.

With his gaze locked intently on hers, he caressed his splayed palm back up her supple thigh, until the tips of his fingers brushed along her sex. At that point, her eyes widened with a sudden bout of vulnerability, and she grasped his wrist to keep him from going any farther.

His groin throbbed, and his entire being shook with the need to be inside her any way he could. "Rachel . . . let me touch you."

She searched his gaze—for what, he wasn't altogether certain. Then, without a word, she released her grip, trusting him with the most intimate part of her body. Softly, leisurely, he traced the petal soft folds of her sex, before sliding one long finger, then two, deep inside her. He heard his own groan of pleasure mingle with hers, felt her shudder and clench against his hand—and wished it was his thick, pulsing cock inside of her instead of his fingers.

She was so tight and hot and slick, gripping him as he pushed in, then pulled out, while stroking his thumb along her clit, over and over again. Her hips rolled and her body arched, seeking something more tangible. Knowing exactly what she craved, he leaned in close and grazed his lips against her damp cheek, then drifted his way up to her ear.

"Come for me, Rachel," he whispered, his voice low and rough and demanding.

She moaned, closed her eyes, and let her head loll against the edge of the tub. He continued to play her body until she finally gave him what he wanted, and what she needed. With a soft cry she came, her orgasm a long, strong release that seemed to go on forever, and gave him an immense amount of satisfaction since he was the one to give it to her.

When it was over, when she gradually opened her eyes to look at him, he reluctantly withdrew his hand from beneath the water, then stood. Her gaze dropped to the erection tenting the front of his trousers, and he felt himself grow impossibly harder, thicker.

"I'm going to go and shower and change in the other bathroom," he said, before he dragged her from the tub and took her right then and there on the floor—which wasn't how he envisioned their first time together again. "When you're dressed and ready for dinner, I'll be waiting in the living room."

She licked her lips, increasing his physical discomfort by a good ten degrees. "What about you?" she asked meaningfully.

He inhaled a deep, steady breath. "I've waited eight years for you, Rachel, I can wait a bit longer." Then he flashed her a wicked smile. "I'll get mine later."

Her lashes fell halfway, and a slow smile filled with promise appeared on her lips. "I'll make sure that you do."

Five

He should have ordered dinner up to the suite. As Luke followed Rachel in her figure-hugging, deep purple dress, all he could think about was getting her out of it, and getting inside *her*. The sophisticated sway of her hips riveted his attention, and when she turned to slide into the private booth that the maitre d' led them to in The Mystic's upscale restaurant, his gaze shifted to the low V-cut neckline displaying an ample amount of flesh and generous cleavage.

Ignoring the flare of heat igniting in his belly, Luke sat next to Rachel and glanced back at the maitre d'. "Thanks, Richard. We'll take a bottle of Cristal when you get the chance."

Richard nodded as he stepped away from the table. "I'll get that champagne for you right away."

Once the other man was gone and they were alone, Rachel slanted him a playful look. "If you're trying to impress me, I have to admit that it's working. Is all this another perk of working at The Mystic?" she asked, indicating the reserved table and the preferential treatment.

He grinned. "You could say that."

She opened her leather-bound menu, but didn't look at

the dinner selections. Instead, her gaze remained on him, her admiration genuine and real. "You've done very well for yourself, Luke. I'm really proud of everything you've accomplished."

Her praise caused something warm and deep to curl through him and settle in long-forgotten places. "Thanks. I have to say, I love what I do. It's a great job, and the people I work with are equally top-notch in the security field." He nudged her menu in an attempt to avert the attention off of him. "The baked macadamia nut sea bass is exceptionally good here," he said, remembering how much she loved seafood.

"I'm sold." She flashed him a sparkling smile. "That sounds fantastic, and I'm absolutely ravenous."

So was he, but not for food, he thought. Their episode in the bathroom was still fresh in his mind, as was their earlier kiss. Both encounters had him on edge with wanting her in the very worst way. Add that sexy, alluring dress of hers to his rapidly dwindling restraint and he hoped to God he made it through dinner without ravishing her in their very private and isolated corner of the restaurant.

He shifted in his seat, and while they waited for their server to arrive to take their order, he asked about her day, even though he knew exactly how she'd spent those hours. Regardless of his own secret knowledge of how she'd spent the afternoon, he listened to her anyway, and realized just how much she'd enjoyed being indulged and pampered.

"Tell me something," she said once they'd ordered their dinner and their Cristal had been delivered. "How did you get a job as head of security for the Mystic Casino?"

He sighed as he reclined against the booth's leather exterior and watched as she took a sip of her champagne. They were back to him again, despite his attempts to steer the conversation away from his personal life. But her questions were relatively harmless, and the fact was, he didn't have anything to hide from her.

"After you left, I was hired on with The Mystic as a valet attendant. I worked the night shift, which left my days free for school and studying."

"You went to college," she said, sounding very pleased with that revelation. "I'm glad you did."

"I always planned on it," he replied with a slight smile. "You know that."

She hesitated a few seconds while her fingers stroked the stem of her champagne glass, much in the same way he imagined her stroking him. Then she spoke what was on her mind.

"During our senior year in high school, we did talk about you going to UNLV," she said, her tone as tentative as her words. "But, quite honestly, after I left for New York with my family, I wasn't sure what you would do."

Falling apart hadn't been an option for him, no matter how devastated he'd been. Instead, he'd channeled his anger and resentment toward something productive, figuring that there was nothing left for him but work and succeeding and making something of himself. That had been the driving force in his life the past eight years, and what had kept him from ending up like his own useless, worthless drunk of a father.

As their waiter arrived to serve them their entrees, Luke realized that his thoughts had taken a dark turn, and he didn't want their discussion to head down that morose path. Not during a pleasant dinner that had the potential of leading to an equally enjoyable evening up at the suite.

So, he kept things light and casual. "Two years after starting with The Mystic, there was an opening in security which I applied for and got. Over the next few years I went from overseeing the money transfers in the casino to working in surveillance. As for college, I started out taking general ed courses, but switched to getting a degree in security services, which helped with promotions. I worked hard, proved myself to all the right people, and when the head of security took a job with another casino I was qualified enough to get the position."

"That's amazing," she said as she took a bite of her fish. "I bet your parents are very proud of you."

"My mother is. As for my father, he died four years ago of liver disease."

Her eyes widened in startled surprise, and she reached out to place her hand over his on the table in a show of comfort. "Oh, Luke, I'm so sorry."

"Don't be." The last thing he wanted was sympathy for a man who didn't deserve it. "Bill was never much of a father to me anyway, and my mother is better off without him and his abuse."

Understanding glimmered in Rachel's eyes. She knew he'd had a rough childhood because of his father, and there was no making excuses for Bill Kincaid's offensive ways. He'd always been a mean, ugly drunk.

"I always did like your mom," Rachel said with an affectionate smile that affirmed her comment. "How is she doing?" She took a long drink of her champagne, but her interested gaze never left his.

"Actually, she's great." He cut a slice of his beef Wellington as he spoke, then pierced the tender morsel with his fork. "She met a really nice man who treats her well. They recently got married and moved to Henderson. He's retired and fairly wealthy, so she doesn't have to work. It's nice to see someone taking care of her for a change."

"I'm glad to hear she's happy."

"It's nothing less than she deserves." He ate a bite of his dinner, then refilled their almost empty champagne flutes. "So, what about you, Rachel? I take it you became the lawyer your father wanted you to be?"

She tipped her head curiously, and a few loose strands that had escaped her upswept hair caressed her neck. "What makes you think that?"

He found her response odd and wondered if he'd misunderstood what she'd said when they'd discussed their invalid annulment papers. "This morning you mentioned working for a law firm."

"I do, but not as an attorney," she said with a shake of her head. "I'm a paralegal."

Luke certainly hadn't been expecting that, considering how adamant her father had been about his daughter attending law school. "What happened?"

"I started school in the fall of the year we moved to New York, but when my parents passed away I had some difficult choices to make." Absently, she pushed her half-eaten food around on her plate, her voice taking on a quiet, reminiscent note. "Since I was nineteen, I was able to become guardian to my younger brother and sister, and that's exactly what I did."

An unmistakable surge of respect made itself known within Luke. He was beginning to see Rachel in a whole new and different light. Where he'd imagined she'd spent the past eight years living an easy, uncomplicated life, it was humbling to discover that she'd been forced to grow up at a very young age. "That's a huge responsibility."

"But well worth it," she said without hesitating. "I wasn't about to let the three of us get separated, or Casey and Lynn end up in a foster home. But that meant quitting school and finding full-time employment, which I did. I was hired on as a secretary at a prestigious New York law firm, and much like you I worked my way up through promotions. I went to night school and took courses geared toward becoming a paralegal, so I'd at least have some kind of career to fall back on once my brother and sister were on their own."

The woman was as smart and determined as she was

beautiful and sexy. It was an amazing, intoxicating combination. "What's up with Casey and Lynn?"

Done with her meal, she set her fork on her plate and pushed it aside. "Despite the upheaval and emotional adjustments we all went through when our parents died, they turned out to be really great kids." She grinned, the love and devotion she harbored for her siblings evident in her expression and her green/gold eyes. "Lynn just finished her second year at Allegheny College in Pennsylvania, and Casey is working for a marketing firm in New York City. He just moved out on his own, which is why I decided finally to sell our parents' place. It's just too big for one person, and lonely, too, I have to admit." She ducked her head sheepishly at that admission.

He watched her take another long drink of the Cristal champagne, understanding the feeling of being lonely all too well. For as much as he loved his job and was surrounded by many great friends on a daily basis, his suite and the house he owned always felt so empty, too quiet, and devoid of the kind of warmth and emotion that exists when you live with someone you care about and love.

That's why he spent most of his time using the hotel suite, because when the solitude was too much for him to bear, and he felt closed in, he could always head down to the casino and mingle with the employees and guests. Surveillance was a twenty-four hour job in Vegas, and sometimes it was also his salvation—from himself, and those old, sweet memories starring the woman sitting across from him.

"What are you going to do now that you've sold the house you've lived in for the past eight years?" he asked, curious to know what she had in mind.

Finished with her second glass of champagne, she set her flute on the table and licked her bottom lip. "I have all of next week off, and as soon as I'm finished here, I'll be moving to the city where I'll be closer to work."

Finished with *him* and finished with their *marriage*. Her words were a stark reminder that their time together was nothing more than a temporary affair, which would eventually end with his signature on the annulment papers.

As the waiter cleared their dinner plates from the table, and Luke ordered a chocolate souffle to share for dessert, they continued with their light, superficial conversation. It didn't escape his notice that they were both careful not to bring up the past, the end to their relationship so many years ago, and the hurt and disillusion involved in their separation. But he knew the painful emotions were still there between them, just below the surface of the tentative bond they'd forged for the weekend.

They might be skirting all the real issues that had torn them apart as young lovers, but there was at least one thing they'd be able to deal with honestly—and that was their undeniable attraction to one another. And tonight, they'd do exactly that.

As soon as they walked into the suite and Luke stripped off his sports jacket then began loosening his tie, Rachel's stomach fluttered with butterflies. Not from anxiety or even nervousness, but rather from pure, unadulterated anticipation. Eight lonely years had passed since she'd been with this man, but her body yearned for his as if she'd never left him behind. After what had transpired in the Jacuzzi earlier, she wanted him with every fiber of her being. Since she wasn't about to leave Las Vegas for good this time with any regrets, that meant indulging in every sensual pleasure the next two nights had to offer.

He tossed his jacket and tie onto a chair in the living room, then silently extended his hand toward her, his eyes warm with promise. It was an invitation she accepted by placing her fingers in his palm and following him into the master bedroom. Once there, Luke turned on the lamp on the nightstand to give the room a soft, unobtrusive glow of light, then he took off his shoes and socks. When he turned toward her with a sexy, disarming smile that made her pulse quicken in her veins, she closed the short distance between them, slid her arms around his neck, and finally gave in to the urge to feel the damp heat of his mouth on hers.

The moment their lips met they parted in mutual accord, allowing her immediate access to the silken depths of his mouth. Tongues touched, tangled, merged, and that's all it took for her to kiss him with all the hunger and desire that had filled her starving soul.

A low growl rumbled deep in his throat, and his arms came around her, warm and strong and secure. His hands slid down her back, over her bottom, and pulled her hips hard against his. There was no mistaking the erection pressing insistently against her belly, or the tingling sensation and slick heat that settled between her thighs.

Suddenly desperate to touch and feel more of him, she tugged his shirt from the waistband of his pants and began unfastening each and every button, all the while indulging in seductive, teasing kisses. Eventually, the lightweight linen parted, enabling her to splay her hands on his bare chest.

His skin was hot, his nipples as firm as her own. Slowly, she dragged her palms down his lean torso, reveling in the warm, firm contours and toned muscles she encountered along the way. Her fingers skimmed across his taut belly before gradually making her way lower, until she finally held the most virile, masculine part of him in her palm.

She stroked the length of him through his trousers and felt him grow harder, thicker. She squeezed him gently, and with a deep, tortured groan he tore his mouth from hers and pulled her hand away from his burgeoning shaft.

Startled by the abrupt move, and certain she must have done something wrong, she glanced up at him questioningly.

A wry smile kicked up one corner of his sensual mouth. "As good as it feels having you touch me like that, we need to slow down or else this is going to be over before it even gets started . . . if you know what I mean."

Oh, she knew exactly what he meant, and it was a heady sensation to realize that she'd brought him to that breaking point.

Before she could kiss him again and resume a slower pace, he strolled across the room, settled himself in an armless, cushioned chair, and sprawled his legs out in front of him. He was sitting in a darkened part of the room, with his shirt hanging completely open so that she had a wonderful view of his bare, magnificent chest. With the shifting shadows casting across his features, along with his dark hair and glittering eyes, he reminded her of the bad boy who'd stolen her heart so long ago . . . and her virginity.

She was no longer a virgin, but a part of her realized that he had the ability to claim her heart once again. Even knowing this, she started toward him with the intention of giving herself over to him more than just physically, but he held up a hand to stop her.

"Stay right there, Rachel," he murmured huskily. "I want you to take off your dress for me while I watch."

She shivered, excited by this sexually demanding side to his personality, and decided to take full advantage of his request to seduce, tempt, and tease him. It was also the perfect opportunity to show him that she could be bold and brazen, assertive even, with him.

Reaching behind her, she easily, but oh-so-slowly, unzipped her dress. The sleeves glided down her arms, and with a sensual shimmy shake, the silky fabric glided down her curves, her legs, then pooled at her feet.

His hot gaze raked all the way down to her high heels, then back up in a lazy, visual caress that didn't miss a thing. "Very, very nice," he said appreciatively.

A rush of feminine power rippled through her, mingling with a potent dose of desire. "I'm glad you approve."

She was equally glad that she'd purchased the pretty lingerie today on a last minute whim—a black lace push-up bra, matching panties, and thigh-high stockings with a lace stretch band. Her undergarments were normally more efficient than frilly, but judging by the lust and need burning in Luke's eyes, the tantalizing ensemble had been worth every penny.

She continued, pulling the pins from her upswept hair until the curly strands tumbled around her shoulders and down her back. Then she propped one heeled foot on the bed, intending to take her shoes, then her stockings off in a sexy striptease.

"Leave everything else on," he ordered, surprising her once again with his request.

Straightening, she deliberately stroked her fingers across her bare, flat stomach, just to increase his internal temperature a few extra degrees. Then she licked her lips for good measure. "So, what would you like me to do now?"

A wicked grin eased across his mouth. "I want you to get down on your hands and knees and crawl over here to me."

She hesitated, at first not sure what prompted this latest command of his . . . until she realized that he was testing her, daring her to do something that might be just outside of her comfort zone. It was a challenge she wasn't about to refuse, since she intended to make this fantasy of his as erotic as possible.

Lowering herself to the plush carpeting, she began moving toward him on her hands and knees at a leisurely and seductive pace. She made the most of her suggestive position, arching her back so that her full breasts swayed forward provocatively and her hips undulated each time she advanced closer. By the time she came to a stop between his widespread legs, his breathing had deepened and he shifted restlessly in his chair.

She tipped her head coyly. "So, you like your women submissive these days, huh?"

"Not at all." He reached out and entwined a long strand of her curly hair around his finger and gave it a gentle tug. "I was just curious to see how far you were willing to go."

Grinning, she came up on her knees and skimmed her palms up his thighs, wishing he wasn't still wearing his trousers. But she'd remedy that problem soon enough. "So, are you satisfied?" she asked.

"Not quite," he replied wryly, the erection straining against the zipper of his pants making a very obvious point.

Her fingers brushed lightly over the masculine bulge, just enough to make him shudder before she unfastened the top button of his trousers. "Then you won't mind if I take over from here, will you?"

Again, he grasped her wrists, holding her off. "I already told you what will happen if you go there," he said meaningfully.

This time, she wasn't going to let him deter her from what she desired. "I just did what you asked, now it's your turn to let me do what *I* want." She leaned in close, so that his shaft was snuggled between the cleavage from her push-up bra. "And if it makes you feel better, I promise not to let you come. That is, if you think you can handle the challenge, and the pleasure."

He shook his head in amusement, and to her satisfaction he released her. "You are a very wicked woman."

And she had to admit that she liked the confident way that made her feel. "Just relax and enjoy yourself," she said, and lowered his zipper all the way down, which enabled her to reach into his briefs and release his solid erection and taut testicles.

She touched the sensitive head of his cock, then wrapped her hand around the stalk, measuring the impressive length with her fingers. "Umm, very, very nice," she purred, complimenting him in the same way he had her.

His low laughter turned into a raw groan when she stroked him all the way to the base, then back up to the plumb tip. He shook with restraint, and she allowed him a brief reprieve as she flattened her hands on his bare chest, then leaned in so she could explore other parts of his body with her lips and tongue.

Closing her eyes and letting other senses take over, she nuzzled his neck and inhaled deeply of his male scent, a dizzying combination of spice and musk, then trailed damp kisses down to his chest and the hard nubs she'd found with her thumbs. She laved first one nipple with her tongue, then the other, savoring the salty heat of his skin as she gradually made her way back down his torso. By the time she'd reached his shaft once again, his entire body was tense, and his need nearly tangible.

Gripping him tight in her hand, she used her tongue to taste the velvet head of his penis with a soft, swirling stroke that had him digging his heels into the carpet and a hissing sound escaping his throat. Emboldened by his response, she took him deeper, swallowing him inch by delicious, maddening inch, then added suction as she pulled all the way back up to the tip of his cock.

He swore beneath his breath, and when she glanced up at his face and saw the sensual anguish etching his features, she realized that he was right on the brink and using every ounce of control not to climax. To toy with him any longer would be nothing less than sheer torture.

"Stand up," he rasped, obviously not wanting to take the chance that she'd resume her lip service.

Without hesitation, she rose so that she was standing in front of him, still wearing her bra, panties, stockings, and heels. He looked his fill of her for a handful of seconds, then sat forward and hooked his fingers into the waistband of her barely-there underwear. He dragged them over her hips, shoved them down her thighs, and let them drop to the floor. Then he pulled her bra straps down her arms, until her breasts were freed from the lacy cups, her nipples already tight and aching for his fingers and mouth.

He didn't touch her just yet, and instead put his knees together and gave her a shameless smile that made everything in her quiver with awareness. "Come closer."

There was only one way to accomplish what he wanted, and that was to widen her stance so that her legs were straddling either side of his thighs. And that, of course, would leave her completely open and exposed to him, as he'd no doubt intended.

She did as he asked, which brought him up-close and personal with her breasts and stomach, and the most intimate part of her poised right over his rigid erection. The position was extremely erotic, and nothing like anything they'd done as teenagers. No, this was all about adult desires and playing risqué sexual games, and she had to admit that it was thrilling, exciting, and more arousing than her wildest fantasies had ever conjured.

He glanced up and met her gaze as he skimmed his hands up her smooth thighs, then over the curve of her bare bottom. His fingers traced the line of her spine to the middle of her back, where he flattened his palm and urged her upper body toward him. The sensitive peak of one breast brushed along his damp lips, and his tongue darted out to lick her nipple before he drew as much of her as he could into his warm, wet mouth. She gasped as his teeth scraped gently across the tip, moaned softly when he sucked her harder, stronger, and felt her legs threaten to buckle when his free hand dipped between her legs to explore her weeping, swollen sex.

With a low, mewling sound of pleasure, she braced her hands on his broad shoulders to steady herself, but he wasn't done making her burn. His thumb strummed her clit slowly and rhythmically as a long, strong forefinger slid deep, deep inside her and stroked. With his mouth latched onto her breast and his hand working the most exquisite magic elsewhere, she panted with the need to grasp the orgasm he deliberately kept just out of her reach. Every time she came close, he'd change the pace—from fast, deep, and greedy, to slow, lazy, and tender.

Desperate beyond belief, she fisted her fingers in his silky hair and tugged on his scalp. "Oh, God, Luke. Please let me come." She was begging and didn't care.

In his own good time, he released her breast and withdrew his fingers, which was the exact opposite of what she'd just pleaded for. She made a sound of protest.

"I want to be inside you when you come." He reached for a sealed condom on the dresser that she hadn't noticed was there until now, then glanced up at her, his eyes blazing with carnal lust and something more visceral.

Before she could analyze that latter emotion she'd witnessed so briefly, he was gripping her waist with his hands and pulling her down so that the head of his erection pressed insistently against her entrance. She was so ready for him, so slick and soft and hot, and he slipped inside her easily, until she was sitting completely astride his hard thighs and his thick shaft was impaled to the hilt.

She closed her eyes, sighed, and shivered decadently, enjoying the blissful moment. He felt so amazing filling her, being a part of her. So good and perfectly right. They were locked together so tightly it was difficult to tell where he ended and she began.

He spread his hands over her bare bottom and pulled her forward at the same time he thrust upward, grinding against her sex in a way that elicited a jolt of sensation that made her breath catch and her nerve endings zing. He grinned too arrogantly, and she countered his move, rocking and rolling her hips against his in an erotic lap dance that earned her a shudder and a groan from him.

Tension and need spiraled between them, and she undulated again, increasing the pressure and slick friction. He shuddered, wrapped one arm around her back, and tangled the fingers of his other hand in her hair, taking control. He pulled her head way back, forcing her to arch harder, deeper into him. Her breasts were crushed against his chest, her lower body at his every command, and she closed her eyes and surrendered to him and the pleasure coiling tighter and tighter within her. She felt his warm, damp lips on her throat, his hot breath, and when he gently bit the side of her neck, everything within her finally unraveled and came undone.

With a soft cry, she gave herself over to the pulsing orgasm surging through her, causing her inner muscles to clench tight around his shaft, over and over again.

"Rachel," he groaned raggedly, his own intense release making him shudder uncontrollably as he came right along with her.

With a trembling sigh, she collapsed against his chest and buried her face into the crook of his neck as he gently stroked his hands down her spine. They were both breathing hard from exertion, and beneath the hand she'd placed on his chest she could feel his heart beating in cadence with hers, so perfectly attuned, as if they'd never spent the past eight years apart.

Her throat grew tight, because for as wonderful as being with Luke was, she was forced to remind herself that her time with him was all a temporary situation. A weekend with Luke for his signature on the annulment papers—a proposition he'd issued and she'd accepted. An eventual end to any ties they had left to one another.

She never wanted anything less.

Six

If Luke thought hot sex with Rachel would get her out of his system, he'd been sorely mistaken. And Lord knew he'd tried his damnedest to accomplish that goal. During the course of the night he'd made love to her three times, and again this morning in the shower after breakfast—with each encounter more intense and passionate than the last. If anything, being with Rachel intimately had only increased his need and desire for her, and he'd never anticipated that unexpected turn of events.

Exhaling a quiet stream of breath, he glanced at the woman who had him tied up in knots inside. She was sitting in the passenger seat of his SUV as he drove them outside the city limits of Las Vegas, taking in all the changes since she'd left eight years ago. Her eyes widened with wonder at all the new casinos, hotels, and condominiums that had been built in her absence. Just before he pulled his gaze away from her profile, he caught sight of a small mark on the side of her neck, evidence of the love bite he'd given her last night. That quickly, that easily, arousal hummed through his veins and settled in his groin.

Obviously, there was no sating his body when it came to

this particular woman, and therein lay the problem, he realized with too much clarity. Because Rachel was entrenched more than just skin deep. And sex, no matter how erotic and great it was between them, wasn't going to expunge her from the part of him that mattered the most—his soul. No, he feared she was there to stay for the rest of his life. Always in his heart and dreams, but never completely his. And by this same time tomorrow, she'd be flying back to New York, signed annulment papers in hand.

Exiting the freeway, he made a left turn toward the house he hadn't seen in nearly a week, which wasn't uncommon for him since it was more convenient to stay at the hotel most nights. It was only because Rachel had asked to see his place that he was heading in that direction now—with very mixed feelings about sharing something so personal and private with her, especially considering he'd never brought another woman there. On one hand he wanted to show her all that he'd managed to accomplish over the years. Yet he knew his decision was going to cost him in the end, because there was no doubt in his mind that Rachel's presence would linger in his house long after she was gone.

He pulled into the circular drive of a large, two-story house. The custom-built, Spanish-style structure was situated on a private lot well away from his nearest neighbor, which was what had attracted him to the house: A good amount of land and a whole lot of privacy. Judging by the awe transforming Rachel's features, she was impressed with what she saw, and that was just the exterior.

They exited the car and collected the few bags of groceries he'd stopped to pick up on the way, since he knew there wasn't much in the house in the way of food. He figured they'd eat dinner there, and with that in mind he'd bought steaks to barbeque, potatoes, the makings for a salad, something for dessert, and drinks.

Once they deposited the groceries in the state-of-the-art

kitchen, Luke gave Rachel a tour of the house, which was open, airy, and efficiently designed. The place was over three thousand square feet of spacious rooms and living area, and it was kept spotless thanks to the housekeeper that came in once a week to clean while he was in the city.

"This place is amazing," Rachel said as they stood outside in the lushly landscaped backyard. She waved her hand from the house to the swimming pool, complete with rock formations and a waterfall. "I don't know why you'd stay at the hotel when you have such a beautiful home."

A beautiful home, yes, but there was too much that was lacking and missing. Like a wife and kids. Like chaos, love, and laughter echoing in the halls and filling the house with life and vibrant energy. Not that he cared to explain any of that to Rachel.

So, instead, he came up with a pleasant diversion from a conversation that had the potential of turning too emotional and revealing. "Wanna go for a swim?"

She laughed and shook her head, her eyes sparkling happily. "You didn't tell me to bring a swimsuit today."

"Who says you need one?" Already, he was imagining her naked—no big surprise there. "Ever been skinny-dipping?"

"Not in broad daylight." She ducked her head sheepishly. "Okay, make that never. Now you know how truly boring my life has been."

"Well, there's a first time for everything." He tipped her chin back up so that she was looking at him again, then flashed her a charming smile, intent on swaying her to be a little adventurous with him. "And since I don't have any neighbors close by, you don't have to worry about anyone spying on us."

She grinned, her eyes suddenly sparkling with a mischievous light. "Okay. Let's do it."

She kicked off her sandals and started unbuttoning the front of her cotton summer dress while he stripped off his shirt and shorts. Within minutes, they were diving into the crystal clear pool—a brisk, refreshing contrast to the dry, one hundred degree plus heat. Rachel came up for air laughing, obviously enjoying herself, the liberating, uninhibited feeling of being naked, and the exhilarating sensation of cool water caressing bare skin.

They frolicked in the pool, playing and splashing and chasing one another, with Luke copping a feel whenever the opportunity arose. They took breaks beneath the waterfall in the shade, where they kissed and teased and seduced one another. Awareness and need built between them, and when Rachel kicked off the edge of the pool to swim to the shallow end, Luke followed at a determined pace.

They broke the surface at the same time, and before she could escape him again, he wrapped his arms tight around her, trapping her in his embrace.

Grinning down at her, he bent his knees slightly, nestling his erection between her sleek thighs. "Gotcha," he murmured huskily.

Her eyes widened in feigned fright, but the arching of her lower body against his gave her away. "Now that you have me, what do you plan to do with me?"

He chuckled. "Do you really have to ask?"

She squealed in surprise as he swept her up in his arms and carried her out of the pool, then laid her down on a cushioned lounge chair on the covered patio. She was wet all over, her skin soft and glistening, her gaze filled with desire and anticipation.

Moving over her, he nudged her knees apart with his own and settled his hips against hers. The head of his erection slid through her slick folds, teasing him with the tantalizing promise of being inside her. Unable to wait any longer, he slid into her with a hard, deep thrust that wrenched groans of mutual satisfaction from both of them.

He dropped his mouth over hers for a long, erotic kiss,

and from that point on nothing else mattered except the sensual pleasure of making love to Rachel. The slow, lazy strokes inside her body, and the hot, slick friction that built to a shattering peak. But mostly, he cherished the sweet, unforgettable sound of his name on her lips as she came.

The afternoon passed much too quickly for Rachel's liking—mainly because for every hour that passed, it meant an hour less she had to spend with Luke. In less than twenty-four hours she'd be back in New York, and her time with Luke would be a distant memory. That dismal thought brought on a pang of sadness she knew would only increase as her flight out of Las Vegas neared.

Already feeling the loss, she snuggled closer to Luke's side, and he automatically tightened the arm he'd tucked around her waist. They were relaxing together on the large, comfortable sectional couch in his living room, unwinding after their day in the sun and their stomachs full from dinner. Her head rested on his shoulder and she'd entwined her legs with his as they listened to the soft, soothing jazz music playing from the stereo system in the oak wall unit across the room.

Closing her eyes, she sighed softly, reveling in Luke's warmth and strength. It had been so long since someone had just held her, and she was beginning to realize just how much she'd missed not having a man in her life the past eight years. Specifically, Luke, because every other man she'd briefly dated hadn't even come close to comparing to him, which was a big reason why she was still unattached. Her heart still belonged to Luke, and probably always would.

They hadn't spoken much about their past, but before she returned to New York and a future without Luke, there was one burning question she wanted, *needed*, an answer to. It took her a few extra quiet minutes to work up the nerve to ask.

"Luke . . . why didn't you try and contact me after I left for New York eight years ago?"

Beside her, she felt his entire body stiffen defensively. She'd known she was treading on a touchy, sensitive subject, but she'd just effectively put an end to their fun, affectionate day together. The mood turned decidedly dark and dismal.

"Your father made that pretty damn hard for me to do, Rachel," he replied gruffly.

The money, she thought, and a huge, painful lump formed in her throat. With their cozy respite shattered, she pushed to a sitting position. He released her without so much as a fighting attempt to make her understand, and for some reason she equated that to the easy, devastating way he'd let her go all those years ago.

Tension radiated off him, and she swallowed hard, hating the emotional walls that Luke had instantly erected around himself. But she was responsible for that change in him since she'd brought up the serious conversation, and she needed to see it through to the end.

"My father told me that he paid you off in exchange for you not contacting me," she said quietly.

A muscle in his cheek clenched and his dark gaze locked on hers. "Did you believe him?"

There was a harshness to his voice that made her shiver. Not because she feared him in any way, but rather she feared where this discussion was going to lead them both. "I believe he offered you money, yes," she admitted, knowing her father wouldn't hesitate to offer him a bribe. "But I never wanted to believe that you'd take it."

His lips twisted into an unpleasant smile. "But you *did* believe it."

She was guilty as charged, but not without a good reason. "I never heard from you, Luke. Not a phone call or even a letter." Her voice cracked with emotion and she managed, just barely, to keep her feelings in check. "Then the annulment papers came in the mail. When I saw your signature on the documents I knew that was the end to us and our marriage, and that you had no intentions of ever contacting me again."

He moved off the couch and paced across the room, his body seemingly vibrating with anger and animosity. When he was a good distance away, he turned around to face her again. "It wasn't money that kept me away, Rachel," he bit out vehemently. "I never took a cent from your father. *Ever.* What kept me away was the fact that your father issued a restraining order against me, forbidding me from calling or going anywhere near you."

She gasped, shocked by that revelation. "Oh, God, Luke. I never knew." But having lived with her controlling, manipulative father and knowing the lengths he would have gone to keep them separated, she didn't for a second doubt Luke's claim.

"As much as I loved you, it wouldn't have done either of us any good for me to end up in jail. I didn't need an arrest of any kind on my record." Then his eyes flashed with barely concealed resentment. "You could have contacted *me*, Rachel, but you never did that either, did you?" he said, making it very clear that he wasn't the only one to blame.

His uncensored words forced her to face those old insecurities and fears that had kept her from standing up to her father, to fight for what *she* wanted, and not what Randall Hudson had mapped out for her life. Unfortunately, her father never could have predicted that his death, and her mother's, would change everything about her life and future. Not that she ever regretted giving up law school to care for her brother and sister. Without question, she'd do it all over again.

But there had been many times when she'd wished that she had had the courage to defy her father, despite his threats and how scared she'd been. Instead, she'd left the fate of her marriage and future all up to Luke, and that had been so unfair and incredibly selfish on her part.

The shrill ring of Luke's cell phone cut through the tense silence that had descended over the room. She watched him shove his fingers through his hair, then walk over to the end table where he'd left the unit.

He flipped open the phone and answered the call in the middle of the second ring. "Kincaid here," he said in a brusque tone of voice.

Less than a minute later he snapped the unit closed again, his features drawn into a troubled frown. "I need to get back to the hotel. A group of guys are passing off counterfeit hundred-dollar bills, and security already has one of them in custody."

With that brief explanation, they gathered up their things, locked up the house, and were on their way back to the Mystic Casino. Luke spent the entire time on his cell phone talking to his security agents, leaving the two of them no chance to finish up their earlier discussion.

Then again, Rachel wasn't sure there was anything left to say.

Seven

It was well after midnight when Luke finally made his way back up to the suite, mentally exhausted from work yet still feeling the sharp emotional sting from his earlier conversation with Rachel. She hadn't known about the restraining order, but neither had she made any attempt to get in touch with him after moving to New York all those years ago. She'd just assumed the worst, without knowing all the facts. Without trusting in him and what they could have had together.

He told himself that it was all in the past, and while they could rehash what was right or wrong, they couldn't change what happened between them, or how their lives had changed as a result of the choices made. Besides, she hadn't come to Las Vegas to ask him for another chance. She'd arrived with a new set of annulment papers for him to sign that would dissolve any chance at a new relationship, or a fresh beginning for the two of them.

Sighing tiredly, he made his way to the master bedroom, knowing he'd give Rachel exactly what she'd come to Las Vegas for, just as she'd given him what he'd wanted: A weekend fling that hadn't even come close to getting her out of his mind or heart. But a bargain was a bargain, and that problem was his to deal with once she was gone. He'd survived the first time after she'd left him, and he knew he'd manage without her again, even though the pain of losing her twice was likely to devastate him all over again.

Quietly, he entered the bedroom and found Rachel sleeping soundly beneath the covers. She looked achingly beautiful, and his chest tightened with longing, because he couldn't help but think that this was where she belonged. In his bed and in his life.

As he began stripping off his clothes, she stirred, then gradually woke up. She sat up in bed, pushed her disheveled hair away from her eyes, and smiled drowsily at him.

"Sorry," he murmured as he toed off his shoes. "I didn't mean to wake you up."

"I'm glad you did," she replied huskily, and released the covers she'd been holding against her chest. The sheet dropped to her waist, revealing the fact that she was completely naked beneath. "I fell asleep trying to wait up for you."

Her invitation was unmistakable, and he wasn't about to refuse something he wanted so badly, *one more time*. His need for her was so strong and overwhelming; he didn't hesitate to take what she was so freely offering him.

Finished removing his clothes, he crawled his way up to Rachel from the foot of the bed. He shoved away the last of the covers, flattened his hand on her chest, and gently pushed her back onto the mattress. For a moment he just stared down at her, taking in the long, curly strands of hair flowing over the pillow beneath her head, the soft desire in her eyes, and the way her lips parted in anticipation.

Emotion welled inside him, along with a primitive hunger to claim and possess her. To take his time and make her irrevocably his, in every way possible, so that when she returned to New York she'd remember their time together and think about what could have been.

Moving downward, he splayed his hands on her knees and pushed her legs wider apart to accommodate the width of his shoulders as he settled in between. He trailed hot, damp, lingering kisses along the smooth skin of her inner thigh. She sighed blissfully, then gasped when he raked his teeth over that same spot. Finally, he reached her sex, and he kissed her there, too—long and slow and deep. His tongue dipped and swirled over and around her clit as he slid one finger, then two, inside her, heightening her pleasure but keeping what she ultimately wanted just out of reach.

She moaned, shuddered, and twisted her fingers in his hair as her hips moved beneath the onslaught of his mouth. With the relentless stroke of his tongue and the slick glide of his thumb over her delicate inner lips, he urged her higher, until she was sobbing and pleading with the need for release. In his own sweet time, when the teasing became too much for her to bear, he finally drove her over the edge and gave her the orgasm she craved.

While she recovered from such an explosive climax, he slowly, leisurely, worked his way back up the length of her body. He worshipped her with his hands and mouth, putting to memory every single thing about her that he could. Her lush, womanly curves and the baby soft feel of her flesh. Especially along her stomach, he thought, as he skimmed his lips over her belly and toward her trembling breasts. Then there was the delicious floral scent that clung to every inch of her skin and how her sensitive nipples puckered beneath the lazy lick of his tongue.

But it was the undisguised adoration he witnessed in her green/gold eyes that unraveled him the most, as he oh-so-slowly sank into her—a long, deep stroke that had her arching up to meet the thrust of his hips. It was the same exact way she used to look at him, and even now, eight years later, it still managed to make him feel as if he meant everything to her.

She reached up and brushed away the strands of hair that had fallen across his forehead, then framed his face in her hands. Their eyes met and held, and she whispered his name like a soft, reverent prayer before bringing his mouth down to hers for a deep, soulful kiss.

He moved inside her, in no great rush to reach completion. Tonight was all about making love to Rachel, and he let the pleasure between them build on a warm, lazy wave of satisfaction. When the end neared, she wrapped her legs around his hips, locked her ankles at the small of his back, and pulled him closer, tighter, against her.

He felt her climax first, her inner muscles clenching and squeezing his shaft as soft moans vibrated in the back of her throat. Only then did he give himself over to his own mindless release.

In the morning, before Rachel woke up, he slipped from the bed, took a shower in the other bathroom, then dressed for the day. He made a quick call to housekeeping with a request, and within five minutes a single, long-stemmed red rose was delivered to his suite—a reminder of sweeter, simpler times with Rachel. And he knew that she'd remember, too.

With one last look at the woman sleeping peacefully in his bed, he left the suite and headed down to the security offices to immerse himself in work, which had been his solace for the past eight years, and would no doubt be for the rest of his life.

There was no need for an awkward farewell scene between them. The signed annulment papers and single red rose he'd left for her on the dining room table said goodbye more eloquently than he ever could.

As soon as Rachel opened her eyes Sunday morning and realized she was alone, a cold hard knot of dread settled in her stomach. Deep in her gut, she knew that Luke was gone. She'd hoped after how incredible and emotional last night had been that there was a possibility things could be different between them this time around. That maybe they might even have a chance at a future together.

But if his absence from the suite wasn't enough to convince her that this was the end, then the note and the long-stemmed red rose he'd left for her on the dining room table clinched the deal. She touched the soft petals, recalling the single crimson rose he'd bought for her on the day they'd gotten married. It had been an indulgence he'd been barely able to afford at the time, which had made the flower one of the sweetest gifts she'd ever received.

Tightening the sash on her robe, she reached for the piece of stationery, her hand already trembling. With a sinking sense of trepidation, she read the words he'd written to her:

Rachel,
Thank you for a great weekend. I've signed the an-nulment papers and I've arranged for a car to pick you up to take you to the airport. Take care of yourself in New York.

Sincerely,
Luke

Devastated by the impersonal note, she let the piece of paper slip from her fingers and flutter back to the table. Pain sliced through her, and she wrapped her arms around her middle to keep herself from falling apart right then and there.

As much as she hurt deep inside, she couldn't be angry with Luke. He'd given her exactly what she'd come to Las Vegas for—and a whole lot more, she thought, remembering every nuance of their sensual weekend together. But she never imagined that she'd fall in love all over again with the man she'd married. But she had, and this time she knew there would be no getting over Luke Kincaid.

She touched the tips of her fingers to the new set of annulment papers he'd signed, and realized she had two choices she could make. She could be on the plane back to New York this afternoon, with every intention of filing the annulment papers, ending any chance at a relationship with Luke. Or, she could do what she should have done eight years ago and fight for what she wanted.

Her mother had left her with the incredible gift of a second chance with Luke for a reason, and this time Rachel didn't want to leave Las Vegas with any regrets or "what ifs" haunting her for the rest of her life. She didn't want to return to New York expecting Luke to contact her, either. She'd made that mistake once, and she refused to do it again.

She was no longer a scared young girl influenced by a controlling father who dictated her life and future. She was a grown woman who deserved to be happy, to take what should have been rightfully hers eight years ago.

And this time, she planned to do exactly that.

From the security cameras in his office, Luke watched Rachel cross the hotel lobby and knew that this was it. He'd already double-checked to make sure her car had arrived to take her to the airport, and in a few hours she'd be on her way back to New York. No matter how much he'd expected this outcome, the realization that he'd never see her again hit him like a solid punch to the stomach.

He exhaled a harsh stream of breath that did nothing to ease the tension within him, though he continued to keep his cameras trained on Rachel as she made her way up to the hotel's front desk. That struck him as odd, considering she didn't need to check out of a room since she'd stayed in his suite for the weekend.

She spoke to the clerk for a few minutes. Luke didn't have the ability to tap into conversations outside of the casino area, so he couldn't begin to guess at their discussion. Finally, the young man on the other side of the counter nodded, then picked up the hotel phone and dialed a number.

Luke jerked in his seat when the phone on his desk rang, startling him with the coincidence. Or was it?

Frowning, he picked up the receiver. "Security offices," he answered hesitantly. "Kincaid here."

"Mr. Kincaid," the hotel clerk replied professionally. "There's a woman at the front desk by the name of Rachel Hudson who would like to speak to you. She asked that you meet her in the lobby."

Luke couldn't believe it. He'd wanted to avoid a farewell conversation with her and had deliberately left the suite early this morning for that very reason. He thought about making up an excuse that he had an appointment or wasn't available, but he found that he just couldn't bring himself to do that to Rachel.

He shook his head and sighed in resignation. "I'll be right there."

Minutes later he was strolling through the lobby toward Rachel, who was biting on her lower lip as she watched him approach. She was wearing a pastel pink summer dress with sandals and she'd left her hair down in soft, loose curls. Her eyes were wide and filled with a vulnerable expectation that he didn't quite understand.

When he was finally standing in front of her, he shoved his hands into the front pockets of his trousers because the temptation to reach out and touch her, pull her into his arms and kiss her, was almost too great to resist.

"Hey, there," he said, and knew he sounded as awkward as he felt.

She tipped her head, and a tremulous smile lifted her lips. "You were going to just let me leave without saying good-bye?"

He couldn't miss the hurt lacing her voice, and an unexpected dose of guilt wrangled with his conscience. "It seemed easier that way." Put into words, his excuse sounded lame even to his own ears.

She shifted anxiously on her feet. "Well, there's some things I really need to say to you, so can we talk in the car?"

His jaw clenched, along with the fists he'd tucked into his pockets. He couldn't believe she honestly expected him to join her on the drive to the airport, when that's the sort of thing he'd been trying to avoid. But he knew he'd look like a certified jerk if he said no, so he sucked up his reluctance and gave her what she wanted.

"Sure," he said, and with his hand on the small of her back, he led her toward the private car waiting curbside for them.

Once they were enclosed in the backseat of the Town Car and their driver had pulled out onto Las Vegas Boulevard, Luke glanced at the woman beside him, anxious to get this conversation over with.

"What's on your mind, Rachel?" he prompted.

She drew a deep breath and met his gaze. "When I arrived in Vegas a few days ago, all I expected was your signature on the annulment papers."

"Which I gave you," he said gruffly.

"Yes, you did." Her hands twisted nervously in her lap, and she swallowed hard. "But I never expected to spend the weekend with you, and I never, ever, would have anticipated that I'd fall in love with you all over again. If I even stopped at all."

He held his breath, stunned by her admission, unable to utter a response.

But his lack of a reply didn't stop her from continuing with what she had to say. "My mother believed in us being together, to the point that she was willing to risk my father's anger when he found out what she had done with the annulment papers, had they lived that long. And that's what I should have done from the moment I married you. I should have believed in us, in you, and our marriage."

Hope tightened his chest. "Rachel . . ."

She quickly pressed her fingers over his lips, keeping him from saying anything more. "Don't say anything, Luke. Not just yet." The look in her eyes darkened with a desperate kind of emotion. "Last night when we made love I felt something between us, and it was more than just lust. What we shared was intimate and tender, with the potential of being something more than just a weekend affair."

Slowly, she let her fingers fall away from his mouth, but her eyes were damp and glistening as they searched his. "I know I might be asking for more than you're willing to give, but do you think that maybe you could give us a second chance and see where it might lead?"

"Yes," he said without hesitating.

Her eyes widened in surprise that he'd agreed so easily. "Yes?"

"*Yes,*" he said, and grinned because she looked so damn adorable. But there was one issue they still had to discuss. "What about your life in New York?"

"It was nothing more than an existence, Luke," she told him and placed her palm on his cheek. "Now that my brother and sister are on their own and the house is sold, there is nothing left for me there. Everything I want, everything I could ever need, is right here with you."

She smiled at him, the emotion in her gaze so sweet and

pure as she gave him what he desired most. Her heart. "I love you, Luke Kincaid."

"I love you, too, Rachel," he said, holding nothing back, because there was no longer any reason to. "I always have, and after this weekend with you, I know I always will."

"Oh, my God," she breathed in awe, then threw herself into his arms, hugging him as tight as she could. "I am the luckiest woman in the whole entire world!"

He laughed, then kissed her, slow and hot and deep. He felt the car roll to a stop and growled as he lifted his mouth from Rachel's, intending to tell the driver to take them back to his *house*, which was where Rachel belonged. Except they weren't at the airport terminal as he'd expected, but parked in front of the same chapel they'd gotten hitched at eight years ago.

He glanced curiously at Rachel.

"I was hoping you still loved me, too." She grinned impishly, her expression soft with adoration and a wealth of devotion. "Luke Kincaid, will you marry me? *Again?*"

He felt his own smile spread from ear to ear. "Oh, yeah," he said, already opening the door to the car, anxious to get this woman to the altar to start their future together. Because this time, she'd be his forever.

Tempt Me, Tease Me, Thrill Me

Tina Donahue

One

Until tonight Cait Campbell had no idea that a black tie dinner could be even more disturbing than an aerobics class filled with a bunch of leering guys.

Of course, as the junior member of Chicago's esteemed Maples & Weiss law firm, she was the sacrificial lamb for tonight's event, which included a charity auction. In no time at all, the leering guys in here would be bidding on one dinner date with her in order to raise funds for a good cause.

God. For this she had graduated first in her class at Harvard Law, then clerked for a powerful Federal judge and now worked eighty-hour weeks that left little time for dates she might actually want. Not that she had had any of those recently, or even wanted to after what she had once experienced with Sean.

Cait closed her eyes and ordered herself not to think about him again. Okay, okay, so she would think of him only until she was auctioned off. *You are hopeless.*

For the last four months she had not been able to forget the man. Memories of Sean Logan flooded Cait's mind before, during, and after just about everything she did with tonight being no exception. How could it be? This dinner was being held in the same ballroom that had hosted the reception for Cait's cousin Julia, who had married Sean's younger brother Tim.

It was at that wedding reception, or rather after it, that everything had changed for Cait.

Uh-uh. She really couldn't think of that now. She really shouldn't think of—

Too late. That night came back with such startling clarity, Cait's breathing picked up. That night, as the other wedding guests were gathering around the lavish buffet and open bars that had been set up in here, Cait recalled holding back. There hadn't been a thing on those tables that would have satisfied her hunger. She wanted Sean. It was a need that was soul deep and one Cait had not been able to deny.

Because of that, she had forced herself to wait. She watched the others eat and drink, then regarded the newlyweds, who were sharing a playful kiss that quickly turned breathless. Before they embarrassed themselves or anyone else, Julia smacked Tim's butt, then pushed him into the hall for some privacy. Cait glanced from that closing door to another bridesmaid who had cornered one of the young servers with her soft voice, sultry look and billowy gown.

Cait knew that whatever the girl was offering him wouldn't come close to what she would give to Sean.

Just a bit longer, she told herself, until she was aching inside. At last, she gave into her heart and glanced past the crowd.

Sean's gaze was already on her.

Liquid heat poured through Cait, making her feel deliciously weak and completely female.

It was a stunning desire she had never really known, and yet experienced the moment she first met Sean only days earlier during the wedding rehearsals. It was as if she had known this man all of her life.

His clean scent was welcome and familiar, his confident

bearing an unexpected comfort, while his masculinity—
wow—made all the other crud in life bearable.

Oh, he was something. Tall, with deliciously male features, dark hair that was silky and thick, and a build that
was lean yet muscular.

No way was anyone gonna mess with this man.

Even his pierced ear, a souvenir from his work as an undercover narcotics officer with the Chicago Police, made him
seem wild, like a pirate, and aroused Cait beyond reason.

As did his approach.

He moved through the crowd that night as if Cait were
his only reason for being.

How she adored that.

When he was finally so close that Cait could feel his heat,
Sean leaned down to her and asked, "Enjoying yourself?"

Her skin tingled. There was nothing like his rich voice
and luscious scent. Turning her face to his, all caution drifted
away. The only thing that mattered was tonight with him.
"Not yet," she murmured, "but I hope to."

Sean's eyes grew hooded as he took her hand, his firm
grip saying he had no intention of letting go.

This was a man who knew what he wanted. He was not
going to be denied.

Minutes later they were upstairs in Suite 854. What happened after that was deliciously wicked, achingly tender
and something Cait just couldn't think about again.

Her time with Sean was beautiful, but over. She had to
get real. Heavenly sex, stimulating conversations, shared
laughter, unyielding desire and a man who seemed to really
want her did not necessarily make for a lasting relationship.

Just look at her mom and dad. Twenty years they had
given each other and for what? Immediately after their own
divorce, they started marrying and divorcing just about
everyone else.

Those romances always started off good until the great

sex wore off, loyalties were broken and the nasty prenups kicked in. And that was an eventuality Cait couldn't face with Sean. From the get-go, she had wanted him too badly. To have him for a time, only to lose him in the future to another woman—uh-uh, no damned way. It was better to simply forget their one night, move on from that fantasy of Forever After and focus on the godawful date she was about to get.

Please, just make it go fast, Cait prayed, ignoring the persistent yearning in her heart as she looked around this table to her boss, his senior partner, and her colleague, Billy Price.

They were all staring at her.

Cait stopped stroking her champagne glass. Had she just spoken her thoughts of Sean aloud? "What?"

Walter Maples, the firm's founder, tapped the linen napkin against his aristocratic lips, which complemented his aquiline nose, silvery hair and pale-as-death skin.

The man was so purebred Cait was always surprised by his startling bluntness, which she knew was coming. *Come on,* she thought, feeling vaguely annoyed, *just spit it out.*

Walt made her wait as he folded his napkin. At last, he said, "You can resume breathing, Cait. We do understand how you feel."

Oh hell. What in the world had she said when she was thinking about Sean? Did these people actually know how his rich laughter stirred something deep within, and how her heart whimpered at the sight of him asleep, his dark hair tousled, his sensuous lips parted in a quiet sigh, his bristly cheeks betraying his utter masculin—

Will you just stop? "You do?"

"Of course. That's why Billy knows to get the ball rolling."

Cait looked at the man. He was thirty-one, the same as her, just as slender, and blushing at the sudden attention, which was no surprise. As much as Cait enjoyed a court battle, Billy had always preferred a behind-the-scenes, non-confrontational role.

Leaning toward him, she asked, "What ball are you planning to roll?"

The skin around Billy's receding hairline turned pink.

Walt answered for him. "The bidding on that dinner date with you."

Ah. She sighed.

That was not lost on Abbie Weiss, the firm's senior partner. "Well, we certainly don't want you standing up there looking like a fool."

As if Billy's bid could change all that? Resisting the urge to roll her eyes, Cait looked at the Princess of Darkness.

In her day, Abbie Weiss had probably been considered handsome, or spooky, what with her penetrating gaze and prominent features. It was her platinum pedigree, however, that got Walt all hot and bothered.

Go figure. Cait made her voice nice. "I certainly wouldn't want to disappoint you."

Walt leaned forward in his chair. "Then don't."

"Especially when it comes to getting that associate judgeship," Abbie said.

Walt put up his hands. "That possibility shouldn't even be considered. Not being appointed would make the firm look bad."

Abbie looked at him. "Everyone would think we made a mistake in bringing her on."

"Exactly." He frowned at Cait. "That has never happened with any other member of the firm. I would hope you don't want to be the first."

She stopped pressing her fingers against her temple and shook her head.

"See that," Walt said to Abbie. "She has no intention of screwing us."

Abbie's dark eyes grew even more intense as if she were as aroused by Walt's bluntness as he was by hers.

Cait wasn't about to consider what happened when the two of them got together.

Abbie tapped the table in front of her. "Doing well tonight will only help your candidacy."

Uh-huh. Cait bet none of the other judicial candidates had a section in their resumés about being auctioned off to the highest bidder.

"Now, you," Walt said, tapping Billy's cufflink with a dessert fork, "remember to start the bidding low. If we can get away with a thousand—"

"Or less," Abbie offered.

Surely they were joking or giving her a way out before she humiliated the firm. Slipping on her reading glasses, Cait scanned the program for tonight's event. As Walt and Abbie kept lowering the bid, she finally interrupted, "What you're proposing won't work. The bid has to be twenty-five hundred—at the very least."

Walt frowned. "By whose authority?"

Cait suspected the sponsors of this loony event. Lifting the program, she pointed out the obvious.

"It is tax deductible," Billy offered as he looked up from the icing that Walt's fork had left on his tux.

The man leaned back in his chair and pouted. "Keep it as close to the required bid as you can."

"There's no need to worry," Abbie said. "Once Billy makes the opening bid it'll be over."

Cait arched one slender brow. Nothing like these two to make her feel attractive and in demand.

Realistically, Billy didn't have much competition tonight. Many of the guys here—and there were attorneys, civic leaders, industrialists, and physicians—were too old to bid on a dinner they wouldn't be able to digest, while the others were currently involved in so many divorces, remarriages and extramarital affairs, their dance cards were already full.

Just like mom and dad's.

They had been divorced a scant twelve years, but already Cait's father had remarried three times, her mom twice and there seemed to be no end to their lunacy. The older they got, the younger their spouses and lovers.

Cait wouldn't have been surprised if her mother was currently dating one of the male servers in this room since she owned the Livingston on the Lake along with most of the other luxury hotels in Chicago. It was how Cait's parents had met. Her dad owned the real estate beneath this building, at least until after they split.

That divorce had been so nasty it was tailor-made for a Donald Trump reality show, and it was definitely something Cait would avoid in her own life.

Sighing, she looked at Billy as he gently tapped her wrist. "What?"

He glanced at Walt and Abbie who were whispering as they plotted their next rendezvous or coup. Turning back to Cait, he kept his voice low. "The MC's on the stage. It's show time."

Cait crossed her eyes. It got a smile out of Billy and went completely unnoticed by Abbie and Walt. They kept up that whisperfest throughout the first thirty minutes of this auction in which an Internet mogul, a female surgeon, and a male real estate developer looked like deer caught in headlights as they faced this less-than-generous crowd.

Cait added up the bids thus far and could see that the sponsors weren't anywhere near their targeted—

Her thoughts paused; her head snapped up as the spotlight suddenly swung to her.

Eww. She squinted.

Walt whispered, "Smile!"

Cait started to, until the MC introduced her as Carmen, not Caitlin, Campbell.

Walt whispered during the scant applause, "Take off those glasses."

"Can she see without them?" Abbie asked Walt, then turned to Cait. "Can you see without them?"

"I only use them for read—"

"Then take them off!" Abbie ordered.

"Do us proud," Walt warned.

Billy patted her arm. "Break a leg."

Abbie pressed her fingers to the inside corners of her eyes as if she expected Cait would.

I wish. Cait figured a few weeks in traction might be kind of nice after working with these two. Removing her glasses, she stood, then began the long trek toward the stage with all the grace she had learned in those dumb social deportment classes that taught little girls how to behave like Stepford Wives.

As she eased past tables, Cait's beaded gown whispered around her, twinkling beneath the enormous chandeliers and that spotlight.

There were a few wolf whistles with one being interrupted by a hacking cough. Cait guessed that belonged to the elderly circuit judge who was expected to appoint her to the bench. That is, if she did well tonight.

Right. The moment she reached the stage, Cait turned and faced this crowd with the same cockiness she used when squaring off against adversaries in court.

Some of the guys must have liked that because those wolf whistles were suddenly prolonged.

The MC grinned so hard it had to hurt. "Now, now," he said, flapping his hands, "let's settle down." When the wolf whistles were replaced by that same hacking cough, he leaned toward the microphone and read from his cue cards. "Ms.

Campbell comes to us from the law firm of Maples and Winters and—"

"That is *Weiss,* not Winters!" Abbie called out.

The MC squinted as he looked into the crowd, then glanced at his cue cards. "Oh yes," he said, "Weiss and Maples. So sorry, Ms. Maples," he called out to Ms. Weiss.

Cait exchanged a look with Billy, then held back a sigh as the MC went into a bio of Carmen Campbell that included everything but her age and measurements.

At last an older man shouted, "Can we just get on with it?"

As the crowd laughed and the MC opened the bidding, Cait's gaze lifted to one of the chandeliers. It was a monstrous sucker that sparkled nearly as much as the engagement ring her father had given to his latest—

"Here!" Billy suddenly shouted. "I bid twenty-five hundred dollars!"

Bless you. Cait lowered her gaze, delicately lifted the skirt of her gown and got ready to get the hell off the stage.

"Three thousand," a male voice called out.

The gown slipped through her fingers. A moment later, Cait's gaze slowly lifted even as her heart paused. She warned herself not to look into the audience. If she did, there would be no turning back.

It can't be his voice. That's just not possi–

"Thirty-five hundred," another man called out.

Cait looked at Billy, who was glancing in the direction of that last voice. When she looked, a middle-aged man wiggled his fingers at her.

Taking a cautious step back, Cait swung her head in Billy's direction. He had to bid again no matter what Walt or the Princess of Darkness said. Billy had to win this date with her.

Come on, damn you, bid!

Billy looked from her to Walt who was finishing his dessert as if this had nothing to do with him. His dough was safe.

"We have thirty-five hundred!" the MC said with the same enthusiasm reserved for a million dollar bid. "Going once, going—"

"Four thousand," that first male voice called out.

Cait's mouth went dry, while her heart raced. Four months ago she told herself she would never forget that voice, nor a touch that caressed her soul and a scent that so effortlessly aroused. Four months ago, she knew she would not allow herself to see him again.

This can't be happening.

Taking a deep, steadying breath, Cait's gaze finally swept the crowd. She glanced at faces she knew and those she did not. She saw bored expressions and questioning gazes. She moved past most quickly . . .

And finally lingered on one.

Sean.

Cait's lips parted in a quiet sigh as his gaze touched hers. In that moment everything else, even the last four months, faded away. Her gaze hungered over him as it had that night, touching his eyes, his hair, his mouth—*oh, his mouth*. It welcomed, it pleasured, it comforted, and healed all the hurt Cait had ever felt, all the loneliness she had endured.

How she had missed him.

Without thinking or pause, Cait stepped forward recalling the last time they were in this room. Then, Sean's hand on hers had sealed the events of the night. Then, his breath had whispered against her cheek, his gaze had demanded and she had willingly followed. His effect on her was that great.

Her need for him was that foolish.

Getting involved with a man who might someday leave her wasn't what Cait was looking for. She wanted forever, which didn't exist. Hadn't her parents' many marriages taught her that?

Better to work eighty-hour weeks and occasionally get auctioned off at stupid events like this than to risk her heart.

Is that why he was here? Is that why he was bidding on her?

Oh, Sean. From the moment they first met, he had captured her soul, and by God Cait wasn't going to risk any more of herself.

Having him, then losing him would simply kill her.

Didn't he know that? Didn't he care? What was the matter with him?

He smiled.

Cait got so quickly dizzy, she lowered her head and closed her eyes.

That was hardly the reaction Sean hoped for. Holy shit, was she going to faint? He was about to leave his chair to go to her, when Cait lifted her head and looked across the room to that balding young guy she had been sitting with.

As they exchanged loaded gazes that had everything to do with him, Sean arched one dark brow. *Do whatever you want,* he thought, *say whatever you want. You are not putting me off this time, Cait.*

Not after what they had shared. Not after seeing her again tonight.

Jesus, she looked amazing. Her dark brown hair was longer than Sean recalled and fell in thick, soft waves around her delicate face to her narrow shoulders. They were bared except for really tiny straps that held up her gown.

Sean had never seen a dress like that. It sparkled wildly around her soft curves and hugged her like skin.

His cock continued to thicken; his breath caught as Cait shifted from one foot to the other. That small movement allowed her left leg to peek through the gown's long side slit.

Sean's gaze rode that satiny flesh, her flat belly, narrow waist, and the swell of her full breasts that were so creamy next to the gown's honeyed color. It matched her eyes. They seemed golden beneath dark lashes and had once given away her desire with a gaze that was willingly vulnerable . . . opened to him, adoring him.

He wanted that again. For four long months Sean had thought of little else.

He had tasted this woman straight to her core and by God, if it took everything he owned he was going to have all of it a—

"Well, it appears we have four thousand!" the MC gushed. "Do I hear—"

"Forty-five hundred!" that balding young guy said.

Sean turned in his chair and looked at him.

The guy's hands were tented; his bony forefingers tap, tap, tapped against each other.

Sean's jaw clenched. He frowned.

That tapping stopped and the guy's gaze zipped to Cait.

"Five thousand," Sean said.

"Fifty-five hundred!" another man in the audience said.

Cait's heart continued to race. Had everyone in here lost their minds?

"Six," Sean said.

Cait moistened her lips.

His gaze lowered to her mouth.

She pulled in her tongue and glanced at Billy as he said, "Sixty-five hundred!"

Walt stared as if Billy had gone seriously nuts.

"Eight," Sean said.

Oh my God, Cait thought. The room started to spin as the bidding got faster and Sean kept going higher. *What is he doing? It's too damned much!* The man wasn't wealthy; he was a detective with the Chicago police. He couldn't possibly have that much money to throw around. She had to tell him that. She had to stop this.

Lifting the edge of her gown, Cait left the stage.

"Miss Campbell!" the MC immediately called out. "Where are you going? We're not finished here. Miss Campbell!"

Around her, the crowd grew very quiet.

As she moved toward Sean's table, Cait felt the spotlight's heat on her shoulders.

Billy called her name. There were sudden whispers and murmurs. None of it mattered. There was no stopping Cait now.

As she negotiated the path around that last table, her gaze lifted and met Sean's. He seemed torn between surprise and pleasure.

Pleasure quickly won out. As Sean pushed to his feet, those murmurs died down. Even the MC finally shut up. At last, quiet surrounded Cait and Sean until all she heard was the rush of blood in her ears from the wild pounding of her heart. It had been four long months since she had been this near to him and it was an effort to contain her excitement.

In the glare of the spotlight, Cait saw the tiny depression in the lobe of Sean's left ear where he had once worn a diamond stud during a narcotics bust. She wanted him to put that damned stud back in. She wanted him to look like a pirate.

God, he was so beautiful.

Already, there was that shadow of beard on his upper lip, cheeks and firm jaw. Cait warned herself not to touch it, or to notice how his blue eyes had already grown darker with need, or to consider the wave of desire that continued to course through her until she was quickly breathless.

I've missed you, her heart whispered, even as her mind warned, *don't do this.*

Sean must have read that on her face as he seemed briefly uncertain, and then he looked down.

When Cait lowered her gaze she was surprised to see that her hand was resting on the sleeve of his tuxedo jacket as if it belonged there.

Before she could take back her hand, he rested his own on top.

Cait swallowed. Her gaze lifted as he gently squeezed her fingers.

It was a small touch, but one Sean knew brought all of the memories back. He saw her gaze turned inward to that moment, months before, when he had taken her hand, leading her from this ballroom to the elevator.

The second those doors had closed, Cait moved into him so quickly that Sean had been pressed against the mirrored wall. Before he could show his surprise, her mouth had been on his, while her hands . . .

Even thinking about that now got him too damned excited. After Cait got through with him on that elevator, Sean didn't even recall making it down the hall to their suite or those first few seconds inside. It was a blur of pleasure until they were both finally nude, flesh to flesh, and he buried his hardened cock within her velvety warmth.

That night had been like nothing else Sean had experienced in his thirty-three years, and it wasn't only the lovemaking, it was everything . . . their weary laughter afterward, their sleepy conversation, the pillow talk, the teasing, and an intimacy that had stolen all thought.

There had been no other women in his life since that night, because none could come close to what Cait had to offer. She was the one Sean wanted, and he intended to be with her for a very long time, starting tonight. "Hi."

Her delicate nostrils flared ever so slightly, while her lips parted in a quiet sigh.

"Ah, excuse me," the MC suddenly said into the microphone, "but we really need to finalize this bid. Now, the last amount we had was—"

"No!" Cait suddenly said to the MC, then turned back to Sean. She looked at him for a long moment, then spoke in an achingly soft voice. "Hi."

He smiled.

At just that moment, the balding young guy suddenly upped the bid again.

To hell with that. Sean called out his newest bid.

Cait cried, "What are you doing?"

"Winning you," he said. Wasn't that obvious?

She gave him a frown, then shot it to the balding young guy and finally the MC who was asking for even more bids.

"Okay, that's it!" Cait said. "Everyone just shut up!" She tried to take back her hand.

Not a chance. Sean gently increased his grip, not letting her go. Not again. Not ever.

She gave him a withering look that he responded to with a smile. Cait's gaze went all blurry again, while her voice got really soft. "Noooo."

Aw baby, don't say that.

"Yo Carmen," a young woman suddenly said to Cait, "if you don't want the guy, I do!"

A female chorus of "Me, too!" quickly followed.

Cait's eyes narrowed. She pulled her hand from beneath Sean's and stepped back.

He followed.

She looked torn between wanting him and whatever the hell else was going through her mind, then continued to step back.

Sean still followed. If need be, he'd track her to the ends of the earth.

She finally backed up into an older man. "Whoa, careful," he said.

Cait gave him a look as she sidled away.

Sean held back a sigh, then figured he better start using reason and the same easy tone he always employed in hostage situations. "There's no need to be upset."

Cait's gaze slid to that young woman who had said she wanted him. "Oh, I'm not."

Uh-huh. There wasn't a bit of softness in her tone now. "We can talk about—"

"No, we can't."

"Well, not here, but we could—"

"No, we—"

"Just let me finish," Sean said, his voice nice as all get out and patient as hell as he continued to follow, "we could go outside and—"

"No, we can't."

He held back another sigh. "It's just outside, Cait."

"I know what's outside and upstairs, so—"

"In the hall, then. We could—"

"No, we can't."

Damn. "Will you just stop?"

She did not.

As the MC tried to finalize the bid and that balding young guy called her name again and again, Cait turned and quickly left the ballroom.

Two

The moment Cait was in the hall she looked over both shoulders, not certain where to go. At last she moved to the opposite wall, pressed her forehead against it, breathed hard, and kicked the molding.

A young male server stopped pushing his cart. "Hey!" He sounded truly offended, as if his wall had been hurt, not the side of her foot—and her heart.

Cait frowned over her shoulder at him.

"Do that again," he warned, "and I'll—"

"Don't even go there," she warned. "My mother owns this place." Cait swung her arm to that super-sized portrait of Lydia Livingston, aka Mom, draped in jewels and silk.

The server's expression said *yeah, sure.*

Damn. "It's not your wall, all right? It's going to be mine, and do you know why?" Cait continued before he could say. "She kept this hotel in the divorce. It was in the prenup. That's love, huh? Putting down what you're going to get when it's over, like that matters. If it's going to be over, why the hell should you even bother?"

"Hey, lady, I just work here."

"Good." Cait went to him. "I need a room. Which one's empty?"

"Empty?" His gaze darted from her to Lydia's portrait as if to compare features.

At just that moment, the door to the ballroom started to open.

"Never mind." Cait hurried past the kid down the hall to the Michigan Room that was reserved for brides and their wedding parties.

Four months earlier, her cousin Julia had used this room. Tonight some other poor girl—who would eventually get her heart broken—had used it to dress for a wedding or a reception or whatever.

There were street clothes strewn about and cosmetic cases opened, but for the moment this space was empty of hopeful females.

Slipping inside, Cait leaned against one of the brocaded sofas, lowered her head and breathed hard.

We can talk, he had said.

Not a chance. Cait knew she couldn't risk that. The sound of his voice thrilled her far too much. No matter what Sean said during that talk, she'd probably end up believing it, then regretting it.

A future with him, no matter how delightful that sounded, had some serious drawbacks, which Cait had witnessed first-hand tonight.

Yo, Carmen, that overly made up and extremely rude young woman had said, *if you don't want the guy, I do!*

Well, duh. What woman wouldn't want a man like Sean? And that, of course, was the problem. For the rest of his days Sean was going to have women throwing themselves at him, and no guy, no matter how honorable he was or how much he thought he loved his wife, could endlessly re-sist that temptation.

Cait had seen it with her parents.

Her dad, a strikingly handsome man, had once adored Cait's mom. They giggled and hugged like lunatics during her childhood, which had always made her gag.

By the time Cait reached her early teens that adoration had grown to a comfortable respect, the kind parents should have since they were far too old to even think about sex.

How wrong that assumption had been. During college, Cait was floored by the news of the divorce and those tabloid accounts of her father's past affairs. When her mom decided to catch up with her own stable of lovers, Cait knew that Forever After was a stupid myth perpetrated by romance writers on a gullible female public.

But not her. No way. Her tastes ran to True Crime, the gorier the better, so she was never going to fall for—

Her thoughts paused; she looked up as the door to this room opened.

Before anyone else gave her a hard time, Cait growled, "My mother owns this place, and I was only—"

"Hey, it's okay." Billy stuck his head around the door. "It's only me."

She sagged against the side of the sofa.

Billy slipped inside and stared at the sports bra draped over the back of a chair. "Should we be in here?"

Cait's gaze slid to him.

"You okay?" he asked.

She arched one brow.

"Hey, I tried my best." He went to her. "Walt kept telling me to shut up and Abbie kept trying to kick me under the table, but she got Walt instead, which at least shut him up."

Cait laughed.

"You sure you're okay?"

Hell no, she wasn't okay. Her laughter had already turned to ragged sighs. "What happened in there after I left?"

"Well," Billy said, then paused so long that Cait lowered her head and breathed hard.

"Nothing happened, really," he finally explained. "Everyone's cool with what you did. In fact, Abbie said that the way you told all of us to shut up showed real authority; the kind a judge would use."

"In a movie of the week or real life?"

"Really, Cait, everything's cool. Walt said you have that judgeship sewn up, because of the bidding. He said he never saw anything like—what?" Billy interrupted himself as Cait lifted her head and stared at him.

Her mouth was so dry she had to lick her lips to get them to move. "What was the final bid?"

Billy licked his lips before he told her.

Oh my God. Cait lowered her head again.

Billy's voice was cautious. "Although it's unprecedented, it is for a good cause, not to mention tax deductible."

Cait covered her face with her hand and asked the question that just had to be asked. "Who made the winning bid?"

Before Billy could answer, the door to this room opened again.

"Just give us a minute, okay?" Cait said.

"'Fraid not," Sean said, his voice much calmer than hers, "I've waited long enough."

Cait's heart paused. Lowering her hand, she turned her head to look at him. God, he was gorgeous and wearing an expression that was all cop. No way was Sean leaving this room until he was good and ready, and Cait could see he wasn't anywhere near that.

He flicked his gaze at Billy. "You're leaving. Now."

The younger man frowned. "I am not. Just because you made the winning bid doesn't mean—"

"Oh yes, it does." Sean spoke to Cait. "We need to talk."

She could barely breathe. He was carrying a single, long-stemmed red rose, the mark of a winner at tonight's event.

Despite that and what Billy had just blurted, Cait asked the obvious, "You made the winning bid?"

"That's right." His voice got husky. "Now, you're all mine."

"That is it," Billy said. "You need to leave." He pointed to the door with more authority than his physical presence allowed. He was a head shorter than Sean, which made Billy as tall as Cait, and to her way of thinking Sean had at least eighty pounds on the guy.

Before she could point that out, Billy plowed ahead. "This is a private conversation."

"Uh-huh," Sean said. "That's why you're going to leave." Billy frowned. "Excuse me?"

"That would be up to Cait." His gaze was still on her.

"Cait?" Billy asked.

As they both waited for her response—as if she could actually talk at a time like this—the door to this room opened again.

A young woman in a pink bridesmaid's gown briefly paused. Glancing at the door plaque to see if she was in the wrong place, she then looked at the police shield Sean was holding up.

"You're a cop?" she asked.

"That's right. You'll have to leave."

Cait noticed she didn't. The girl's gaze went from that shield to his naked ring finger.

"Would you like my name and phone number?" she asked.

"I'd like you to leave."

She looked disappointed, before noticing Cait and Billy. With her gaze still on them, she asked Sean, "Has something happened in here?"

"Not yet," he said, gesturing her outside.

Once the door was closed, Sean leaned against it, tapping that single red rose against his leg as he looked at Cait.

Despite her flushed cheeks, her voice remained on the cool side. "Not yet?"

Well, no. Not with her way over there and him way over here and Buddy Boy chaperoning this whole mess. "You don't approve of the way I handled that?"

Cait's eyes narrowed slightly, though her mouth was starting to turn up in a smile. "It worked."

"Then I'm right."

"About getting rid of that girl?"

"About everything."

"I didn't say that."

"You will." He was going to make certain of it.

Those delicate nostrils were flaring again. "Pulling rank?" she asked.

Now, he smiled. The last time she had asked that was the one and only night they made love. Then, Cait had insisted on stripping him bare—making him wait for her—making him want her until Sean thought he'd go fucking nuts.

Each time he had reached for her, each time he told her that he wanted her *now,* she had murmured, "Pulling rank?"

She hadn't given him a chance.

The moment she had put his gun safely to the side and then had his trousers and briefs puddled around his ankles, she had knelt before him, taking his stiffened cock in her palm with such reverence—with such love—it had stolen Sean's breath.

After that, breathing wasn't even an option as Cait ran her sweet little tongue up and down his length, while cupping his tightened balls in her other hand. Faster than Sean thought possible, and certainly faster than he wanted, he was hers. "Only if you let me," he said.

Her eyes sparkled.

Buddy Boy cleared his throat. "Cait, do you know this man?"

"You're kidding, right?" Sean turned to the guy. "So, who are you?"

He frowned to Sean's tone, but did take a cautious step back. "Billy Price. Cait and I are colleagues. So, who exactly are you?"

"Sean Logan," Cait answered before he could and seemed to be waiting for Billy's response. When it didn't come immediately, she frowned. "Surely you've heard of him."

Billy looked confused, then worried. "He's one of our clients?"

"God no." Her frown deepened. "He's a detective with the Chicago police. I can't believe you haven't heard of him."

Billy looked at Sean. "You're in some kind of trouble with the—"

"No!" Cait interrupted and talked fast. "He was recently cited for the Arlington standoff. It was all over the news. Where were you?" Before Billy could answer that accusation, she continued, "Sean saved two lives that day. Prior to that he worked in the gang unit and narcotics. There was the Rogan bust and the Hayworth affair and—"

As Cait went on and on, Sean's eyes continued to widen. Damn, he had forgotten about most of that stuff. He wasn't certain he had ever had as many details about it as she seemed to. At last, he interrupted, "Who told you all that?" He pushed away from the door. "Have you been talking to Tim?"

Cait hesitated before meeting his gaze. "Your brother was the one who got you into tonight's event, correct?"

Well, the fact that Tim was an attorney with a couple of free tickets certainly helped, not that Sean was about to admit to that. "Tonight was open to the public, and that's a good thing since I could hardly wait for you to invite me, correct?"

Cait's face flushed.

Sean moved closer. "You've been following my career."

Hell, she had a photographic memory when it came to his career. "Why?"

Her color deepened as she regarded him. At last, she glanced at Billy.

He looked at her expectantly. Cait frowned. Billy blushed like a virgin, lifted his hands in surrender and left the room, leaving her alone with Sean.

It was a moment before Cait could look at him. When she did, her heart whimpered. She wanted him so badly she could barely speak. "Why are you doing this?"

Sean crossed the room to her. "Talking to you?" His voice was all innocence.

She arched one brow. He arched one right back.

Damn you, Sean Logan. Cait lowered her head so he couldn't see her smile. "You're doing this because I rejected you, aren't—"

"Excuse me?"

Cait looked up. She took a step back.

Sean followed.

Hmmm. "You're just not used to it." She stepped back again.

He continued to follow. "Used to what?"

Cait moved back again, this time circling the sofa so it would be between them. "Being rejected."

"Just a minute, sweetheart, you ran out on me, you hardly rejected me. As I recall, when we were on that elevator going up to our room, you were the one who stopped it. Several times, in fact." He went around the sofa to her. "I had no idea that such a small woman could overpower me and so easily, too. Not that I'm complaining," he interrupted. "Hell, I didn't even mind the fact that you tore several buttons from my shirt to get it off of—"

"Yeah, yeah, yeah," she interrupted, "I know. I was there, remember?"

Sean grinned. "Believe me, that is one night I will never

forget." He lifted the rose, then drew its dewy head across the base of her throat as he murmured, "How about you?"

She was having trouble getting through a full day without thinking of that and him, while that rose was driving her over the edge. Stepping back, she said, "And that's why you're here tonight, making such a ridiculous bid."

"Whoa." Sean lowered the flower. "A bid for you is not ridiculous. And that much money is never—"

"Don't I know. Do you even have that much?"

He frowned. "I'm not a man who promises something I can't deliver, Cait."

She paused to his tone and the look in his eyes. There was strength and hurt. When she spoke again, her voice was contrite. "I know."

Just like that the hurt vanished and his gaze softened.

Cait held back a sigh. It was just so easy for men. They lived in the moment and simply hoped everything would be all right. Broken hearts were something they figured only happened to women.

But not this one.

"Sean, why would you bid on me at all?"

"Well, actually, I thought I was bidding on Carmen Campbell."

She laughed.

"But I really wanted you," he said.

Her laughter paused.

He moved closer. "You never returned my call."

His comment was so unexpected, not to mention vulnerable, Cait didn't know what to say. For the first time she actually considered what courage it took for him to do this. Despite Sean's great looks and obvious success with women, he had put his ego on the line tonight and months before, after their night together.

There hadn't been only one call that she hadn't returned, there had been several.

When his calls finally stopped, she had never felt lonelier.

"You left that night while I was still in our bed, Cait. You never gave me a good reason why you would do such a thing."

"Sean, you—"

The door behind her suddenly opened and yet another bridesmaid was about to come inside.

"Hold it right there." Cait went to that young woman. "You'll have to leave."

Unlike that last bridesmaid who had been fairly docile, this one frowned. "Says who?"

Cait pointed to Sean. "He's a detective. I'm an attorney. And we are very busy."

"Yeah, I can see that."

Cait looked over her shoulder at Sean. His long fingers were stroking that velvety rose as he studied her butt.

"My mother owns this place," Cait informed the young woman. "Go to the desk and tell them that Caitlin Campbell has authorized an all-expense paid weekend in the Campbell Suite for you and a guest of your choice."

"Yeah, right."

"Do you want that weekend or not?"

"I want you out of here. I'm going to the desk and having you and him arrested."

"You do that." Cait swung the door closed on her, then looked over her shoulder at Sean.

A moment passed before his gaze lifted from her butt to her eyes. "Go on," he said, then smiled, "you have my full attention."

Cait's gaze fell to his mouth, while a wave of tenderness hit so hard she nearly moaned. She liked seeing him like this, little-boy mischievous. She needed that and didn't want to consider why. "Where were we?"

"Looking for a logical reason why you left our room so abruptly that night."

Cait went to him. "You know why."

"I know what you said after I woke up and saw you getting dressed. You don't want to get involved, because it'd only end up badly."

That didn't begin to describe what she would face if she allowed herself to fall even more deeply in love with this man.

"How can you be so sure?" he asked.

"History."

"Okay. Whose? Yours, mine, ours, the world's?"

"Don't tell me I'm the first woman you've gotten involved with so quickly."

Sean didn't admit to anything at all. He took a step back.

Uh-huh. Cait finally had him, and this time she followed.

Sean arched one dark brow. "You wanted me to be a virgin?"

"Were you ever a—"

"No," he interrupted, then quickly added, "I've never gotten involved so quickly with anyone as I did with you."

Cait's eyes widened in surprise, before they narrowed. "Not even with another bridesmaid when your cousin Dylan got married?"

"He eloped."

She wasn't about to comment on that.

Sean worked his mouth so he wouldn't smile. "What's this really about? Is it because I'm a cop?"

"God no." Cait actually liked the way he was commanding with others and yet achingly tender with her. He seemed dangerous and wild—a true bad boy, but also a man of integrity with rock solid principles.

She bet that cheating wouldn't come easily to him. Oh no. First, he'd consider divorce, and even during those proceedings he would be honorable, and no way could she live through that.

Simply leaving him that night had been impossibly hard,

while watching him sleep was a pleasure Cait would hold in her heart for a very long time. Despite his bristly cheeks, heavily furred chest and that thatch of dark hair above his wonderful penis, he had seemed so much like a little boy. Content and peaceful, without a care in the world.

Their son, if they were ever to have one—which they would not—would look like that all grown up.

She sighed.

"You're sure?" he asked.

Cait looked at him. "About what?"

"That this isn't about my being a cop."

She shook her head. "I told you, no. Besides, you're not just a cop, you're a highly decorated detective, and," she added when he smiled, "very foolish with your money."

He sobered. "To hell with that. I've missed you, Cait."

Her face flushed, but she didn't comment.

She didn't have to. Sean saw the need in her eyes and what he sensed was the beginning of love. She might be able to fool herself, but she was never going to be able to do that to him.

Earlier, when she had seen him from the stage, her expression had filled with wonder. When she had stopped at his table, her gaze had caressed. She wanted to touch him then and had.

She wanted to be with him, no matter how much she fought it, while Sean wasn't about to resist what he felt.

Loving a woman as deeply as he did Cait was something Sean had never experienced before. It was exhilarating, kind of frightening and fucking frustrating, but not something that could be denied.

Before Cait, he had always been the casual lover, enjoying women, but never committing to them, no matter how badly they wanted that.

And now that he had finally found a woman he did want, she was afraid to want him.

What a world. He sighed.

"I've missed you, too," she said.

Sean's eyes widened. "What?"

"You heard me."

That he did. "About our dinner."

"No. Not a good idea. You shouldn't have bid for me."

"You gave me no choice. You can't keep avoiding family functions in order to avoid me."

"I have not been doing—"

"So, you are going to my brother's birthday party next Sunday? The one that's being given by his wife, who also happens to be your favorite cousin? You remember, Julia?"

It was a moment before she spoke. "Uh-huh."

Sean looked skeptical. "Uh-huh, what?"

Cait took a moment to lick her lips before answering, "I'll be there."

Damn. He certainly hadn't expected that. She was just full of surprises tonight. "You're sure?"

Cait's gaze lifted from his mouth to his eyes. "If my being there will prove that I haven't been deliberately avoiding you, and if it will settle everything between the two of us, then yes."

"Oh, honey, that doesn't begin to settle anything," Sean said. He leaned down to her until their lips nearly touched. "Our dinner will be the time to start doing that. Time, I might add, you forced me to pay dearly for. But," he added before she could speak, "it's only dinner . . . unless you want it to be more. It can be the beginning or the end. That will be up to you."

Her breathing picked up. She looked like she wanted to run. "Up to me?"

"That's right."

She swallowed, then joked, "No more pulling rank?"

"I never did that and never will." He straightened. "What happens is up to you. The beginning or the end."

Cait's gaze lowered; she breathed hard. Didn't help. It was impossible to think. Sean's words were simply too disturbing. His height and build too comforting. His maleness too heady.

Cait warned herself to leave this room and never look back. She lifted her face to his instead.

In that moment, Sean saw her need. It was as overwhelming as his own, and the very same as that last time, before she had so abruptly left.

Because of that, he forced himself to temper his response. Until she was ready to fully commit, he would be patient. He would move slowly, he would make her wait and want as she had so surely done to him. He would give her a taste of heaven, but no more. He would make her come to him.

As he held her gaze, Sean lifted his free hand to her lush hair. It was soft beyond belief and perfumed with a provocative fragrance that recalled roses more succulent than the one he held and rain-freshened air. Working his fingers inside those incredible curls, Sean used that as an anchor as he tilted Cait's head even further, exposing her throat.

A soft moan escaped her, and then her breath caught as Sean lowered his head and pressed his lips to her flesh.

It was fragrant, moist, hot.

It was everything he had dreamed of for four long months and each part of him demanded more, wanting it, needing it.

Later, he promised himself. For now, he had to go slow.

He ran his tongue over her heated flesh.

Cait trembled.

He kissed the base of her throat, the soft swell of her breasts, the lobe of her right ear, her temple, that wondrous hair.

Breathing hard, aroused nearly beyond control, Sean buried his face in her hair, inhaling deeply of that incredible scent.

He adored her beyond reason. He had loved her for so damned long.

But, by God, if it killed him, he was not going to rush this.

Swallowing hard, Sean finally lifted his head from hers and opened his eyes.

It was a moment before Cait's lids fluttered open. Her hazel eyes held a question she wouldn't ask.

Sean looked at her until she seemed unable to bear this separation. Only then did he lower his mouth to gently brush her lips with his. Her mouth was so warm and silky, her breath so sweet and hot, his head swam.

Cait inhaled sharply and moved into him.

Sean suppressed a growl of delight, and nearly groaned in frustration, but still warned himself that what they both needed would have to come later.

For now, he ran his tongue over the seam of her lips; he tempted, he teased, not yet ready to thrill.

Cait was beyond ready. She whimpered as Sean lifted his head, depriving her of his mouth. Those delicate nostrils flared as she breathed hard. At last, she opened her eyes.

The need in them, the wanting of him, touched Sean in a way he never believed possible. If this woman approved of him, if she required him, nothing else mattered.

This was life. She was his world.

But completion would have to wait. Commitment was the goal. *Later,* he promised himself again, then finally lowered his mouth to give her a taste of what was to come.

Cait moaned. It was a greedy, wanton sound as Sean's mouth covered hers and his tongue plunged inside.

He tasted of champagne, chocolate and a flavor that was his alone. In this moment, Cait felt more alive than in all the months that had passed. Sean's touch, his unashamed need brought a response she could not resist. Wreathing her arms around his neck, she ran her fingers through his silky hair, leaving them there so that he couldn't lift his head from hers. So that he simply could not end this kiss.

Sean deepened it, pulling her so close that Cait knew the power she had over him. His rod was thick and hard, his broad chest pushing against hers with each strained breath.

Cait allowed it. She welcomed it.

Her tongue swirled around his as her body yielded to his touch. That acceptance made him tender. That tenderness made her wild.

Wrapping one leg around him, forcing him even closer, Cait pushed his tongue away, then thrust her own into his mouth.

Sean growled in pure delight, then moved her right arm down so that he could ease the strap from her shoulder and lower the gown, exposing her right breast.

Cool air kissed her nudity, making Cait feel deliciously female, and more daring than she had ever allowed. At any moment someone might come in.

That thought fueled Cait's passion and made Sean very protective. Turning her away from the doors, he kept her close so that his body was blocking hers from view.

Cait adored him for that, and the new pleasure he gave as his palm warmed her flesh, while his long fingers shamelessly used it.

His touch was that of a man who had been denied far too long. Her response was equal to his.

She was so dizzy with need, time passed without notice. She was so weak from desire, she finally rested her face against his neck, content to have Sean draw his thumb across her tightened nipple again and again.

When, at last, he was momentarily sated, Sean eased her gown over her breast and slipped the strap back to her shoulder.

Cait lifted her head and looked at him.

His lips were still damp from their kiss.

As he moved back, Cait quickly frowned and followed. Cupping his face in her hands she brought his mouth right back down to hers, shamelessly. When Cait finally ended the kiss and eased back her face felt hot.

If Sean noticed her blush he didn't let on, nor did he look away.

Cait's heart started beating out of control again. "What?"

He took a deep, steadying breath, then said, "Our dinner will be two weeks from today."

Cait opened her mouth, then closed it without saying a word. She had expected him to invite her upstairs as he had during Julia's reception. She had been ready to say yes.

Of course, she could always invite him, but for some reason Cait sensed he would turn her down.

Wait a minute, are you nuts? What had just happened here shouldn't be repeated. They couldn't keep rushing into each other's arms every time they saw each other. They had to keep their distance, or at least she did.

"On a Saturday," he finally added.

Tell him no. Tell him you can't make it. Tell him you'll reimburse him for all the money he spent. Now was definitely the time to do that since they were obviously not going upstairs.

"Cait?"

Tell him, she thought. "Two weeks?" she asked.

Sean drew that rose over the swell of her breasts and smiled. "Yeah. Two weeks. It's the only time you have free on your calendar, at least this month."

Cait didn't understand. "How did you know that?"

"I called your secretary."

He did? And she gave him that information without once warning Cait that he was asking for it or that he would be here tonight? She frowned.

"Don't worry," Sean said. "It's not all that long for you to wait, and it will be well worth it. Besides," he added, before she could speak, "I'll be seeing you well before then at Tim's birthday party." He leaned down to her again and murmured, "You do remember Tim, right?"

Cait wasn't about to comment on that.

Giving her a playful wink, Sean gently kissed her lips, handed her the rose that said she was now his, then left the room without a backward glance.

Three

Tuesday afternoon found Cait in her office scarfing down a hoagie with four different meats, every cheese imaginable, and two creamy dressings that possibly weighed in at three thousand calories and it still wasn't enough.

What she really wanted was something far richer.

The taste of champagne and chocolate.

The taste of Sean.

She sagged in her chair and continued to gnaw on that sandwich when she should have been focusing on work since the Villabous suit wasn't going to settle itself.

How could it? Victor Villabous was the most helpless, demanding and unrealistic client Cait had ever come across.

Not only that, he didn't sound like, look like or behave anything like Sean.

Will you just stop? Already she was a month behind in her work because she kept daydreaming about Sean. Her computer screen was currently displaying one of those recent newspaper articles about him, while a Google search had produced quite a few from the past, though her search of his high school and college databases had yet to bring up all the possible hits.

She was hopeless, but now knew the hospital where Sean had been born, how much he had weighed at birth, his social security number, current zip code, previous addresses and just about everything else. Except a way to get out of that party this weekend, and after that, their dinner date, which he had paid thousands for.

If Cait hadn't already loved him, good manners would have demanded that she get started on that affection and let him do whatever he wanted with her heart.

You are so screwed. She pressed her fingers to the inside corners of her eyes.

At just that moment the Princess of Darkness decided to barge into the office. "Cait."

Crud. She lowered her hand, then froze as Abbie came around the desk to look at the computer screen. Cait moved so quickly to close it her hoagie dripped dressing on Abbie's high heels.

"Sorry." Cait handed her a napkin.

Abbie's jaw continued to clench. She buzzed Cait's secretary.

"Yes, Ms. Camp—"

"This is Ms. Weiss. Tell Fred to bring his cleaning equipment into my office immediately."

"Yes—"

Abbie cut her off and glared at Cait.

Her mouth paused around the hoagie. Did Abbie expect her to clean those shoes? Even if she were a junior member of this firm, no way was Cait going to do that. Hell, she had said she was sorry, hadn't—

"You need to quit screwing around," Abbie warned.

Cait pulled the sandwich out of her mouth. "Excuse me?"

"Not if you keep this up. You only put in ten billable hours yesterday and God knows how little today. Quit surfing the net looking for stories about that man." Before Cait could even think to respond, Abbie stormed out of her office.

Cait's secretary, a motherly woman who was far too nosy, leaned inside the door. "Want me to surf the net for you?"

"No."

Mildred looked disappointed, but quickly brightened. "I'll do it tonight on my own time."

Before Cait could respond, Mildred closed the door.

Lord, this was like being a horny teen all over again with Mom One bitching, while Mom Two was enabling.

Time to put an end to this nonsense.

Cait closed the screens that had stuff about Sean, pausing only once—okay twice—to read the articles and look at his photograph.

In the last two days Cait had seen so many, she had pinpointed exactly when he had gotten his ear pierced for that undercover—

Her thoughts paused at a small rap on her door. Had to be Billy, since Mom One and Mom Two never knocked.

"What?" Cait shouted.

Billy opened the door and poked his head inside. "You okay?"

Cait looked up from the ribbons of lettuce she was brushing off her skirt. "Do I look as if I am?"

He came inside and shut the door. "Actually, you look kind of aroused."

Cait arched one brow.

Billy lowered his voice even more, as if he suspected the place was bugged. "Don't play innocent with me. I just heard what Abbie said and," he continued, interrupting Cait, "I saw how you looked after the auction when Detective Logan wanted to be alone with you, and you obviously wanted to be alone with him."

"That's something that's definitely not going to happen again."

Billy lifted his brows and rocked on his heels. "Planning on going to a really busy restaurant with him, are we?"

"Actually, I'm going to cancel on him."

Billy stopped rocking. "Are you certain you should do that?" He went to her desk, sitting against the edge of it. "The man is armed and potentially dangerous, correct?"

Billy had no idea, especially when it came to the danger Sean posed to her heart.

"There," Billy said, pointing to her face.

Cait's eyes crossed as she looked down at it. "What?" Did she have dressing on her chin?

"You're aroused again." He moved his leg before she could smack it. "Beat me up all you want, but you want that guy and man, does he want you."

Cait mumbled, "For now."

Billy fell silent, then cleared his throat as if he were embarrassed. "I'm so sorry. I had no idea he's a two-timing, no-good bum. I should have guessed it given the way he acted, but—"

"What are you talking about?" She frowned. "He is not a bum, Billy. He's a good man. The very best there is. And don't you dare say otherwise, understand?"

"Actually, I'm confused. He's all that and you're still canceling?"

"It's complicated," she said, then quickly added, "he'll just have to understand. I'll reimburse him for what he spent."

"Thousands and thousands and thou—"

"I know," she growled. "I was there."

Billy nodded agreeably, pulled out his cell phone and punched in a number.

Cait hoped that call wasn't going to Mildred so that her gossip machine could get the latest installment of the Cait & Sean Love-a-thon.

As the call started ringing on the other end, Billy offered Cait the phone.

She leaned away from it. "What's that for?"

"To speak to another human being across long, long distances—believe me, it's all the rage. Take it," he insisted at her look. "Please, just trust me on this."

She rolled her eyes and took the damned phone. "Who are you calling?"

"Detective Logan." He spoke above her.

"What, are you nuts?"

"You need to cancel and get back to work like Abbie wants, so she'll get off my ass. No, no, no," he said, moving away from Cait's desk when she tried to give the phone back. "You need to focus, so you need to can—"

"Logan," Sean suddenly said on the other end of the call.

Cait started sweating as she brought the phone to her ear.

"Lo-gan," he repeated, like he was starting to get pissed.

Just end the call, she thought. "Hi," she said.

There was a momentary pause, then his voice—deep, rich and bearing the gentleness he reserved only for her. "Cait?"

Her belly fluttered. "Uh-huh . . . hi."

His voice smiled. "Hi, baby, how you doing?"

He would ask that. Billy was currently pointing to her face and mouthing *aroused.*

"Just a sec," she said to Sean, then covered the phone with her hand and growled at Billy, "Out! And close the—"

He did before Cait could finish. Returning the phone to her ear, she spoke in a lowered voice, "Are you still there?"

"Of course. I'm not going anywhere, Cait, you can count on that."

Uh-huh. She sagged farther into her chair, wondering how to begin her speech about not being there for him.

After a moment of static-filled silence, Sean asked, "Did you call just to listen to me breathe?"

Cait smiled. "I have done that before, you know."

"No kidding?" He sounded genuinely surprised. "So those calls I got months ago weren't crank ones after all, but—"

"I listened to you breathe after you had fallen asleep that night."

"Our night?"

Who else's? "Yes, our night."

"Were you afraid you had killed me with all that great sex?"

Cait laughed, then leaned up in her chair and sagged against her desk. "You?" She lowered her voice to a husky murmur, "Those multiple orgasms nearly put me into a coma."

"Just so long as you had a good time."

It was like nothing Cait had ever experienced in her life. She murmured, "It was wonderful."

"Yeah, I know, I was there."

She smiled.

"You're not calling to cancel, are you?"

Cait's smile paused and her stomach fell. Was she that transparent? *Are you serious?* How often in the last four months had she initiated a call? Hell, she hadn't even initiated this one; it had been Billy's idea. Even so, Sean didn't have to be so damned blunt about it. Now she had to say what needed to be said, and quickly, too.

"Ah, Cait," Sean said after a lengthy silence, "are you still there?"

She held back a sigh. "Uh-huh."

"So, what's the deal? You want to listen to me breathe a little longer before you cut out on me,—"

"No."

"Oh hell, my breathing doesn't arouse you anymore?"

She laughed.

"Cait?"

"I'm not cutting out on you, okay?"

"That would depend. Are we speaking about Tim's birthday party?"

"Yes."

"Uh-huh."

Cait waited for him to ask *and what about our dinner?* He did not. He was waiting for her to bring it up, only she couldn't find the words. Damn. She sighed.

"What was that?" he asked.

She arched one brow and decided to play dumb. "Tell you what, if I don't show up you can have an ASA contact a judge and have a bench warrant issued for my arrest with you taking full custody."

"Oh, baby, don't think I haven't thought of that."

She murmured, "Sean Logan, you just don't play fair."

"You got that right."

His voice was so husky it was making her bones soft.

"Gotta go," he suddenly said in that same teasing tone. "See you this weekend, baby."

When the day in question arrived, baby was unfashionably on time despite the fact that it took her far too long to get ready (she still looked like hell), and she had more than a few reservations about seeing Sean again.

I've missed you, he had said. *I'm not going anywhere . . . you can count on that.*

Every promise he made and certainly every encounter with him was sucking her deeper and deeper into a romantic vortex that she really didn't need.

And yet, here she was all ready to party.

Holding back a sigh, Cait finally spotted Julia and Tim's house that looked like all the others in this new, suburban development except for the helium-filled balloons, a huge sign that proclaimed THE PARTY'S HERE!, and all those cars out front.

And here Cait thought she was on time.

As she searched for a spot to park, she noticed a Harley that was all muscle.

Had to be Sean's. It just looked like him—wild, free and driven to perform.

Knock it off, Cait warned herself as she parked her car, shut off the motor, grabbed Tim's birthday present, but didn't budge. Instead, she looked back at that Harley.

A number of images flooded her mind. First she saw Sean's powerful thighs hugging that purring machine, and then her far more slender thighs hugging him as she rode from behind.

Her arms were around his waist, her hands pressed to his chest. She felt the wind in her hair, the sun in her face, his gaze on hers before they kissed. There was hot desire in his eyes as he stripped her bare, then bent her over that impressive machine. Without direction she parted her legs even more, lifting her buttocks to give him full access.

It was a gift Sean quickly accepted as he touched her plump, moist lips that simply ached for him. As he expertly used her flesh, Cait whimpered in response until she cried out to him mounting her, his stiffened rod plunging so sure and deep in—

"Stranger!" a kid suddenly yelled.

Cait flinched. Her head jerked to the left as that little girl kept screeching at the top of her lungs, "Stranger! Stranger!"

Cait turned around looking for the—

"Where?" Julia shouted.

Cait's gaze snapped back to the front of the house. Julia was running across the lawn with a baseball bat in her hand.

"Where?" she shouted.

"There!" The little girl pointed at Cait.

Huh? "Wait!" she shouted through the tinted window before Julia could smash it with that bat. "It's me!"

Julia paused, then frowned at the dark sunglasses and baseball cap Cait wore.

"Get the stranger!" the kid shouted. "Get the—"

"Quiet!" Julia yelled, then ordered the kid to the backyard.

Thank God. With Tim's present in hand, Cait cautiously left her car.

Julia hugged Cait with her free arm, then stepped back. "I didn't recognize you."

"Obviously." She glanced at the bat.

Julia swung the weapon back and forth as if it were a fairy wand. "I'm a member of the neighborhood watch."

"Obviously."

Julia frowned. "So, what's up with you? Why are you dressed all gangsta today, of all days?"

Cait closed her eyes. That's what she loved about Julia— the girl was even blunter than Walt, Abbie and now Sean. "Sorry, I didn't realize this was a formal affair." Opening her eyes, she looked at Julia's naked feet, flowered shorts, that hot-pink tank top and her mussed blond hair.

"Insult me all you want," she said, "I've already got my guy." Running her arm through Cait's, she leaned into her and murmured, "Lock, stock and—"

"Aw, gawd. You're not going to talk about your sex life again, are you?"

"No." Julia sounded offended. "I've got it posted on my website."

Cait laughed.

"Come on," Julia said, pulling her toward the house, "I'll bet Sean can't wait to see you."

"Whoa." Cait pulled away. It was one thing to fantasize about them on his Harley or talk to him on the phone, and another to actually see him, again. Suddenly, being here seemed like a very bad idea. "Maybe I should leave. You have Tim's present. I should leave."

Julia frowned. "You look bad, but not that bad. Let me see what I can do with your hair."

Cait held onto her cap as Julia tried to snatch it. "That's not why I want to leave."

"No?" She leaned closer and squinted at those shades. "What are you doing?"

"Trying to see what's wrong with your eyes."

"Besides them being crossed because you're too close?'

Her cousin stepped back. "You are wearing mascara, aren't you?"

Almost a tube of the stuff since Cait had had a hell of a time getting the lashes on both lids to look balanced. Right now, her makeup looked worse than Tammy Faye Bakker's ever did, which was why she was wearing the shades.

"Relax," she said, "I've got on everything but a diaphragm."

Julia snickered. "Living dangerously, huh?"

"Nope. Virginally."

"Now that Sean's back in your life?" Julia laughed so hard her face got red.

"Get real. That man's waited four months for you. He's not going to settle for a good night kiss after—"

"Whoa," Cait said again.

Julia's glee finally dimmed. "What's wrong?"

This conversation, what else? "Sean hasn't been talking to you about us, has he?"

"God no." Julia's small hand went to her equally small chest as if she were pledging allegiance to the man. "He hasn't said a word, I swear."

Cait figured as much since gossiping just wasn't like Sean. "Then how do you know about him and me? Recently," she added.

Julia arched a brow. "Tim told me. One of his attorney friends told him." Her giggles were lusty. "Hey, you and Sean really made an impression at that auction. The way he won that dinner with you, well, it's been the talk of the—"

"I'm not going," Cait blurted. "I'm canceling on him."

Julia started to nod, then paused and frowned. "What?"

"I'm canceling."

"Are you kidding? How can you—oh my God," she interrupted herself, "you're not going to do that today at this party? You're not going to ruin Tim's—"

"No—no!" Cait said, since she had fully intended to ruin Sean's plans, not Tim's celebration. Not that that was even an option anymore, given the look on Julia's face and that baseball bat in her hand.

Her cousin's brows drew together. "I don't understand."

Well, hell, she didn't either! Her heart wanted one thing, while her mind kept repeating, *you'll only regret it.* "It's complicated." She held up her free hand. "And that's all I'm going to say on the matter."

Julia's green eyes narrowed even more. "Sean's in the backyard with the rest of the guests."

"Yeah, I already guessed as much."

"You be nice to him."

Like she hadn't already during his numerous orgasms? "I'll kill him with kindness."

"I mean it, Cait. He's Tim's favorite brother. He's my favorite brother-in-law."

"I swear I'll be nice and I won't say a word about canceling."

Julia shook her head and led Cait toward the backyard that smelled of smoky barbeque and newly mown grass.

The half acre was decorated with crayon-colored balloons and streamers, filled with tables that simply groaned with food, and stuffed with people of all ages that were eating, drinking, playing games, talking or laughing.

At least, until a few of those adults noticed Cait.

Oh damn. She had met most of this group at Julia and Tim's wedding and they certainly remembered her. She saw in it their eyes. One after the other seemed to be recalling the way she and Sean had exchanged all those longing gazes before they disappeared from the reception. Unless, of course, Tim had told everyone what had happened more recently at that loony auction.

God, God, God, Cait thought, wishing everyone would just look away.

Some did as they glanced to the right, before returning their gazes to her.

Holding back a sigh, Cait finally forced herself to look where they had and saw five of the most handsome men in Chicago, the Logan brothers.

Kyle, who had taken over their late dad's construction company, had dark brown hair and eyes. Tim, Julia's new husband, had reddish hair and a freckled face like their mom, who had passed just last year. There were the twins, Patrick and Quinn, who each had light brown hair, blue eyes and dimpled grins that most likely excited all those young women in graduate school where they were getting their MBAs.

And finally there was Sean, who was the best-looking of the lot and watching Cait like he expected her to run.

She would have, too, if his gaze hadn't so easily held her and Julia hadn't been blocking her escape.

"Go on," Julia hissed from behind. "And be nice."

Cait was about to say *sure,* but didn't as Julia suddenly swiped that cap from her head.

As Cait's hair spilled over her shoulders, Sean stopped lifting his bottle of beer.

Wow, she looked gorgeous. He even liked her springy hair, which she obviously did not since she kept jerking her fingers through it.

Not that he minded. Oh no. That movement caused her breasts to bounce up and down beneath her snug black T-shirt. Damn, it was cute. It had little cap sleeves, a plunging neckline and ruffled edges that fluttered in the hot, humid breeze.

Nice. Sean's groin continued to ache as his gaze prowled lower. Beneath that adorable tee, she was wearing black shorts that bared most of her very long legs, open-toed sandals and a glittery bracelet around her left ankle. Was she trying to kill him? His gaze jumped up as Cait finally headed his way.

For some reason, Julia wanted to get there first. She ran around Cait and headed straight for Tim.

"Excuse us," Julia said to Sean and his brothers as she pulled Tim to the side.

Cait had already stopped. She looked down at the present, then watched Julia whispering to her husband.

Kyle elbowed Sean. "What's going on?"

Who knew? Who cared? "They're newlyweds." His gaze remained on Cait.

She was still watching Julia and Tim.

"I meant with Cait," Kyle said.

Who knew? Now that Julia had stopped whispering to Tim, they both leveled their gazes on her.

What in the hell was going on? What in the hell was the matter with them, especially Tim? He was the most laid-back of Sean's brothers and never had a bad word to say about anybody.

He sure as hell better not have one to say to Cait.

Sean was about to go over there and have a talk with little Timmy, but didn't get the chance as Cait finally approached the couple.

After she dropped that gaily wrapped box in Tim's hands,

Cait kissed his cheek, backed away from Julia's scowl, then turned and wore an expression that said she didn't know what to do or where to go.

Sean sure as hell didn't want her to go home, so he crossed the yard to her. "Hi."

She continued to glance at the other people here.

Sean looked over both shoulders and was surprised that a lot of the crowd were looking from him to Cait, then back, like they were celebrities or something. Maybe his little brother Tim had told them about that auction.

"Hi."

Sean looked at Cait with that delayed response. She was staring at his beer. He offered it to her.

"Thanks." She guzzled most of it before coming up for air.

"Birthday parties usually this hard on you?" he asked.

Her bottom lip briefly stuck to the edge of that bottle as she lowered it from her mouth. Her head inched down as her gaze drifted over his navy blue T-shirt to his jeans, where it briefly lingered, then finally to his biker boots. "Only when you look so freaking good."

"Excuse me?"

Her head edged back up. "What?"

Sean held back a smile. "That's what I'd like to know."

Cait took another healthy gulp of that brew, swallowed, then licked her lips. "About what?"

"You two okay?" Julia suddenly asked.

Sean looked at the girl. Julia was closer than any chaperone should be and shooting loaded gazes at Cait. "Well, I am," he said. "How about the two of you?"

Both women looked at him, then glanced away.

Hmmm. As Julia was forced to return to one of the other guests, Sean leaned toward Cait and murmured, "You've been talking to Julia."

She lifted her face to his. "Of course I have. She's my cousin."

"Yeah, I know. She married my brother. What I meant is, you've been talking to her about me."

Cait brought that bottle back to her lips even though it was empty.

Sean eased it from her and placed it on a table to the side. "You're not thinking of canceling our dinner, are you?"

"No!"

He paused at her shout, then glanced around the yard. Too many sets of eyes stared back at him, then Cait, then—

"Everything okay here?" Tim suddenly asked.

Before Sean or Cait could respond, Julia ran back up. "We should all play a game."

"How about Truth or Dare?" Tim asked, then looked at Julia as she smacked his arm. "Hey," he said to her, "I'm only trying to get it all out in the open."

"Get what out in the open?" Kyle asked as he joined them.

Cait looked over her shoulder to where she had parked her car, like she was getting ready to bolt.

"Never mind." Julia offered a fake laugh. Sobering quickly, she elbowed Cait.

She remained turned away. "What?"

"Do you know how to play horseshoes?"

"Horse—"

"That's okay," she interrupted, "Sean will teach you."

Cait looked at him. "Horseshoes needs to be taught?"

"Only if we play the blindfolded version."

Kyle turned away from them as he laughed.

"Come on." Sean took Cait's hand. "You're about to get your first lesson. In private," he added to Julia, then gave his brother a look that said *keep her here.*

Tim slung his arm around Julia's shoulders and barely winced as she elbowed his side.

As Sean led Cait away, she said, "That was slick."

"Whatever it takes to keep her there and you here."

"Knowing Julia, you might have to use your handcuffs."

"Oh no, honey, I'm reserving those for you."

Cait looked at him.

Sean gave her a wink, then led her toward the horseshoe area that was currently unoccupied and secluded behind several weeping willows.

As his fingers played with hers, she murmured, "Careful." Her voice was husky, thinking about those cuffs. "We are being watched."

"Only by each other. Everyone else would need a telescope to see us from here."

Cait arched one brow.

Sean arched one right back.

Bad boy. His tempting gaze, coupled with all that beer whizzing through her system, the heavy sun, and those prying eyes behind them made Cait a bit giddy. "Okay, where's my blindfold?"

Lifting her hand to his mouth, Sean brushed his lips over her knuckles. "You'll get that when we go to bed."

The kiss made her swallow hard. That, and his hot breath and his choice of words. Not *if,* but *when.* "I thought you weren't going to pull rank."

He stopped at the edge of the horseshoe area. "I'm not." His gaze lowered to her breasts, lingering there, before he met her gaze once more. "You'll get to choose whether we use my cuffs or not."

Cait's gaze hung on his, before turning inward to the thought of securing Sean to her bed—or maybe even that Harley—so that she could pleasure herself with his stiff, hot rod and tight balls for as long as she wanted. Damn, but that sounded nice. She moistened her lips as she imagined stroking him, licking him, arousing him beyond reason until she, at last, took him fully into her—

"But first, horseshoes." He picked one up.

Cait looked from it to the playing area. "This is only a guess, of course, but I take that," she pointed to the horseshoe in his hand, "and throw it there," she swung her finger to the iron post that was several yards away.

"That's the easy way."

She laughed. "There's a hard way?"

Sean looked at her.

Her laughter paused, while her cheeks flushed. The desire in his eyes was unmistakable, as was his determination to have her no matter how difficult she was making it. "Anyone got their telescope out yet?"

His gaze flicked to the side. "Even better. A camcorder."

Cait looked over her shoulder. "Julia!"

She pulled the camcorder away from her eye. "Don't worry, your hair looks nice. Go on both of you, play."

Cait mumbled, "She has no idea what she's asking."

Sean worked his mouth so he wouldn't smile. "Don't you worry." He handed her the horseshoe. "I'll keep it R-rated for the most part."

"What? Wait—where are you going?" She looked over her shoulder as he went behind her, then chastely slipped his free arm around her waist.

To anyone who might come this way—(like Tim, who was pulling Julia back to the rest of their guests)—it seemed as if Sean was simply guiding his pupil through the proper stance to throw that first horseshoe.

To him and Cait it was far different. As Sean slid his fingers down her silky arm to her hand, he eased her against his erection.

Her breath caught.

Only Sean heard. Everyone else was simply too far away and finally involved in their own pleasure. The adults had resumed talking and laughing until the din rose above the children's noise as they played.

As the world continued around them, this space was reserved for him and Cait alone.

Already she was soft and yielding, her breathing lazy as she turned her head to the side and spoke in a voice only he could hear. "Play fair."

Not a chance. Pressing his face into her hair until he was consumed by its provocative scent, he then moved his mouth to her ear and whispered, "Just pay attention and follow me."

For the rest of her life Cait would recall the following moments as Sean's body hugged and thrilled hers, while he helped her throw that first horseshoe.

A moment passed before it thudded to the ground.

Cait sighed.

Sean murmured, "You missed."

Well, yeah. Her eyes were closed, her muscles relaxed and her bones damn near melted by his touch. "Darn."

Sean's shoulders and chest trembled with his suppressed laugh.

How wonderful that felt. So wonderful that Cait turned her face to his and asked, "Want to play again?"

Sean's laughter turned into a prolonged sigh. At last, he nodded as if he were too aroused to speak.

For the next half hour, Cait enjoyed horseshoes like it was never meant to be enjoyed.

As the trees' slender branches swayed in the balmy breeze, she and Sean engaged in lingering gazes, quiet sighs, and prolonged touches. Through it all Cait was helpless to resist.

She had loved him from the start and adored him now. She didn't want to think about tomorrow, much less next weekend's dinner or that endless, worrisome future.

Instead, she stroked sunscreen on the tip of Sean's nose and his bristly cheeks, after which he coaxed her to remove those shades. Nice guy that he was, Sean didn't say word one about her Tammy Faye eyes. He concentrated instead on the sunscreen he was easing across her lower lip.

Before he could take his finger back, Cait gently bit it.

For the rest of the afternoon, straight through the off-key singing of "Happy Birthday" to Timmy, the cutting of the cake, and the opening of the presents, it went like that. Tempting, teasing, thrilling.

It went far too quickly.

At last, Cait knew she had to leave. There were hours of work yet to be done before court tomorrow.

Julia was not impressed. "Tim doesn't have court tomorrow."

Cait pulled out her car key. "That's because it's the day after his birthday."

Sean laughed until Julia leveled her gaze on him. He lifted his hands in surrender. "I've got to be going."

"No!" Julia looked from him to Cait and back. "You can't leave."

"Ever?" Sean asked.

"Yet," Julia hissed as she gestured Cait away. "Go on. Leave. I'll call you later."

Before Cait could move an inch from him, Sean captured her hand. "If I didn't know better," he said to Julia, "I'd think you didn't want Cait and me to be alone."

She doesn't, Cait thought, especially if it were off these premises. Julia probably guessed Sean was going to hear some very bad news about next week's dinner date the moment they hit the street.

Julia frowned. "Why should I care?"

Sean looked at Cait for an answer.

Not a chance. Not tonight. "Gotta go," she said to Julia, then leaned over to kiss her cheek after which she whispered, "I'll be good."

As Cait pulled away, Julia smiled. "Go on you two." She flapped her hands, gesturing them away.

On the way to Cait's car, Sean asked, "Are you really going to be good?"

She smacked his arm for eavesdropping, then giggled as he hauled her close. Resting his arms on her shoulders, Sean said, "And here I thought you were going to be good."

"I let you win at horseshoes, didn't I?"

He frowned. "When did we play horseshoes?"

Her laughter was unrestrained and lusty just the way Sean liked it. Of course, that was right now because she had promised Julia to be good.

It didn't take Sherlock Holmes to figure out what that meant, or that if he wanted Cait's lusty laughter and wicked smile permanently in his life, he had to make her come to him.

With more control than he thought he had, Sean moved away from her fragrant softness and heat.

She seemed surprised by that abruptness. "We're leaving?"

"You're leaving," he corrected, then casually added, "and I'm leaving. Separately."

"I get it, all right?"

Actually, it wasn't. She sulked to her car. After she was inside, Sean rapped his knuckles against the window.

Cait lowered it and looked at him expectantly.

"Drive carefully," he said.

Her brows drew together. She turned away. "I'll be lucky if I can drive at all."

Welcome to my world. "What?" he asked.

Cait looked at him, then closed her eyes and parted her lips as Sean cradled the side of her face in his hand.

Her skin was hot from the sun and so unbelievably soft

he very nearly lost his resolve. "I'll call you next week to finalize our dinner plans."

Cait's lids fluttered open. She glanced at his hand as he took it back.

Before she looked up or had a chance to comment, Sean left her side and went to his bike for that lonely ride home.

Four

True to her word, Julia called later that night. "What happened?" she asked in way of a greeting.

"Not much," Cait said. "I wanted to run over his Harley, but—"

"Be serious."

Cait was being serious. She had wanted to run over Sean's bike so that he had no way to get home, except with her, which was no big surprise. The man was driving his way through her resistance straight to her heart and soul. First it was the wedding, then the auction, then horseshoes. Where in the hell was it all going to end?

"Hey, you still there?" Julia asked.

Of course she wasn't all there. Her body was at work, her soul in romantic limbo, her heart in her throat and her mind on Sean. "I'm a little distracted."

Julia's breath caught. "He's there with you."

"Would I be talking to you if he were?"

"I would hope not," Julia shot right back. "Of course, you are kind of weird when it comes to men."

"I'm careful."

"Yeah, right. Careful is not signing up at the Boston

Strangler website for a date, *or,*" she quickly added, "not jumping into a new relationship before you've gotten over the last one. Far as I can see, you don't have any—"

"Okay, okay, okay," Cait said, then sighed. "I'm kind of scared."

"Kind of?"

"Look, I don't want what happened to my parents happening to me."

"How could it? You don't even date."

Maybe not, but that didn't mean her life was totally bland. After today's horseshoe-fest with Sean, Cait was still having trouble uncurling her toes. "I'm handling this in my own way, thank you."

"Not if you hurt Sean."

"Hurt him? What about my getting hurt?"

"He won't do that," Julia assured, then interrupted, "He's like Tim. And Tim wouldn't do that."

"Well, no, not with another woman, but hon, statistics do point to the fact that Tim will be leaving you one day."

"Not a chance. He knows that if he dies before me, I'll kill him."

Cait wasn't certain whether to laugh or sigh.

"Don't cancel," Julia said, her voice suddenly serious. "If nothing else, at least have this one dinner with him."

By Monday morning Cait had more or less decided to do what Julia asked, not that that had actually been a factor. Cait was already so goofy that by the time court ended Monday afternoon she was practically drooling as she waited for Sean's call.

By Monday night she still hadn't received it.

By Wednesday afternoon Cait was beginning to wonder if the man was going to cancel on her. Maybe he was having second thoughts, with those having started at Tim's birthday party. Maybe that's why Sean had left so abruptly.

Or maybe he was just too busy to call because he had to go to a second job to pay for that outrageous bid.

Either way, Cait couldn't stand the suspense any longer and called Julia to get Tim's office number.

"No, you can't have it," she said, then asked, "why do you want it? Don't tell me you're canceling!"

Cait didn't. She had something else in mind.

Sean had just pulled off his shirt and was tossing it to the side when Matt, his partner on the force, stopped dribbling the basketball. "Hmmm," the guy said, putting that ball under his arm, "now there's something interesting."

The other cops on this court glanced to where Matt was, the public street bordering this area.

Sean pulled off his sunglasses and tossed them on top of his shirt. "Are you goons gonna play this game or leer at jailbait?"

"This babe's a little older," Matt said.

"Not too old," Nathan said.

"Actually, just right," Charlie said.

Sean rolled his eyes. Despite the waning sun it was still too hot to play anything but dead. Still, he needed to run off some steam, if the guys would just focus.

They huddled together instead.

"Why isn't she moving?" Nathan asked.

Sean went to one knee on the toasty concrete and tied the laces on his right Reebok. "Could be she's a crime scene."

Matt shook his shaggy head. "Nope. This babe's definitely alive."

"And staring at Logan," Charlie said, then asked Sean, "you being surveilled?"

He hoped not. As he ran a list of former girlfriends through his mind, Sean pushed to his feet, looked over his shoulder and felt his heart instantly pound. *Cait?*

She remained framed in the driver's side window, her

hair gently stirred by the scant breeze, her lips parting as her gaze trickled down him, lingering on his naked chest, then lower to his running shorts.

Whoa buddy, Sean warned his quick erection, *not now.* What was she doing here? How in the hell had she even found—

The basketball hit the side of Sean's head. He glared over his shoulder at Matt, who was not intimidated.

"Who's the babe?"

"Babe?" Sean growled.

Matt's expression finally went *uh-oh.* "Lady?"

Much better. "None of your damned business."

Charlie started humming "Love is in the Air," until Sean glared at him.

"Hey Logan," Matt said, "she's getting out of her car."

Sean's knees went instantly weak, while his head swam. Cait's being here just couldn't be good; but if she thought he was going to make this easy on her, she was dead fucking wrong.

He wanted her, he was going to have her, and she just better understand that.

As he finally faced her, Cait paused. In that moment, the edge of her beige silk blouse and oatmeal-colored skirt fluttered in the breeze, while her expression grew downright scared.

Aw hell. Sean's heart demanded he offer some comfort. Thankfully, his resolve said *no fucking way.* If she had come here to cancel, he was not going to make it easy on her.

As the guys shifted from foot to foot behind him, Sean held his ground. He didn't move. Hell, he could barely breathe.

At last, Cait reached him, but remained on the other side of the chain-link fence. "Hi."

Sean's heart ached with her vulnerable tone. "Hi."

Cait glanced at the guys, then back at him. "Can we talk?"

Not here. Not now. Didn't she know that? Probably not. He held back a sigh. "Sure." Before Sean went around the fence he glanced at Matt and the others.

They looked intrigued, but also embarrassed. At last, they moved away and started playing their game.

The moment Sean reached Cait he took her arm, leading her farther down the street until they could not be overheard. Releasing her, he asked, "How'd you know I was here?"

"Tim."

That was a surprise. "Is he all right? Is Julia all—"

"They're fine. I came about our dinner."

Okay, that was no surprise, so Sean didn't comment. No way was he going to make this easy on her.

"You didn't call," Cait said.

Huh? That's why she was here? "I had planned to call you later tonight."

"To tell me what?"

Wasn't it obvious? That he adored her, that he needed her, that he was going nuts not being with her. "That I've arranged for a table at the Lilac River Inn."

"Kyle's place?"

"Well, more like his, mine, the rest of our brothers and the bank since we all own a stake in it."

That's what worried Cait. The Lilac River Inn had been their dad's dream before he died, and his boys had put their hearts, souls and most of their available cash into that beautifully romantic inn, which was a reasonable drive from Chicago.

She rested her fingers on Sean's bare chest. "Please tell me that's not where you got the money for the bid."

He looked up from his quivering pec and shook his head.

"Your savings?"

He moistened his lips and shook his head again.

Oh my God. "Your house? You actually mortgaged your house to—"

He finally interrupted. "No. And don't worry about the money. I'm not."

She could see that. Unlike Walt, her father, and nearly every other man Cait had known, money wasn't what mattered to Sean. For the first time in her life a man—this man—put her above everything else.

She stroked those short dark hairs on his chest. "You spent far too much on me."

His gaze lifted from that stroking. "It was all for a good cause."

Mmmmm. "Did I thank you?"

"Do you want to?"

Oh yes. Lifting her hand from his chest, Cait cradled the side of his face. His cheeks were lightly stubbled, his beautiful eyes hooded as she tilted her face and gently touched her lips to his.

The moment was so tender and intimate Sean felt it clear to his soul and wanted more, but told himself that would have to come later.

As Cait eased back, her eyes sparkled. "I've got to go. I'll see you—"

"Saturday," he said, then told her the time the car would come to pick her up.

Those sparkly eyes got kind of cloudy. "Car? You're not picking me up?"

Sean wanted to, but told himself he had to be patient. His future and hers rested on this. "I'll meet you at the inn."

She seemed to want to question that, but finally nodded, then turned to go back to her car.

Sean remained where he was, watching her, wanting her

more than he ever believed possible. At last he moved forward, unable to help himself. *Look at me,* he thought, willing her to stop and meet his gaze one last time. To let him know that her need was as overwhelming as his.

She stopped and looked over her shoulder at him.

Sean ached to say how much he loved her. Hell, he wanted to shout it at the top of his lungs and whisper it to her for the rest of their days. He didn't give a damn about anything else, only that and her lingering resistance. She was finally sharing a meal with him, sure, but what about everything else?

With no answer to that, Sean warned himself not to push it. "Drive carefully," he called out.

Her eyes widened and then her gaze questioned as if she had expected more.

Later, he thought.

If he was trying to tempt her, it was surely working. If he was teasing her so that she'd want more, it was also working.

By Saturday night Cait was in the back seat of the car in which she was being driven, stroking the soft petals of the lone red rose Sean had delivered to her, while her gaze kept going to the speedometer.

"Excuse me," she said to the driver, an older man who was probably the father of one of Sean's friends, "but can't you go a little faster?"

"Detective Logan wants you to get there in one piece," he answered, keeping his speed steady and slow.

Cait chewed her lower lip as her belly continued to flutter and her breathing picked up. She felt as she had the night of Julia and Tim's reception when she had made the decision to sleep with Sean.

That thought certainly crossed her mind now. Surely, he

had every intention of sleeping with her tonight, right? Surely, he wasn't going to simply share a meal and some conversation with her, then roar away on his Harley, right?

He sure as hell better not. She asked the driver to please put a move on.

"We'll be there shortly," he said.

Twenty minutes later they were, with him insisting on helping Cait out of the car.

As she straightened, her gaze went to the three-story Victorian mansion that Kyle's company had renovated and expanded. The graceful structure was painted a deep lilac with snowy white trim and decorated with hundreds of tiny white lights. Cait smiled. It looked like something out of a fairytale, and was definitely a vacationer's dream. There were rooms for at least a hundred guests, a lovely dining area, and graceful porches bordered with lilacs and white roses, while the rest of the grounds were flanked by massive oaks and scented with pines.

Inhaling deeply of the fragrant night air, Cait sighed.

"You all right, miss?" the old guy asked.

She looked at him. "Oh yeah."

"Good to hear. Now you be sure Detective Logan shows you a nice time."

"Don't you worry." Cait fully intended to see that Sean showed her a very nice time.

Her thoughts paused as the front doors to the mansion opened. The strains of a soft ballad floated outside as Sean came onto the porch.

Behind her, Cait heard the driver getting back into the car and leaves being rustled by the gentle wind. Next, she heard her own sigh as her gaze drifted over Sean's dark blue suit and azure blue tie and shirt.

Wow. He looked luscious. Cait smiled.

It brought Sean a step closer. His gaze lowered to her mouth and lingered, before returning to her eyes. He extended his hand. He wanted her to come to him; or at least to meet him halfway.

There was absolutely no hesitation in Cait's response as she moved across the drive to the front steps.

Sean's heart soared, but he wanted more. He needed it all.

For now, he contented himself with simply gazing at that amazing halter dress she wore. It recalled the one Marilyn Monroe made famous in that old movie *The Seven Year Itch*, only Cait's version was a rich coppery color that complemented her high-heeled sandals, hazel eyes and that cloud of thick, dark hair.

Those silky waves tumbled over her naked shoulders, while the dress swirled over her curves as she moved up the steps to him.

The moment their fingertips touched a wave of raw desire hit Sean with such force that his stiffened cock ached for her tight, wet warmth.

Cait knew. It was in her gaze as she touched his cheek with that lone red rose. It was in her voice as she murmured, "Hi."

Sean cradled her face in his free hand and gently pressed his lips to her temple. It was scented with female arousal and heat. "Hi."

She trembled.

His heart smiled to that response. He teased, "Cold?"

"I guess I should be." She turned her face to his and whispered, "I'm not wearing any underwear."

He stared as she eased back. Taking his hand, Cait glanced at the entrance and spoke in her normal voice, as if not wearing underwear in public were an everyday occurrence. "We are going inside, aren't we?"

It was a moment before Sean could speak, his balls ached that badly. His gaze drifted from her pebbled nipples to the full skirt that hid whatever was—or wasn't—beneath. "Are you trying to kill me?"

Turning into him, Cait again rested the rose against his cheek, then drew it along his jawline. "Would I do that to you?"

Sean arched one dark brow at her playful tone. This, when his own voice sounded strangled. "If you did, I'd have to arrest you."

Her cheeks flushed and her voice lowered. "Now there's an idea—did you bring your handcuffs, Detective?"

"Never leave home without them."

"And your concealed weapon?"

"That depends. Which one would you be talking about?"

Cait's answer was to ease into him, not to mention his erection, as she lifted her face.

There was enough seduction in her body and gaze to make a grown man cry. And enough to make this man even more determined to have what was beyond that seduction. As far as Sean was concerned, he would settle for nothing less than love. Regaining his composure, he asked, "Are you ready to go inside?"

Ever so discreetly, so no one could possibly notice, Cait's hips pressed against his as her skirt fluttered around them both. "Are you?"

Given the look in her eyes, she wasn't talking about him entering this establishment. Damn. She was trying to kill him. He smiled. "Only if we go by my rules now."

Cait's gaze hung on his, while her voice grew a wee bit hesitant. "Sure . . . as long as you play fair."

Not a chance. Not if it meant he might lose her heart. Leaning down to her, he whispered, "Who said I'd be playing?"

She trembled once more.

He straightened. "Does that mean you agree?"

Her face lifted to his. "I do."

Now there were the words Sean had waited to hear for a very long time, though not in this context. Even so, he counted his blessings as he laced his fingers through hers. "Our table's waiting."

Cait held back. "We're going to eat?"

Sean looked over his shoulder at her. "I'm going to feed you. Trust me, you'll need the strength to keep up."

Those delicate nostrils briefly flared as Cait allowed him to lead her inside.

If the exterior of this inn was a fairytale come true, the dining area was an unexpected confection. Cait's lips parted in sheer wonder as they were led to an outside table that overlooked the river.

Fireflies danced in the balmy night air and stars dusted the darkened sky. Each railing surrounding this area was strung with those same tiny white lights, while Victorian-style lamps added a rosy allure to the tables that were clothed in snowy linens, fine china, sparkling silverware, crystal and fragrant centerpieces. They were also appropriately spaced so that private conversations could not be overheard.

As wonderful as that was, their table was even better. It was closest to the railing that overlooked the river and well removed from the rest of the diners. There was even a bank of decorative trees to further protect them from prying eyes.

An island of seclusion, Cait thought. Good thing, too. After Sean helped her with the chair, he leaned down and murmured, "Seat too cold?"

Cait suppressed a smile as she looked up at him. "Your body will certainly be warmer."

His eyes grew hooded.

Cait wanted far more, and had every intention of getting it. The moment Sean eased into his own chair, she slipped off her right high heel and worked her bare toes up the inside of his thigh.

His gaze snapped up, then went right back down to the napkin he just dropped.

As he leaned over to retrieve it, Cait eased her skirt up

her naked thighs, giving Sean a view of what no one else could see, and certainly what no other man would have this night.

His fingers paused on the napkin as his gaze touched her toes, calves and finally the inside of her thighs.

"Do you see it?" she asked.

He straightened. "What?"

"The napkin," she said, her voice all innocence despite the look in his eyes. "Did you see it?"

He held it up for her to see.

She took it. "Let me help." She wiggled her forefinger, gesturing him closer.

Once his chair was next to hers, Cait draped that napkin over his lap. "That better?" She stroked his stiffened cock.

Sean captured her hand. His lowered voice was husky as all get out. "What has gotten into you?"

"Nothing . . . yet."

His gaze lifted to hers as he ran his tongue between her fingers.

Cait swallowed at the sensation of wet heat.

"How are we doing here?" a waiter suddenly asked.

Cait looked at the twentynothing boy, then Sean, a real man, as he pressed his lips to her knuckles. "Really good," she said.

The boy pretended not to notice that Sean was now kissing the inside of her wrist. "Would you two care for a drink?"

Cait's gaze remained on Sean. "Champagne would be nice."

The waiter gently bounced on his heels. "Would we be celebrating something?"

"That would be up to you," Sean said to Cait.

Her cheeks flushed. "Champagne it is." She looked at the waiter. "Two glasses here, and before dinner's over I'd like a bottle sent to our room."

"Very good," the waiter said and turned to Sean. "Your room number, Detective Logan?"

Sean arched one brow as he looked at Cait. She arched one right back, then glanced at that napkin covering his erection.

"Suite three fifty-eight," Sean said to the boy, which admitted to her that he had gotten a room.

Cait smiled as if she had always known a night of wild lovemaking would be a part of their plans. "Have room service bring something chocolate, too," she said to the waiter, then looked at Sean. "I'd like to have dessert in our room."

He suppressed a smile. "What else would you like?"

Cait leaned toward him. "You decide."

A wave of warmth hit him in the chest and groin.

The waiter asked, "Would either of you care to see a menu?"

"I think we know what we want," Cait said. "Don't we, Detective Logan?"

Oh, she was something. With his gaze still on her, Sean told the boy to bring them two filet mignons with all the trimmings.

"We're very hungry," Cait added, "so please see that we have it as soon as possible."

"Yes ma'am," the boy said. "Would you two care to begin with an appetizer?"

To Sean's way of thinking, her verbal foreplay was appetizing enough. He smiled.

Cait returned it.

Damn, she was definitely something. "What would you like to whet your appetite?"

"What do you suggest?"

"Surprise us," Sean told the boy, just to get rid of him. When they were again alone, he regarded Cait.

She saw heat in his eyes that was stronger than anything

he had shown her before. After a moment of his quiet scrutiny, she murmured, "What?"

Leaning toward her, Sean spoke in a voice only Cait could hear. "Don't think I'm waiting until we're in that room to touch every last part of you."

Heat rose to her throat and cheeks. "I would hope not."

Sean's gaze remained on hers.

The inside of her thighs continued to ache, though she kept her voice calm, even nonchalant. "So, where do you intend to frisk me?"

"You'll know when we get there."

Cait's skin tingled at the look of delicious need in his eyes, while her mind considered all the possible locations where he might also strip, lick and mount her.

"The elevator?"

"Too far."

Really. She glanced over her shoulder and between those decorative trees to the rest of the crowd. "This dining area?"

"Too busy."

Uh-huh. So he was thinking of someplace close, but even more secluded. "The river?"

Sean laughed. "Too cold."

Cait looked at him. "Not to mention very, very wet."

He smiled his agreement.

She murmured, "Wherever you enjoy me will be amazing and exactly what I need."

"You mean that?"

Cait spoke from the heart. "I have full confidence in whatever you do. You're an amazing man."

"You haven't seen anything yet."

"Oh, but I have." She gently touched his smooth cheek, then placed her hand in his. "You brought me here." Her gaze drifted to the beauty surrounding them. "This place is simply incredible, Sean. You should be very proud."

He seemed amused. "I didn't build it, Cait."

"You helped make it happen." She looked at him. "You supported Kyle and the rest of your brothers in it."

"Only because they kept whining about—"

She gently interrupted, "Joke all you want, you risked a lot for them."

"It's only money. Besides, that's what families are for."

Maybe his family, she thought, but hers? No way did she want to recall all the divided loyalties in the Campbell clan. "You're very lucky," she said.

"Well, I hope to be." He played with her fingers.

Cait's eyes brightened as hers played right back.

They were still whispering naughty nothings to each other when a server appeared with the appetizers. On the tray were savory stuffed mushrooms, specialty cheeses, fresh fruit and shrimp cocktail.

"Enjoy," the young woman said.

Cait fully intended to. Spearing one of those jumbo shrimp, she slowly licked its length, then swirled her tongue over the rounded end.

"My God," Sean said.

Cait pulled in her tongue. "Don't tell me I'm embarrassing you."

"I won't. You're about to give me a stroke."

Poor baby. "I'll be good." Before he could comment, Cait brought the shrimp to his mouth, then gently drew it across his lips, coaxing them to open.

At last they did.

Never had Cait seen a man chew so slowly. It was as if Sean wanted to savor every moment of pleasure. As he finally swallowed, she asked, "More?"

"Later. Now, it's my turn."

She expected him to spear a bite of that shrimp or perhaps offer her one of those succulent grapes.

Instead, Sean motioned for the waiter.

The boy hurried to the table. "Yes, Detective Logan, what do you need?"

"Have the appetizers, champagne and chocolate brought to the suite immediately," Sean said, then looked at Cait.

"And the main course?" the waiter asked.

Sean kept his gaze on Cait as he said, "That, too. We'll be dining in our room."

Before she could comment, Sean was leading her from the dining area.

Cait's heart raced. She recalled his words.

Don't think I'm waiting until we're in that room to touch every last part of you.

"Where are you taking me? That is," she quickly amended, noting Sean's mischievous expression, "where are we going if not the room?"

"Just come with me."

Cait fully intended to, and wondered if they were going to his car . . . unless he had brought his Harley. She looked in the direction of the parking lot until Sean led her away from it and deeper into the inn.

It was enchanting. Glittering crystal chandeliers illuminated the large and elegantly appointed lobby that led to a bank of wrought iron elevators on the right and a closer, secluded hall to the left.

Cait looked over her shoulder at the other guests, who seemed very far away as Sean brought her down the hall.

She turned back to Sean at the sound of a door being opened.

Without comment, he led her into that room. Before Cait's eyes could adjust to the darkness, he had already locked the door and was backing her into the wall, then blocking her escape with his powerful body.

"Not a sound," he whispered, his lips close to her ear, his breath hot and sweet. "There's staff in the next room."

Cait was about to ask *what staff?* but could not. Her mouth had already opened in soundless delight as Sean slipped his hand beneath her skirt to touch bare flesh.

She inhaled deeply, luxuriously, as Sean pressed his hot palm against her naked belly, while his long fingers stroked those delicate curls between her legs.

Her breath caught as his hand moved to her vaginal lips.

Cait whimpered. She might have even moaned if not for Sean's mouth to her ear. "Quiet," he warned.

She bit her lower lip and nodded. She wouldn't make a—

Cait nearly cried out as Sean slipped two fingers inside her opening with a boldness that said this was his right . . . one she had given to him. Before she was able to catch her breath, his thumb found her clitoris and teased it.

She pressed the heels of her hands to her temples as his fingers stroked and played with her feminine core, tempting, teasing until she had to bite her lower lip to keep from crying—

Completion hit so quickly and hard, a strangled moan escaped the back of Cait's throat. Before she made another sound, Sean's mouth was on hers, his tongue plunging inside to silence and own.

During this, he continued to stroke her clit.

Cait tried to shake her head, she had to let him know that the feeling was too intense, but there was no escape from this man's touch or his kiss.

Sean worked her flesh until Cait's only choice was to yield still further.

The sounds of her ragged breathing filled this darkened space, while muffled voices could be heard on the other side of the wall. A male said something that made a female laugh. An object was dropped on the floor. More words, more laughter followed that.

Through it all Cait willed herself to be quiet as Sean left a trail of kisses over her cheek, ear and finally her throat where his mouth lingered. She felt that wet heat clear to her soul, and then his free hand on her halter top, easing the stretchy fabric over her left breast to expose it.

Cait's nipple puckered in the room's cool air, then tightened even more to Sean's hand as he covered this part of her flesh. His touch was both shameless and tender. He took precisely what he wanted, while delivering pure pleasure.

At last, he lowered his mouth to her breast, flicking his tongue over her nipple before he drew it into his mouth.

Her back arched to that wanton suckling. She inhaled sharply as Sean slipped his free hand from her breast to her buttocks, roughly fondling them.

His touch, scent and heat drove Cait to the edge once more, only this time Sean made her wait for release. His fingers slowly enjoyed her flesh, using it, playing with it, until she was straining to be closer to his touch, her body begging for fulfillment.

When he finally allowed that, Cait shivered to its intensity as she slumped against the wall.

Sean took just that moment to sink to his knees.

Oh my God, not that . . . not yet. She needed a moment to catch her breath.

Sean was not about to allow that. Bunching the skirt to her waist, exposing her nudity to the room's cool air and his touch, he kissed her navel, then that expanse of flesh above her curls before burying his face in her womanly fur.

The room spun. It was an intimate moment like no other as he inhaled deeply of her female scent, lingering, wanting, loving until unbearable desire flowed through her. She trembled.

Sean's response was quick and effective. Lifting his hands to her buttocks, he used that embrace to keep her close and vulnerable to his will.

As more sounds came from the next room, Sean licked

her curls until they were fully damp, and then he pressed his mouth to her clitoris.

Cait shook her head. That part of her was still deliciously sensitive.

Sean knew. His grip tightened, his mouth caressed as his tongue leisurely licked her flesh until Cait couldn't breathe, she could no longer think. Fully yielding, she delivered herself to him.

He enjoyed her for a very long time. When he was finally satisfied, Sean pushed to his feet and moved into her until Cait could feel the impressive beating of his heart.

Lightly touching her mouth with his, he whispered, "Now, we leave."

Her lids fluttered opened. The muted light showed her that this was a small office. "Leave?"

Sean pressed his finger to her mouth. "Quiet," he ordered.

Cait sucked his finger into her mouth and gently bit it. The second he pulled his hand away, she brought his head down to hers and whispered in his ear. "I am not leaving. You're not leaving. Got it?"

"'Fraid not," he whispered right back. "The night manager should be here any minute."

"I'm not leaving this inn," she whispered. "Neither are you."

"Well, I would hope not," he said, easing back. "Our room should be ready by now."

Oh . . . *oh*. Cait smiled, then grabbed his hand and headed for the door.

"Just a minute," Sean said.

"Uh-uh. I don't want to wait any longer."

"Maybe not. But you need to fix your dress."

Cait looked down, covered herself, then slapped Sean's arm as he quietly laughed.

His response was to use his superior height and weight

to trap her against the wall again. "Now, you be nice," he warned.

She murmured, "Screw that."

Sean's shoulders shook with suppressed laughter, though not for long. Pulling her into his arms, he kissed her savagely, while Cait kissed him right back.

When they were both pretty damned breathless, he led her from the room and past two staffers in the hall.

"Excuse me!" the female desk clerk called out. "Guests are not allowed in this part of the—"

"Quiet," the male desk clerk said.

Cait leaned into Sean and spoke in a subdued tone. "He must know you. He talks like you."

Sean lowered his head to hide his smile.

"If anyone tries to stop us," Cait said, "I want you to put them under arrest."

He turned his face to hers. "To hell with that. I'm not using my cuffs on anyone but you."

That got her cheeks to pink up. Giving her a wink, Sean led her to the elevator.

Cait suddenly held back.

He looked at her. "Change your mind already?"

"Hardly. But aren't you forgetting something?"

Since he was here and she was here, Sean couldn't imagine what she was talking about.

And then he did.

Leaning toward her, he whispered, "You are protected, aren't you?"

"Very, but don't we need a room key?"

It had been in Sean's jacket pocket well before her arrival. "You know we don't."

Cait gave him a wanton smile. "You're right. Bad boy."

She had no idea. Though she sure as hell was about to find out as he led her into the elevator.

The damn thing was older than his Great-aunt Sarah and filled with too many other couples as it slowly wheezed from floor to floor. During this, Cait leaned against the far right wall, while Sean leaned against the left. Not once did he take his gaze from her. Not once did she look away.

Her gaze was ballsy as all get out, while her expression said she was his equal in whatever was to come.

That, as much as her intelligence and beauty, stirred Sean until he could barely maintain control.

But control himself, he would. Tonight had to be more than just great sex that had been too long denied. Sean needed an intimacy with this woman that he had wanted from no other. And, by God, he wanted her to feel the same.

It's only dinner, he had once said, *unless you want it to be more. It can be the beginning . . . or the end. That will be up to you.*

When they finally reached their destination, Sean continued to regard her.

Cait's color heightened under his scrutiny, while her quickened breathing betrayed her need.

Even so, Sean made her wait a moment more before offering his hand.

With no hesitation whatsoever, Cait pushed away from the wall and accepted it.

"My rules." His fingers encircled hers.

"I'm all yours."

You will be. From this night forward, Caitlin Livingston Campbell was never going to get away from him again.

Their suite was at the end of the hall, secluded from all of the others, just as Sean had planned. When he opened the door he was pleased to see that the room had been prepared to his specifications.

Rose-scented candles in Victorian holders gave off a sensual fragrance and cast a glow on the period furniture that included a large canopied bed, a dresser with an oval mir-

ror, another cheval mirror to the side, a marble fireplace
and dainty rose-printed wallpaper.

As Cait's gaze lingered on the bed that had been strewn
with hundreds of rose petals, her fingers clasped his. The
French doors that opened onto a small porch with the river
below and countless stars above made it seem as if they had
left the real world and entered one of their own.

Releasing her hand, Sean slipped his arm around her
waist and pulled her into himself so that she could feel his
body's need.

Cait turned her face to his.

Her gaze was so unbelievably soft, while her body had so
easily yielded to his passion, it was a moment before Sean
could speak. "Uh-uh-uh," he said, removing her hand from
his shirt that she was trying to unbutton. "My rules, remember?"

Cait glanced down, then looked back at him. When she
spoke, her voice was very soft. "You might have to keep reminding me."

"Believe me, I will."

She laughed.

Smiling, Sean led her to a small sitting area where their
meal had been set up. Pouring a little champagne into a
fluted glass, he brought it to her lips. "Drink."

Her throat quivered as she swallowed. He licked a drop
of champagne from her lips.

Her lids fluttered and finally closed as Sean fed her a
grape, then a chocolate truffle. At last, Cait licked the chocolate that remained on his fingers.

Sean allowed that intimacy for only a moment before
pulling back his hand.

Cait looked at him from beneath her lashes. "When are
you going to let me touch you?"

"Later."

She looked disappointed. "How much later?"

"That will be up to you."

"I'm all yours."

That truth was in her voice and gaze. It was such a gift, Sean could barely wait to have her. But wait he would, until she wanted him so badly she could think of nothing else.

He led her to the mirrored dresser. When Cait turned into him, Sean shook his head. "Face the mirror."

She did so without pause or question.

"Bend over," he said.

Now, she hesitated, but only briefly before doing as he asked. With her hands gripping the edge of the dresser, she bent at the waist and watched Sean's reflection as he moved behind her.

"Arch your back," he said.

Cait immediately obeyed until her raised buttocks seemed to beg for his touch.

Easy, he warned himself. He had to take this slow, he had to make it last.

With great care, and more slowly than he would have liked, Sean lifted her skirt until that coppery fabric was draped over her waist, exposing her nudity.

Another woman might have resisted at this point, feeling embarrassed, but Cait remained perfectly still, allowing Sean precisely what he wanted.

He took it. With his gaze on her reflection, he rested his hands on the insides of her thighs.

She inhaled sharply to that and to the way he spread her legs so that he had full access. But he wasn't through yet. Oh no. Slipping one hand to her flat belly and the other to the small of her back, he said, "Lift your ass."

His tone was commanding, his choice of words deliberately coarse, with each exciting Cait beyond reason.

She did as he asked, and in that moment felt more exposed, more vulnerable than she ever had in her life. Her skin tingled with excitement. Her heart raced. She wanted him to mount her, to use her, to love her now.

Sean had other plans. *My rules,* he had said.

Cait's mind rebelled even as her body yielded. Her gaze followed Sean's reflection as he stepped back, leisurely regarding her naked flesh, those hidden areas only he could see.

More than once, he touched her there, his gaze flicking to her reflection to gauge her response.

Each time, Cait's gaze softened, while she lifted her body to meet his touch, wanting more, begging for more.

In time, his expression answered.

Despite her body's need, Cait accepted this, waiting for him as he had once waited for her.

At last, Sean removed his suit jacket. As he tossed it on a chair, his gaze remained on her legs and buttocks, the position that left her so completely opened to him and made her feel more female than she could have believed possible.

The insides of her thighs ached as Sean removed his tie and unbuttoned his shirt. Her opening grew even wetter as he took off his gun, placing it on a table to the side.

When he turned back to her, Cait drew her tongue across her lips.

Sean's gaze remained on her mouth as he removed his shoes and socks, then, at long last, his shirt. His chest was all male, nicely furred and deliciously muscled, while his right biceps sported a tattoo from his undercover days.

As arousing as that was, Cait knew there was something far better awaiting her.

Her gaze trickled past his navel to his fly as Sean lowered it, then pushed his slacks and briefs down and stepped out of them.

His cock was thickened and stiff, the blunt head dark and his sac tight.

Cait ached to feel its heavy warmth in her hand, to press her lips to that fragrant, wrinkled skin and those thick dark curls above his shaft.

But this was his show, his rules.

Positioning himself behind her, Sean rested his hands on her naked buttocks.

His hands were heavy. Hot. His touch unrestrained as he roughly fondled her flesh, while his cock pressed against the inside of her left thigh.

Cait strained to see more, but the dresser's mirror wouldn't allow that. Turning her head to the cheval mirror, she received an unrestricted view of Sean's body pleasuring hers.

It was a scene Cait would never forget. With one hand on her buttock's left cheek, Sean used his free hand to explore her hot, wet opening.

When he stroked her clit, Cait's breath caught. When he stroked again and again her thoughts cried *enough!*

He paid no heed. As Sean worked her body, his gaze caressed. As her vaginal lips grew plumper and slicker it was finally time.

He did not rush.

Lifting his beautiful cock in his right hand, Sean placed his left on her hip to keep her still. From him, there was no escape.

Cait wanted none. *Now,* her thoughts cried, while her mind whispered, *please.*

No matter. Sean took his time, bathing his cock's silky head in her womanly moisture, gently prodding her opening with his stiffened shaft, but not entering just yet.

Cait's fingers tightened into fists as her anticipation grew. Her body strained to reach his, to envelop him, but each time she tried Sean gently eased back.

My rules, he had said.

Cait accepted this. She had no choice. Her body was his to use and to pleasure, she had given him that right. And so she remained opened and vulnerable. She waited, then finally cried out in raw delight as he mounted her, plunging fully and deeply inside.

He filled her as no man ever had. He touched her core. They were flesh to flesh, hair to hair, his sac tapping against her nakedness.

Thus joined, Sean ran his left hand down her belly to her clit. As he stroked it, Cait whimpered. Soon, her wiggling buttocks told him he just had to stop. It was too damned intense.

And precisely what Sean wanted. He didn't miss a beat as his fingers stroked Cait's feminine core. He gently eased his cock from her then thrust back inside, imprisoning her in his strength and heat, demanding her response.

Her body molded to his; she willingly followed his lead. Nothing else mattered. Cait no longer felt the cooling night air or heard the soft music playing from the terrace below. Her reality was this room, this man; his hot, hard cock; those relentless thrusts as his fingers continued to stroke and stimulate and—

Pleasure shuddered through her with such force, Cait could scarcely breathe. She tried to gulp air, but was soon whimpering as Sean pumped for a moment more before allowing his own release.

It was pure male, unashamed and proud, though hardly the end.

Even as Sean bent over her, his chest still heaving with his own response, he slipped his hands beneath her halter to capture her breasts.

Cait softly moaned.

Sean kissed her back.

For that, and everything else, Cait wiggled her butt into him.

Sean's growl was one of pure contentment.

Now, she had him. "My turn," she finally gasped.

His voice, though weary, held a smile. "You are ballsy, you know that?"

"I want to show you that."

God, did she ever. When Sean finally turned the reins over to her, Cait had him on a pile of cushions in front of the fireplace, which she had lit. As the light from those flames danced over their nudity, Cait straddled him, driving his cock deep within herself.

Before Sean could begin to catch his breath, she brought him to climax. While he was still gasping, she cradled his face in her hands and simply looked at him, as if she needed to memorize his features, as if she needed to remember this night.

As if she were reluctant to see morning come.

Five

Come it did, and after only a few hours of sleep that they both tried to fight off.

During those last quiet moments, Sean vaguely recalled telling Cait that he loved her, though he couldn't recall receiving a response.

Maybe he had only dreamt that he declared his heart.

He looked at her now. Cait's lush, dark hair tumbled over the startlingly white linen, while the sheet hugged her naked hips. To Sean's delight, the rest of her was clothed only in rose petals and kissed by the morning sun.

His gaze moved from her sleek thighs to her velvety nipples to her plush lips that were parted in sleep and contentment.

Sean watched her for a long moment that felt oddly sacred, he loved her that much. It had never been in question, not from the first moment they had met. He just knew.

And now, he waited.

As the morning light touched her lashes, Cait's brows finally drew together. Minutes later she turned away from the sun and forced her lids to part.

Her gaze went to Sean's side of their bed even as her

hand plowed through the linens to find him. Failing, she finally turned her head to the foot of the bed and stared.

God, I adore you, he thought. "Morning," he said.

Cait pushed to a sitting position, then rubbed her eyes and ran her tongue around her mouth. "What are you doing?"

Sean's voice was all innocence. "Nothing . . . yet."

Once her hands were lowered, she ran her gaze up and down him. "You're dressed."

"It's morning."

Her brows drew together again. She glared at the sun as if she hated it. "Yeah, I know, but you're dressed." She paused, then looked worried. "Are you leaving?"

"I have to."

Her eyes widened. "Why? Were you called back on a case?"

"Nope." Sean's gaze lowered to her bare breasts.

"I don't understand."

He nodded. "I know."

"What I meant is—why are you leaving?"

"Because I love you, Cait." He lifted his gaze to hers. "Didn't I tell you that last night?"

She looked too stunned, or perhaps worried, to speak. She slowly shook her head.

Then he had dreamt it. And now that he was awake, he was getting the same response from her: panicked silence. Holding back a sigh, Sean went to the dresser and returned with a hand mirror that he offered her.

Cait seemed reluctant to take it. "What's that for?"

"Look at your expression," he said, "that's why I'm leaving." He turned to do just that.

"Wait!"

Sean's heart paused when he heard the raw need in her voice. Even so, he wasn't yet ready to take that as an answer or let her off the hook. It killed him to do this, but she had put him through hell these last four months and now he wanted to be sure. Looking over his shoulder, Sean forced his voice to be casual despite his thudding heart. "Don't worry, Cait, I've arranged for Matt's dad to pick you up and take you back to your—"

"To hell with that." She tried to get out of bed but couldn't; the sheets were tangled around her legs.

"Careful," Sean said as she slipped over the side of the mattress and sagged to the floor.

Cait shot him a look as she struggled to free herself. At last, she pushed to her feet and went to him.

Sean regarded her nudity.

She slapped his arm. "Will you pay attention?"

His gaze jumped to hers. His voice was all innocence. "Who says I'm not paying—"

"Sean, don't leave."

She meant it. Never had he heard passion like that in her voice, not even during their adventures last night. Still, it wasn't the total answer he wanted or deserved. No way was he going back to seeing her once every four months. "I have to. You have to. We can't stay here forever."

She gave him a soulful look. "We could stay a little longer."

"No."

Her eyes widened at his sharp tone, while Sean's finally narrowed, because she just didn't get it. Or more likely, she simply refused to get it. "I'm not interested in now and again sex with you, Cait, despite how much you enjoy it. I love you," he said, interrupting her, "and, I want you to love me. I want you to be my wife with all that that entails, you know, the unthinkable. We live together in the same house, we have a few kids—the number of which will, of course, be up to you since you have to do most of the work. We grow old and ugly together, fight on occasion, just like everyone else does and," he said, interrupting her again, "take a risk on each other. There are no guarantees. There are no perfect marriages, just that messy stuff most people call life."

"And lots more call divorce."

"Fine," he said, grabbing his jacket. "You gave me your answer."

"Sean, wait."

This time, he didn't.

"Dammit," she cried, "don't you dare leave this room! You can't leave this room—I love you!" She breathed hard and lowered her voice. "I've always loved you."

Sean's heart caught, but he remained facing the door.

Cait crossed the room to him. She touched his arm and softened her voice even more. "Didn't you hear me?"

He looked at her. "The kitchen staff probably heard you."

"To hell with them." Her ballsy attitude was back. "I love you."

"Are you sure?"

She seemed surprised by the question. "Of course I'm sure."

"Really sure?"

"Dammit, yes!"

He leaned down to her until their lips nearly touched. "Then convince me."

Her frown faded. "What?"

"Convince me." He straightened. "Like I've been trying to convince you ever since we met that I won't run out on you and I sure as hell won't cheat on you. Yes, I have been doing that," he interrupted, "and you're damned lucky I don't take rejection that easily."

"Whoa, whoa, whoa, I never rejected you. You even said at that charity auction that I never rejected you."

"That's right, you ran out on me."

Her cheeks colored. "Only that first time."

"Only?"

"Sean, you know what I mean."

"Sorry, sweetheart, but I'm afraid I don't."

"What do you want me to do?"

"I've already told you that, Cait. I want to be convinced. I want to know that you want me more than any man on this earth. I need to know that you can't live without me, that you're willing to share your future with me. Uh-uh," he said, resting his forefinger against her lips to stop her from interrupting. "Think about what that means. You have to be so certain of your own feelings that you can convince me, and not just because you want me to stay in this room. When you're finally ready to do that, you know where to find me."

Before she could offer any comment or argument, Sean forced himself to open the door, then left without a backward glance.

The rest of that morning and afternoon were worse than all the heartache and fear Cait had ever experienced.

Convince me, he had said.

How? He refused to believe that she loved him no matter how many times she might have said it. He refused to listen to her, even though she needed to argue her case.

He knew she was scared, but it no longer mattered—it was no longer an excuse. Nothing had stopped him from pursuing her. Not fear, not ego, not even money he didn't have.

He had convinced her of his love. He had proven his commitment. And now he wanted her to do the very same.

But how?

Cait fretted over that for hours, then finally called Julia. The girl was family, not to mention still happily married, and Cait needed some serious guidance.

"You're way beyond any help I can give," Julia said, "but damn—good for him."

"What?"

"I told you once before, Sean's my favorite brother-in-law. So, what's next? You gonna sign up for romance on the Marquis de Sade website?"

"Screw you."

"No need to get nasty. It's not my fault Sean dumped you."

"He hardly dumped me. He gave me an ultimatum."

"Uh-huh. Anyway, now that he's free—"

"Whoa. Hold it right there. He's not free."

"Come on, Cait, I know you, remember? You're definitely not the type to cave to commitment or ultimatums."

"You haven't seen me at work."

"Maybe not, but I have seen you with a few men."

"Sean isn't just any man. I adore him."

"Well, given the way you've avoided him until now, you'd have to convince me of that. Or better still," she said, interrupting Cait, "get down on your knees and convince him."

That night when Sean finally got home, he wasn't foolish enough to hope that Cait would be waiting for him on the front porch.

She wasn't. Nor did he see her parked anywhere close and waiting in her car.

Of course, he had expected that she would at least call, but there were no messages from her on his answering machine. His first reaction was to call her, but he told himself no. He had provided the opening, now she had to come to him. There was simply no other way.

His brother Kyle thought he was nuts.

"Of course there's another way. There's always another way," Kyle said the following day when Cait still hadn't called, shown up or even sent a Dear Sean version of a Dear John letter.

Sean simply couldn't believe it. How could he have been so wrong? She said that she loved him, but was refusing to convince him of it? This, when he had gone to that charity auction and practically bid himself into the poor house just to have one night with her? Damn.

"If there's another way," he muttered, "what is it?"

Kyle lifted his shoulders.

Sean crossed his arms over the edge of the bar's counter and lowered his head. "You know, all I wanted was that she be sure. Was that too much to ask?"

"Of course it was. She's an attorney." Kyle gestured for the bartender to bring them two more beers.

Sean wasn't following. "What's her being an attorney got to do with anything?"

"Attorneys aren't like you and me." He popped more peanuts into his mouth and talked around them. "They have to be sure beyond a reasonable doubt."

Oh, please. "She's not a juror at my murder trial, fool. I just wanted her to be sure about us. How hard could that— you think this is funny?"

Kyle continued to laugh. "Yeah. I think all those babes you loved and left would probably think so too."

"I never loved them. I love her."

"So, you keep telling me. Why, I don't know, since I can't do anything about it. So, tell her."

"I did, repeatedly." And now she had to come to him. There was simply no other way.

When Sean returned home that night the light on his answering machine was finally flashing.

"Sean," her voice said.

His knees went weak, until she paused. What? Sean thought, leaning closer to the machine. *What?*

"You asked me not to rush into this."

"No, I didn't. I asked you to be—"

The recording of her voice went on. "That's why I haven't called until now. I've been thinking about that and convincing you and everything else you said."

"Aw, Cait. I just want you to be sure. Is that so much to—"

"I need some time," her voice said.

"What? Why?" After all he'd done, after all they had shared, she still didn't know if she loved him enough to convince him? She still didn't know if she was going to marry him? She still didn't know how many kids she—

"Why are you on the phone?" another voice suddenly asked on the recording. "Walt wants you in his office, now."

"I'll be right there," Cait said to that person.

Sean heard a door slamming.

"That was the Princess of Darkness," Cait said, then swore. "I'm sorry, but I've gotta go. But I will convince you. I do love you, Sean . . . I've always loved you. I just need to take some time like you wanted me to do."

"Dammit, Cait, I didn't say I wanted—"

"Please give me that time. Please give me the opportunity to really convince you. Bye."

All that night and the following day, Sean honestly didn't know what to expect. Was she going to send him flowers? Candy? Herself?

Two days later, Sean was still looking for an answer, not to mention appreciating how women felt when they waited fruitlessly for a guy to call just because that guy said he would. *Sure.* Hell, Cait hadn't even gone that far. She had misinterpreted what he had asked, then promised she would convince him, but only after he gave her more time.

Given the last pause in their relationship, this one might take them well past retirement, and Sean was not about to wait that long. Nor was he going to contact her.

He called Tim instead. "What's Cait been up to?"

"Hi to you, too. How should I know?"

"You're an attorney, Tim, just like she is."

"Actually, she's a civil litigator and I'm—okay, okay," he said to Sean's swearing. "Do you have any idea how many attorneys there are in the greater Chicago area?"

"You're married to her cousin," he growled. "Now, have you been talking to—"

Julia interrupted from the extension. "Is that you, Sean?"

"Yeah. Has Cait been talking to you?"

"I'll take this," she said to Tim. "Go back to your movie." The moment Tim hung up, she said, "You wanted her to convince you, right?"

Well yeah. "Is she going to start anytime soon?"

"Don't you know?"

"What is this, a freaking riddle?"

"You love her, right?"

Holy fuck. Sean covered his face with his hand. "Would I be taking this abuse from her, you, and the rest of my family if I didn't?"

"Poor baby. If you love her, then you'll wait for her."

Hadn't he been doing that already, not to mention endlessly? "So that means she's at least started to—"

"You gave her an ultimatum, Sean. Now, you'll just have to see how it turns out."

That hardly made him feel better. When four more days passed with no word from Cait, Sean figured she was no longer afraid to love him, she was simply too busy.

Two days ago, Tim had given him the news that Cait had been selected for that associate circuit judgeship. Julia added that that was a good thing, since Cait no longer had to deal with the Princess of Darkness.

"Give her my regards and congratulations," Sean had said, figuring he better get on with the rest of his godawful life that he was obviously spending alone.

"Hang in there," Tim said.

"Remember you love her," Julia said.

"Good-bye," Sean said, and had been ready to hang up when he heard their giggles.

At the time, he wasn't sure whether they were laughing because they knew about Cait's plan to convince him or because they were tickling each other.

You're losing your fucking mind. But, at least, he still had his pride. And then he remembered; he had lost that at the auction.

Not that it mattered, since Sean honestly didn't regret a bit of it. Cait had been worth everything he had, and more, even if she refused to understand that.

I do love you, she had said. *I've* always *loved you . . . I will convince you.*

By Saturday afternoon Sean was still waiting for that as he got ready to polish his bike. In fact, he was so deep in thought about Cait that when a car door slammed nearby, his gaze jumped up.

To his surprise there was a patrol car in front of his house and two of Chicago's finest headed toward him.

"Detective Logan," the first officer said. She was a very pretty young cop who looked vaguely familiar, though Sean couldn't put a name to that face. Oddly enough, though, she kept reminding him of running across a beach.

He nodded to her, then looked at her female partner who was also vaguely familiar, though far taller. "Officers."

"Nice bike," the pretty one said.

Sean looked at his Harley.

"We need you to come with us, Detective."

He looked at the tall one. "What for?" He frowned. "Is this about one of my brothers?"

"Not at all," the pretty one said. "This is about you."

"You'll need to close your garage," the tall one said.

"Excuse me?"

The pretty one came forward. "You need to come with us, Detective. If we have to take you by force we—"

"Excuse me?"

Her perfectly plucked brows drew together. Her voice got kind of nasty, too. "We have a warrant for your arrest."

Sean took a step back. "Matt put you up to this, didn't he?" That nitwit was always getting his new girlfriends to do stuff like this.

"Judge Campbell has issued a warrant for—"

"Cait?" Sean couldn't believe it. "She's having me arrested?"

Both young women narrowed their gazes on him. The pretty one spoke first. "You are coming with us."

Sean was speechless, at least until the tall one pulled out her cuffs. "You're cuffing me, too?"

She muttered, "Judge's orders. We were told you might resist."

"Are you kidding?" Sean laughed. Hell, Cait had been the one doing that. And now she was doing this?

I will convince you. I do love you, Sean . . . I've always loved you.

Hot damn! She was finally showing him that, too. Unless . . .

He quickly sobered. "You're absolutely certain it was Cait who told you to do this? Caitlin Livingston Campbell," he added. "About five-six, dark hair that smells like roses and—" Sean finally paused as the uniforms exchanged a glance. "At least give me a minute to change," he said, "and shower again." He felt his cheeks. "I really should shave again, too."

"No time for that," the tall one said. "The judge wants you now."

Sean's fingers paused on his cheek. "Cait actually said that? Okay, okay," he said, at their impatient looks. "Just let me lock up my bike."

Faster than those two might have believed possible, Sean put his Harley inside, closed the garage and assured his neighbor that this was just a police exercise.

As that old lady returned to her house, Sean put his hands behind his back. "Come on, what are you waiting for? Cuff me."

While that was being done, Sean recalled that phone conversation when he had questioned Cait's sincerity about attending Tim's birthday party.

Tell you what, she had said, *if I don't show up, you can have an ASA contact a judge and have a bench warrant issued for my arrest, with you taking full custody.*

Oh, baby, he had answered, *don't think I haven't thought of that.*

I will convince you, she had said.

With him cuffed like this, that wasn't the only thing she'd be able to do.

"Let's go," he said.

Minutes into the drive, Sean noticed they weren't headed for any courthouse. He wondered if they were taking him back to the Lilac River Inn, the so-called scene of the crime, until they headed in the opposite direction.

At last, they entered an exclusive area of the city where the quiet streets were lined with trees and the stately homes were set back on expansive front yards.

This sure as hell beat a crowded inn. Sean leaned up in the seat. "Can't you drive a little faster?"

The tall one looked over her shoulder at him. "And break the speed limit?"

"I don't want to get another ticket," the pretty one said.

Huh? Were they kidding . . . or had Cait told them to act like this?

Settling back into the seat, Sean told himself to cool it, then felt his heart thudding as the patrol car pulled up to a two-story corner house constructed of dark red brick with white columns and numerous porches. Given this area, it probably cost several million bucks.

"Nice," the tall one said.

"Yeah, maybe," the pretty one said. "But it still ain't LA."

The tall one rolled her eyes. "Look, if we gotta be here, I'm calling my realtor."

Like she could afford this on a cop's salary. "Your daddy rich, too?" Sean asked.

Both women looked over their shoulders at him.

"Now that I have your attention," Sean said, "Let. Me. Out."

At last they did, leading him to the front porch. The tall one pressed the intercom button.

Cait's voice was surprisingly businesslike. "Yes."

"Hi," the tall one said, then frowned as the pretty one elbowed her. "That is," she said in an official voice, "Officers Talbot and Reeves here. We have Detective Logan in custody."

Cait was momentarily silent, then asked, "Is he cuffed?"

Her voice was so sultry Sean's knees sagged.

"Yes, ma'am," the tall one said.

"The door's opened," Cait said.

The pretty officer giggled until she noticed Sean looking at her. "This way," she said in a fake hard voice.

Like a good little boy he followed, then stared at all the marble and crystal in the foyer. He knew Cait was rich, but had no idea how—

"There's a door to your right," Cait's voice suddenly said over the intercom. "Please bring Detective Logan to that office. I'll assume custody at that time so you officers can leave."

"Ah, ma'am," the tall one called out as her gaze continued to search for the source of Cait's voice, "should we un-cuff him?"

"No," Cait said.

The pretty one giggled again.

Sean stared at her, then the room he was led into. Law books and legal journals lined every wall from the floor to the ceiling, but there were also some soft touches. Like the sumptuous burgundy leather sofa that was built for two and strewn with hundreds of rose petals.

"Be very bad," the tall one said to him. "Have fun," the pretty one whispered.

Sean turned and watched them leave. A moment later, the front door slammed.

"Detective Logan."

He felt faintly dizzy at the sound of Cait's voice. During these past days there had been too many times when he feared he'd never hear it again or see her even once more.

He looked over his shoulder now, then turned completely around as she stood in the other doorway to this room.

Her gaze caressed him.

Sean spoke first. "Judge Campbell."

Cait's cheeks flushed. She seemed embarrassed. "Well, not quite yet . . . not officially."

Okay, there was a surprise. Sean looked at the judge's black robe she wore and thought about the cuffs he wore.

"I still need to be sworn in." She gave him a look that was all innocence. "A mere formality. Besides, I had to get you here some way so that you'd start to be convinced. So, let's get rolling on that." Reaching up, she unzipped her robe and let it slip from her shoulders to the floor.

Sean stared. She was beautifully bare except for her black high heels.

"Are you all right?" she asked.

His gaze jumped to hers, then went right back down to

her rosy nipples and those dark, delicate curls between her luscious legs. "What?"

"I'll take that as a yes," Cait said as she went to him.

Sean inhaled sharply as she ran her finger down his cheek to his jaw, then to his chest, then still lower to his jeans and fly that she casually stroked.

It was a moment before he could speak. When he did, his voice sounded strangled. "What are you doing?"

Cait lifted her gaze to his, then looked back down to his jeans. "Convincing you."

He swallowed. "Of what?"

"My intentions." She unsnapped his jeans and lowered his fly.

He inhaled sharply. "What else?"

"My need."

He moaned softly as she ran her forefinger beneath his briefs' elastic waistband. "What else?"

She lifted her face to his. "My love, Sean." She cupped his face in her hands. "I want to be with you. I just have to be with you. I need to share your life and have you share mine. There's no turning back now. I can't. I won't."

Her words were magic; her gaze a gift. Sean could see that all hesitation was gone. In its place was adoration and a peace born of love. This time, she wasn't about to let him go. Her kiss told him that too. It held a tenderness unlike any in the past.

As that kiss lingered and deepened, Cait wrapped her arms around him, covering his hands with her own. Once she had, she gave the cuffs a sharp tug.

Sean stopped kissing her.

Cait eased back.

It was a moment before he seemed to understand what had happened, and even then his expression said he didn't quite believe it. Bringing his hands to the front, he stared at the cuffs dangling from his left wrist. "How'd you do that? Wait a sec," he said before she could answer, "these aren't real?"

Cait slowly shook her head.

Sean frowned. "Those cops weren't real?"

"When they film that new series in the city they'll pretend to be."

"What? They're actresses?"

"Not very good ones, I'm afraid. Their last series—"

"That stupid beach thing." He laughed, remembering, then hauled her into his arms and playfully smacked her bare butt.

"Mmmm," Cait said, snuggling into him. "Now we're cooking."

Sean pressed his mouth to her ear. "I should arrest you."

"And have all your buddies on the force find out about your arrest?"

He eased away and looked at her. "You're not playing fair."

"Who said I was playing?" Cait ran her fingertip down his briefs, then smiled to his sharp intake of breath. "Of course, if we were married, you could arrest me all you wanted and I couldn't say a thing . . . there would be spousal privilege."

"You think?"

"I know." She gently pressed her lips to his. "You'd have all sorts of privileges then."

He started to smile. "Like what?"

For the next few hours, Cait showed him.

Later, as their limbs remained entwined on that petal-strewn leather sofa and their breaths mingled, Cait whispered, "I did good, huh?"

Sean patted her bare butt. "Any better and this'd be a crime scene."

She giggled, then hushed, "I finally convinced you, right?"

Sean yawned.

Cait's heart sank. "I didn't?"

He opened his eyes and looked at her for a long moment. At last, he murmured, "Ask me that again in about fifty years, Mrs. Logan."

Cait smiled. Oh, she would. She most definitely would.

THE INVITATION

Sharon Cullars

One

"Mmmm . . . What's this?" From the door, Jeralyn spotted the long-stemmed rose that lay on the center of her desk. She walked over, placed her briefcase on an adjacent chair, and picked up the flower. Closed and virginal, the scent of the unbloomed petals permeated her office. The unusually pungent smell put her in mind of something or somewhere that she couldn't recall.

"That came along with the envelope there," Ann said, pointing her head at the small cream-colored square that had been beneath the rose. Jeralyn laid the flower down and picked up the envelope with her name inscribed in gold on the front.

She could feel Ann's anticipation from across the room. Her assistant wasn't usually nosy, but it was rare that Jeralyn received flowers. Or in this case, a very lovely, lonely bloom.

Jeralyn opened the seal, pulled out a cream, gilt-edged invitation with florid script. Another scent touched her nose, this one more subtle. A cologne. A men's cologne. Quiet, seductive. And again, familiar.

"Someone you know?" Ann's voice pulled her from her study.

Jeralyn read the invitation out loud.

"'You are invited to a private gathering at Avalon Hall on Saturday, July 21, at 8:00 P.M. Formal dress required.'" She turned the invitation around to the back. Blank. "Hmmm, there's no name."

Ann whistled beneath her breath. "Avalon Hall. Isn't that one of those mansions along Pacific Heights? Yeah, it is, it is. I just read about it a few weeks ago in the Sunday 'Homes Section.' There's a group trying to get the home put on some historical register. Maybe that's a fund-raiser they're inviting you to?"

"Then they need to say so. This is the most incomplete invitation I've ever received. And if it is a fund-raiser, why're they inviting me? I don't have anything to do with building preservation or anything historical for that matter."

"Yeah, and what's with the rose? It's such an intimate touch. So, are you going?"

Jeralyn sat down behind her desk, kicked off her shoes, looked at the invitation again. "It says the twenty-first, eight P.M. That's this Saturday. Talk about short notice. Anyway, the only thing I'm going to be doing at eight o'clock this Saturday is soaking in a hot bath and catching up on my novel."

"You're not even a little curious? I mean, that's a beautiful mansion. The article says it's nearly one hundred and seventy years old. Built by some old rich guy, a sailor or something doing with the sea. He supposedly killed himself up there after his chippy wife left him for a younger guy. Aren't you even a little tempted?"

"As interesting as that sounds, I think I'll pass. Besides, if they're looking for money out of me, they're woefully deluded. I'm down to my last twenty and that's either going toward food or the mortgage, I haven't decided."

Ann laughed and gathered up a stack of folders that sat on top of Jeralyn's file cabinet.

"Stop pretending you're so piss-poor. No one is poor who can afford that beautiful condo you're in."

"Sweetie, that beautiful condo is why I'm so poor. The assessment fee alone is cutting me down to a financial nub."

"Your fault then."

"Right-o."

"So move."

"Nope."

"'Cause you love it."

"Yep."

Ann just shook her head in mock consternation and left, making sure she closed the door behind her.

Jeralyn shoved the rose to the corner of her desk, then for the next hour concentrated on completing the two briefs for her upcoming sessions in appellate court next week. The first was iffy: A nineteen year old who had killed his girlfriend after stalking her for months. The evidence was damning, but still she felt the pictures of the victim's body had been too inflammatory and shouldn't have been allowed in. She was arguing that the photos had prejudiced the jury. The second case was a little better, but not by much. At least here the judge's error was more obvious. He should have allowed the lesser charge to be considered by the jury instead of only allowing first degree murder. And at least in this case, she believed the client was innocent.

Going over the briefs, she pored over the sentences, trying to see where she could bolster her arguments. After she was satisfied that she was indeed finished, she sat back and sighed. And thought for the umpteenth time that she needed a change. These cases were emotionally draining to her soul.

She had no one to blame but herself. She should have closed up shop a long time ago, about the time she lost her idealistic and quite misguided vision of providing an avenue of justice for the misunderstood and the wrongly accused. She had soon come to realize after her first year that the ratio of guilty among her roster of "innocent until proven otherwise" was comparatively larger than she would have liked.

And yet they had the money to keep her in her condo on the bay as well as pay her expenses. Most of her clients now weren't the unfortunate who had to be appointed defense attorneys by the courts. No, her clients resided at swanky addresses and had the money to obtain someone with a good track record. And she had built up an excellent win record over the years. She was as good as their money could buy.

She closed the door on that thought. She couldn't afford to go there, not if she didn't want to bring on another round of the guilts. She wanted to avoid that familiar pique that told her she was whoring herself for luxury. But sadly, she had no other measure for success in her life. No close family. No significant other with whom she could share walks on that same beach she was paying a mint to see from her ceiling-to-floor condo windows. Although she had a few close friends, she no longer mentioned her work to them because she had tired of seeing their eyes become distant and disapproving as she talked about defending people they considered scum. She refused to listen to their silent indictments.

It was enough she indicted herself whenever she looked in the mirror.

The phone buzzed on her second line and she saw Ann's number on the display. Her first line was blinking on hold. She picked up the second line.

"There's someone calling for you," Ann declared with a hint of girlish mirth in her voice. "A Mr. Valmer who wants to know whether you received his invitation."

Jeralyn peered over at the forgotten card. "Did he say what organization he's with?"

"Uhn-uhn. Tried to get the info, but he insists on speaking with you personally. Sounds very distinguished."

"Distinguished, huh? Okay, I'll get it."

She picked up the blinking line. "This is Jeralyn Harris. How may I help you?"

"Ms. Harris, thank you for taking my call. My name is Andrew Valmer and I'm chairman of the Wright Association. Wright with a 'W.' We're a philanthropic society head-quartered here in San Francisco and we were given your name as someone who might be interested in joining."

Ann had been right about the voice. There was a clipped formality, tinged with a faint accent she couldn't pinpoint. Actually more like a blending of accents, as though he had traveled extensively. Yet she could swear she'd heard his voice before.

"Wright Association? I've never heard of it. Who did you say gave you my name?" In her job, suspicion was nurtured and honed. It was dangerous to be without it.

"I didn't. Although I can tell you he is a mutual friend."

"I'm sorry, Mr. Valmer, but thank you anyway for your invitation. I'm busy this Saturday, so I won't be able to attend. And unfortunately, I'm not able to donate anything at this time. Although, you can send me a brochure, and I might be able to do so in the future."

The laughter was soft and unexpected. And it raised her hackles. She was positive she knew his voice, and it was killing her trying to remember from where.

"Actually, Saturday is not a fund-raiser. It's a private gathering, a small get-together for a select number of our associates. It's also a rare open-door event for possible new members. We're very circumspect about whom we invite and I guarantee you that you will not encounter the usual or the mundane."

Despite her misgivings, her curiosity was piqued.

"And what exactly does this philanthropic society do?"

"We fund a number of organizations that provide for the

indigent and homeless. We like to help the underserved instead of the undeserved. Money can make the difference whether a man lives or dies, can it not?"

She didn't know why that last question sounded a little accusing, personal.

"Yes, it can. It often does. So I'll be happy to donate money . . . when I can."

"And again, I'm not looking for your money."

"Then what do you want?"

"I want you to attend Saturday. I want to see you there, Ms. Harris. I think the evening would be advantageous to you."

"In what way?"

"Networking, for one. A successful lawyer like yourself probably has aspirations about moving up. Who knows who you might meet? Unless, you're satisfied with your station in life."

Station. What a strange word to use. "I'm fine with my position. . . ."

"But you could do better, couldn't you, Ms. Harris?" She heard a mocking tone when he said her name.

"Do I know you, Mr. Valmer?"

"Like I said, we have a mutual friend."

"And why won't you name this 'mutual friend'? You know, never mind. I've already told you that I won't be attending. And I don't see the point in arguing the matter. Now if you want a future donation, then I would suggest you send me literature about your . . . philanthropic society. You can get my office address from the phone listing. Now, I really have to go."

"I didn't mean to upset you, Jerri."

No one had called her by her shortened name in years. And not with the intimacy she heard in his voice. He did know her, she was sure of it. And he was playing games.

"You haven't upset me, Mr. Valmer—or whoever you are. If this is some sort of joke . . ."

"It isn't."

"Then why do I get the feeling that we've met before? And not under pleasant circumstances?"

"Maybe you are thinking of someone else then. I assure you, I'm not pulling a hoax on you. The invitation is a legitimate one. I hope that you can attend, but I'll understand if you choose not to. I won't take up any more of your time."

"Thank you, Mr. Valmer."

She hung up, exasperated. But she had to admit to herself that she was also intrigued. Her curiosity had been whetted by his voice and in the hours afterward, as she finished up various projects, she tried to attach a face to it. For some reason, an image of dark hair and dark eyes emerged, but did not fully crystallize into full features.

Outside the window, another late evening fog was rolling in. The Inner Sunset district was famous, or infamous, for its hazy days. Sunshine was a rare commodity, and days morphed into dusk with only a slight dimming of light. Still, as she stepped out into the chilly evening after locking up the office for the night, she saw that the streets were only just starting to fill with tourists and early diners seeking the various fares offered by the numerous ethnic restaurants and cafes. Down the street was San Tung's, so popular that even a little before seven the parking spaces out front were gone. Actually, she didn't feel like Chinese tonight. Maybe she would just pick up a bagel at Noah's and head on home. She was more tired than hungry. She needed to be rested for a full day in court tomorrow.

Walking to her car, her spider senses came alive, always a warning that she was being watched. She looked around at the network of townhouses, some of them residences, a few, like her law office, discreet businesses that melded into the surrounding neighborhood. People were walking, strolling under the streetlights. A few young kids were rollerblading down the path. Everything seemed normal, yet she couldn't shake the feeling.

She turned and spotted someone standing in a doorway, hidden by shadows. The silhouette was tall, masculine.

Though she couldn't see his face, she knew his eyes were trained on her. He was observing her much as a predator scoped its prey. There were so many people around, she should have felt relatively safe. She didn't.

She got into her car and pulled off, turning east at the light. Noah's was scratched off her itinerary tonight. She wanted to get home, to the safety of her building and behind the security of her deadbolts.

At every light, she glanced in the rearview mirror to spot the cars behind her, to see if any one car might be following her. By the time she pulled in front of her building, she felt a little better. But she did a cursory check up and down the streets before unlocking the entry door and slipping in quickly.

Adrian watched her from his car window as she shut the door. Then he started the engine to the Jaguar, pulled out of the parking space just a few doors up from her building and maneuvered down the lane of condos on either side of the street. The neighborhood was upscale, nice, safe. The kind of area that lent to the illusion of being secluded, a place where one didn't have to deal with any ugliness or the inconvenience of other people's pain and poverty.

The same poverty he had grown up in. The poverty that had led his brother to the streets, even as Adrian escaped and found an avenue to a life that the two young boys had only dreamed about.

That poverty, that ugliness, had turned Amil's soul, had led him down darker paths.

Adrian drove down Mason heading toward a hotel in central downtown where he was holed up in a suite. He turned into the entry leading to the underground parking bank, and pulled into his reserved space. Money bought a lot of amenities.

He knew he wasn't alone as he got out of the car. He had half expected to see the silhouette emerge from one of the columns separating lanes.

After four years of avoiding each other, they were now in each other's shadow, tracking, stalking.

As Amil approached Adrian, Adrian noticed that his brother's cheeks were more sunken than they were a couple of weeks ago. And the dark long coat didn't hang as squarely. Amil wasn't eating, or was eating very little. He was on a mission and rudimentary things like food were not high on his priority list.

"What do you think you're doing?" Amil said without greeting, his accent reverting to its Bronx past. "You're following her? Why?"

"And how do you know what I'm doing . . . unless you're having me followed, too."

Amil didn't bother denying it, which was an affirmation in itself. "What d'you think you're going to do?"

"I don't know, Amil. Maybe stop this before it goes too far. She's become your obsession since . . ."

"Since I was released from purgatory? Actually, she was on my mind even before then. She's what got me through it."

"You need to give this up."

"Not going to happen. And you need to step out of my way. This is none of your business."

Adrian stared into eyes like his own but deader. "Then I guess we're where we were four years ago, standing on opposite sides."

"That's because you always choose to go against me."

"I'm not going to let you destroy yourself . . . or me . . . or her."

"And why do you care? What's she to you . . . now?"

"My question exactly."

Amil's face hardened more, if that were possible. "She's my reason for living this long."

"And killing her will do what? Bring you peace."

"Yes." The finality of the word, the quiet tone in which it was spoken, let Adrian know that Amil had already passed the point of rational thought. There would be no reasoning with him now.

"Are you willing to do whatever it takes to stop me?" Amil challenged.

"Yes."

The invisible gauntlets crashed to the ground as Adrian and his brother locked stares. Then Amil turned abruptly, his coat swinging like a black phantom behind him, and strode away. Adrian headed for the elevator, determining that he may have to kill his brother for this sick game to end.

Two

"I'm not going to tell you again, Mr. Ballard, sit down!" the judge warned, her eyes glaring behind the bifocals. Jeralyn pulled at Steve Ballard's arm, venomously whispering for him to sit down.

"Counselor, control your client or I'm going to have him booted from this courtroom and held in contempt."

"Yes, your honor."

Jeralyn's grip tightened as she pressed nails through the cloth of his tailored suit. She knew he felt them, and for a moment, thought that he was going to ignore her silent entreaty. But then he jerked his arm away, straightened his tie, and took his seat beside her. He looked at the witness as though he were imagining his hands around her throat. Which wasn't good for the jury to see, especially since he was on trial for strangling his wife. The witness was the victim's sister.

Only after Jeralyn was sure her client wasn't going to create another scene did she approach the stand to cross-examine. The woman was visibly shaken by her brother-in-law's outburst, her eyes darting from him to Jeralyn and back again. Jeralyn suppressed a sigh. A sympathetic prosecution witness was a case killer—and Deborah Trenton was sympathetic: Petite, blond pixie-cut, baby blues that appeared guileless, overwhelmed. The pastel blue dress with a white Peter Pan collar added to the effect. The D.A. John Weaver knew how to set a backdrop and how to arrange the props. But Jeralyn's bit of digging into the woman's background was about to throw Weaver's carefully set tableau into disarray. She was going to have to work this carefully, though. Any aggressive move on her part would alienate the jury; they were already throwing daggers at her client as it was. Be a lady, not a bitch.

"Ms. Trenton, you say that you feared my client, were frightened by his temper, and that you never wanted to be around him. Is that correct?"

The witness nodded, followed the action with a demure "Yes."

"And it's his temper that leads you to believe he killed your sister, is that also correct?"

Another soft "Yes."

"Again, you tried never to be alone with him?"

The eyes widened this time, as though a sudden prescience had finally given her a clue where she was being led with these questions.

"Yes, that's correct." This time her voice was strained, a little shaky.

Jeralyn walked back to the folder on the table where her client still sat, still glaring. She wished he'd stop that. He was fucking up the case just by acting stupid.

She pulled out the credit card receipts from the motel. Also, there were pictures that the deceased had had taken by a detective she'd hired. The detective was just outside the courtroom doors, waiting to be called in if necessary. These photos had been a last-minute coup and weren't on the list of exhibits to be presented. She knew the other side would object vehemently, but the damage would have already been done. The pictures wouldn't improve her client's image, but it would definitely shatter the Little Ms. Poppins illusion that the other side was trying to perpetrate with Deborah Trenton. The photos had been taken with a zoom lens pointed at the window of a particular first floor motel room where Deborah and Steve Ballard had met repeatedly. Jeralyn was pretty sure the state didn't know about the evidence, otherwise they would have already taken measures to do some damage control.

"Ms. Trenton, I have copies here of several credit card transactions for the Harbor Motel over on Eleventh Avenue. Do you recognize the signature?"

Deborah Trenton paled and her eyes blinked rapidly as she viewed her own signature on the indicting copies. As expected, the D.A. began a series of objections about being unduly surprised with the new evidence, but after Jeralyn explained the relevance to the witness's testimony, the judge allowed it. And in the next few minutes, Jeralyn laid out the scene of an adulterous husband and a sister's betrayal. The judge subsequently allowed admission of the photos and the detective, blowing away the façade and leaving the issue not of a cad and the demure, innocent sister but two flawed people, one who was accused of murder, one now proven a liar and perjurer.

By the end of the day, the prosecution was barely limping, but they weren't walking as steady as they had at the beginning of yesterday's trial. They didn't have concrete evidence linking the husband to Linda Ballard's death and they hadn't been able to show that he had been anywhere near the murder scene at the estimated time of death. Jeralyn had already called two witnesses who had seen her client in a bar, drinking himself into a stupor. He'd gone there after a violent argument with his wife, but had already testified that he'd had nothing to do with her death. His lengthy time in the bar put the murder timeline set up by the prosecution in question. But the real question hanging over the proceedings was if Steve Ballard didn't kill his wife, then who did? Hopefully the jurors had enough reasonable doubt to wonder whether the prosecution had jumped the gun.

The case would go to the jury tomorrow after the summations. And Steve Ballard would finally know whether he would spend the next twenty to thirty years as a free man or behind bars, not eligible for parole for another fifteen years. By then he would be sixty-eight and a good chunk of his life would be over. A travesty—if he were innocent.

Jeralyn just wasn't sure. And again, she didn't really want to know.

She walked out with her client and attempted to encourage him with the customary assurances. She was rewarded with a smirk that brought his lips together in an ugly line. "You really showed that bitch up to be the liar she is. Pretending like she and her sister were so close when she bad-mouthed Linda every time we were together. At least the jurors know that I'm not the monster Deb tried to make me out to be."

Jeralyn didn't say anything, but simply nodded her head as she told him to be on time tomorrow. As for the monster bit, her client had already shown the jury his volatile temper. And it didn't help that he was a hulky figure with meaty hands that even she could imagine around his wife's throat. The problem was that he could very well be convicted not on the evidence, but because of what the jury perceived him to be—a belligerent bully who had cheated on his wife. A wife who had died under violent circumstances. And with no other suspects even considered.

He walked toward one bank of elevators and she headed toward another, ready to go back to her office. It was a quarter after four and she was tired. Weary tired. Leaving the crowded elevator, she passed the security station, her briefcase in one hand, her blazer in the other as she walked through the doors leading outside the justice hall. It was late afternoon and the temperature was still above ninety. The heat settled on her like an uncomfortable wool blanket. She started walking east to the parking garage, and got swallowed up in the rush hour stream of bodies heading toward cars, buses, and trains.

Someone called out her full name and she turned. In the flurry of people passing by, a man stood just at the edge of the sidewalk a few steps away. Tall, dark hair, looking impossibly cool in a charcoal gray pinstriped suit, black shirt and silk gray tie, his cosmopolitan looks were out of place here. Sunglasses hid his eyes. Everything about him said money, including the insignia on the car keys in his hand: Jaguar. She watched his approach, noting the long stride. He reached her in three steps. Caution stiffened her joints, made her clutch her briefcase tighter.

"Yes?"

"My name is Adrian Vance. I need to speak with you."

His tone was sober, quiet. And just like the call from yesterday, it stirred something in her memory. Yet the voices weren't the same. Still, there was something to the timbre . . . why did she know it? She did a mental shake; she didn't have time to figure it out or talk shop on the street. He probably wanted to retain her services.

"If this is about a case, I'm swamped with work right now. I'm not taking on anything for the next few weeks."

He shook his head. "I'm not here about a case. I'm here about you."

Her internal bells were jangling, warning lights flashing. She hadn't forgotten last night's shadow, the man who seemed to watch her from a doorway. Just as the man in front of her watched her now behind those dark glasses.

"You're here about me? Why?"

"There's someone who wants to hurt you . . ."

The late afternoon sun blazed hot, brightening everything below to a stark summer white. Yet his words hovered like a dark cloud. She might as well have been standing in an unlit alley where menacing figures leaped out from shadows. And he was one of those figures.

"Is this a threat?"

"No, a warning. I'm not the one you need to be afraid of."

"But you were following me last night." This wasn't a question. She was sure he was the one.

"I was making sure you got home safely."

"Why would someone want to hurt me? Who? A former client?"

"This has nothing to do with your job. This is about something that happened nearly fifteen years ago. When you were seventeen."

"Seventeen? I wasn't even in the city then. I was down south . . ."

"Yes, in Florida. Naples. You lived there before you came up here to attend law school."

To hear her history come from a stranger's lips disconcerted her.

"What do you know about me?" The question came out an accusation.

"I know more than you obviously remember, Jerri."

The intimacy with which he said her name made her stomach flutter.

"How do you know me?"

"I know you well. So does my brother."

"Your brother?"

"He goes by Amil now. But you used to know him as Drew. Andrew."

All she could do was shake her head. For so long, she'd struggled to remember the years that constantly eluded her whenever she sought to chase them. It was as if her life hadn't begun until the year she turned eighteen. Before that, images were blurred and voices muted. The only certainty gleaned from her past was that she had been alone in the world for a long time. And now that past was pursuing her and she didn't know why.

"How do I know you or your brother?"

A hand came up, touched her cheek, made her catch her breath. For some reason she didn't pull away even when his thumb began lightly stroking her jawline. It was a familiar touch. "You really don't remember, do you?"

She couldn't explain her sadness, but she refused to let it show. "No, I don't."

"We need to go somewhere where we can talk privately. Where I can tell you what you're facing. If you don't come with me now, you won't live to see next week."

She finally pulled away from the seductive touch. "Go with you, where? I don't know you. How do I know you're not the one who wants to hurt me?"

"Because if I had wanted to hurt you, I could have done so last night on the street. Or better yet in your office after your secretary left you alone. I know it's a lot to trust me, but I'm asking you to do it."

Again, she didn't understand why she was standing here listening to him. And why, against her common sense, she was starting to believe him.

"If someone's after me like you say, then why not just go to the police? You can tell them what you know."

He shook his head. "Amil has ways of avoiding the police . . . and getting what he wants."

"I don't understand. What could I have possibly done at seventeen that would make someone want to kill me years later? It doesn't make sense. What did I do to your brother?"

"It's not just what he thinks you did to him. Someone he cared about died."

The implication brought a chill to her flesh even under the hot sun. "Because of me? But I swear I don't remember."

"I can see that, Jerri."

The question stirred the cloud in her mind as she tried to reach for something out of her grasp. And the futility made her angry.

"I don't care what you say. I'm not going anywhere with you. I have briefs to work on tonight and I have a case to finish up tomorrow. You can't disrupt my life like this."

He grabbed her arm before she could move away. "And I'm telling you you won't have a life to disrupt if you don't come with me now. I know Amil and what he's capable of. I also know how to stop him. The police won't be able to and before they can even try, they'll be fishing your body out of the bay. So if I'm frightening you, good. You need to be frightened."

She stood frozen by a wave of emotions: Fear, anger . . . and curiosity. Yes, he was frightening her. But he had also awakened questions that she thought were stilled a long time ago. He knew about her, about her past. Maybe he could tell her things, give her back a part of herself she thought was lost for good.

"My car . . ."

"Don't worry about your car. My car's over here."

He took her arm and led her to where a sleek black Jaguar was parked. He opened the door and waited for her to get in. She hesitated, but his proximity didn't allow her an option. She could feel his eyes boring into her, demanding compliance. After a few seconds, she sighed and slid in. The motion made her skirt hitch up and she quickly pulled it down, but she had the uncomfortable feeling that he had gotten an appreciable eyeful and that he had not looked away.

He finally closed the door and as he walked to the driver's

side, she felt a sudden compulsion to jump out, find a cop, anyone who might help. But in an instant he was beside her, and the opportunity was gone. He turned to her for a moment, and she could feel his eyes through the glasses, but when she turned to look at him, only her reflected image stared back at her. The reflection looked uneasy. She opened her mouth to ask why he was staring, but he turned away and started the car.

She wanted to believe she hadn't made a stupid mistake, that her instincts weren't so skewed that she had let danger walk right up on her. Stupidity aside, the issue was a moot one. She was here now, and if it turned out he meant her harm, then she was going to have to fight with whatever she had handy. Unfortunately, the only thing she was carrying was her key chain pepper spray that she had bought after being mugged last year. She slipped open her purse, felt around for her keys, found them at the bottom.

"You won't need that," he said as he maneuvered into the lane going north.

"Need what?" Her heart was lodged in her throat.

"Whatever you're looking for. Gun?"

She started to correct him, then thought that maybe it was better if he thought she had something lethal. "I'm an attorney. It would be stupid of me not to carry protection. And if your brother's after me, as you claim, I don't want to be caught off guard."

"You won't be caught. You'll be safe with me for right now."

"Until when?"

He didn't answer immediately, making the lining of her stomach burn. A pre-ulcer courtesy of her job and too many nervous nights.

"Until the situation is taken care of."

No, this wasn't going to work. "I can't just go missing indefinitely. I have cases, people I need to see. People who will miss me. You can't just take me out of circulation like this. I'm closing a case tomorrow."

"Then I guess you'll have to call in, say you're sick, ask for a continuance. Tell me, have you had any strange calls recently, something out of the ordinary?"

She didn't have to think more than a few seconds about that one. "There was an invitation yesterday . . . followed by a phone call, but what does . . . wait, are you saying that the caller was your brother?" She had to catch her breath. She'd been suspicious of the caller from the beginning. But to think that he meant her harm . . . to kill her.

"Most likely it was him. Who did he say he was?"

"I don't recall. The name was Valmer or something like that. He sent me an invitation."

Adrian Vance nodded his head. "Valmer is one of his aliases. He uses it quite often. You said he sent you an invitation? To what?"

"Some gala thrown by an organization I never heard of. Wright, I think he said. Supposedly it's a philanthropic society, but he wouldn't explain any more than that or why he'd sent me the invitation in the first place. I had the feeling he was playing with me but I didn't know why at the time. All I knew was that I'd heard his voice somewhere." She remembered something else. "He called me Jerri. Like you did. No one calls me Jerri, just Jeralyn."

"Jerri, with a J, not a G. You were always picky about that. You never liked your middle name either—Alicia. Your grandmother's name."

They were passing the Convention Center. She watched the tourists blankly, too wrapped up in her private misery. "So I killed someone?" she asked after a few moments. "Who?"

"Her name was Sarah. You didn't kill her. But Amil blames you for her death anyway."

She took a deep breath, shored up her strength to ask the next question. "Why can't I remember any of this?"

"Because of the accident. You were hurt for a long time. The police believed Amil was responsible for all of it. And he went to prison. He was released a little over four years ago. Since then, he's been searching for you, trying to track you down. I knew he would come after you eventually, but I only found out about his vendetta a few weeks ago and I tracked him here. And then I found you."

They were moving through downtown traffic which had become snarled bumper to bumper. She felt uncomfortably sticky, felt a bead of sweat tickle the skin between her cleavage as it coursed down.

"Where are we going?"

"I moved out of my hotel this morning to the Serrano. I had to take measures to make sure my brother wasn't following me again. They've probably been trailing you, though. Which is why we're going to another hotel where I'll register us, then we'll take another car over to the Serrano. That should temporarily throw them off."

"Sounds like we're in an espionage movie."

He smiled then. It transformed the lines of his face, made it less intimidating. An afternoon growth highlighted the angles of his jawline, added depth to a dimple. Should she really remember this face? Had she seen him smile before?

"Pretty much. Amil is a big aficionado of spy movies. Fancies himself some sort of underground boss. Even has some flunkies working for him. People he met in prison."

"He went to prison because of me," she said almost to herself.

"Don't think he didn't deserve to. He's more to blame for what happened than anyone alive."

"And you're going to tell me everything?"

"Yes, Jerri, I'm going to tell you everything. And we're

going to figure a way to keep you out of my brother's clutches."

"Seventeen . . . that was so long ago. And I only remember parts of that time and even less before that; I haven't been able to remember things, people. Certainly not you . . . or your brother. All I know about that year is that my parents were killed."

He nodded. "Yes, they were killed the day you were hurt, the day you almost died."

He pulled into an underground parking enclosure next to the Grand Hyatt, slipped into a space near the elevator bank, and turned off the engine. "We're going to the registration desk to get my name into the system. I'll use another name, one that I often use when I'm in town. A name that Amil will know if he's hacking into the system. For right now, that should throw them off temporarily. I'm sure we're being watched, even now. So we'll have to wait in the suite, change our clothes; I bought you a dress to change into. Hopefully, I got the size right. In another hour or so, we'll take the garage elevator down again. Another car will be waiting. My brother is not a fool, but the people working for him aren't all that shrewd."

"I don't understand. If your brother wants me dead, why doesn't he just take a long-range rifle and shoot me while I'm walking near my office or grabbing a coffee? It would be easier. Why all the subterfuge to get me alone?"

Adrian turned to her. "He wants to do it up-close and personal. Hands on. He wants to make you suffer."

Her breath caught in her throat, and her stomach burned. She closed her eyes to try to calm herself, to steady her breathing.

"He really hates me then," she said quietly.

He was quiet for a moment. "No. He loves you that much. And it's driven him crazy."

"Love?" If she thought her world had become unsteady in the last minutes, it was now whirling out of control.

"At seventeen, you ran off with Andrew. The two of you eloped, but you left him on your wedding night. The night you got hurt and your parents were killed. A few days after Sarah died."

"Wait a minute, are you telling me your brother is my—"

"Yes, Amil's your husband."

She stared at him, trying to find something in his face that said he was lying, that he was playing some sort of sick joke on her. That he was trying to hurt her for whatever reason. But she couldn't read anything there. His face had become a mask again.

Somewhere inside, the absurdity of the moment began bubbling, wanting to burst forth. And she found herself giggling. Which caused him to cock his eyebrow.

"This is hardly a laughing matter."

"Yeah, it is," she said as the giggles turned into uncontrollable laughter. "This morning I woke up single, alone, worried about this damnable case that I'll probably lose, wondering what I was going to pick up for dinner, when I was going to have time to finish my novel, catch up on some sleep—and now you're telling me I have some crazed husband that I can't remember who wants to kill me 'up-close and personal' for something I did years ago. And that he's responsible for my parents' deaths and is the reason I haven't been able to remember a whole chunk of my life. And you're my—brother-in-law, who comes dashing to my rescue—in a Jaguar no less—ready to protect me from my said crazed husband." She caught her breath. "You know, I couldn't sell this plot in a book. Oh God, this isn't happening. This is . . . this is . . . oh God . . ." The laughter ebbed as the fear began creeping in again.

"C'mon, we don't need to be sitting here. We don't know

what Amil has planned." He got out of the car, walked to her side, and opened the door. He held out a hand and she took it. For a second, his hand closed over hers, a small warmth countering the chill of fear in her whole body. Then he released her, and there was no comfort at all.

But an arm went around her shoulder as he walked her to the elevators. As they waited, she noticed his subtle scope of the garage, his head barely turning as he cased every direction, watching, anticipating. She also noticed that he stood at her back, shielding her with his body. She didn't like the idea of him getting hurt because of her. And, if what he'd told her was true, she didn't want to be responsible for another death.

Sarah. Who was she?

The elevator pinged and the doors opened. His hand did not leave her back as they walked in and he pushed the lobby button as the door closed. She realized the illusion of safety that he provided was just that, an illusion. She'd seen too many cases where all measures had been taken to protect an innocent, only for that innocent to still meet with his or her fate.

If she was destined to die, there wasn't a thing this man, this stranger who said he was her brother-in-law, could do about it.

The elevator opened onto the main lobby. She'd never been in the San Francisco Grand Hyatt and under any other circumstances, she might have been impressed with its grandeur, the Chinese artifacts and intricate vases lining the aisles. Instead, she found herself looking among the masses of bodies, checking in or out, milling around with their luggage, laughing or gawking, her eyes seeking out someone whose face mirrored, even slightly, the man beside her. A stranger who supposedly was her husband. The thought was so ludicrous her brain fought to register it. Surely, she would remember someone she loved enough to run away with. And why would she have left him on their wedding night? And why had he killed her parents? Who was Sarah and how did she die?

Adrian escorted her to a closed registration window, bypassing the regular line, which was lengthy, snaking down an aisle. He pulled out a cell phone, dialed a number.

"Elaine, this is Allen Martins, I need you to come up front and give me the key to the suite upstairs."

Shortly, a door behind the window opened and an auburn-haired woman with a dark blazer sporting the hotel's insignia stepped out. She saw Adrian and gave him a luminous smile.

"Mr. Martins, I didn't know you were in town. You should have called in advance and I would have made sure everything was ready for you when you arrived."

"I apologize, Elaine, for showing up without notice. Would you register us so we can go right up to the suite?"

At the "we," Elaine looked at Jeralyn for the first time and raised an eyebrow. "Of course, I'll take care of that for you." Her smile wasn't as wide as she took two key cards and swiped them through a coder.

"Here you are." She handed him the cards, the smile back on her lips, but her eyes reflected some other emotion than joy. Jealousy? Or maybe she wasn't used to seeing an interracial couple . . . although they definitely weren't a couple. She wondered how Elaine would respond if she told her that Adrian was "just family."

Adrian took her arm, led her through the throng of bodies. She noticed he was peering around as she had done, looking for his brother. Or someone sent by his brother. His eyes locked on a lone man standing just at the far end of the register's desk. The man was dressed in a black jacket, white wifebeater, and jeans. He appeared to be reading a magazine while waiting for someone. Still, Adrian's grip tightened as they reached a lone elevator just off the traffic path.

A short ride later, they were standing in front of a door at the end of a long corridor. The door opened onto a comfortable, but conservative-looking suite with a beige divan and chairs, set off by black and gold-trimmed lamps, and a glass table. The master bedroom was off to the left, a smaller room to the right.

She nervously looked away from the large bed visible in the master bedroom.

What had she gotten herself into?

"Feel free to relax," he said, taking off his jacket and arranging it around the back of one of the chairs. He took off his sunglasses to reveal grayish blue eyes. They were an interesting clash against his coloring and dark hair.

"Hardly likely." Still she took a seat facing a large window looking out on the downtown skyline. Impressive view.

"Well, try to not to be too nervous. You're going to need your wits about you if we're going to get out of this situation. You want anything to drink?"

She shook her head. "I don't drink."

That smile appeared again. "I remember. You never had a taste for it. Used to grimace trying to force down champagne. Let me see. There's some Sprite in the refrigerator. I remember you either liking that or was it Seven-Up?"

Sprite had been her favorite. But not anymore. "I'll take a Pepsi, if you have it."

"Got it." He walked over to the huge honor bar, opened it and pulled out a sweating can of Pepsi. He walked over to where she sat, handed her the can. She looked up to find him staring at her face.

"What? Have I changed much?"

"Yes and no," he said quietly before walking over to a chair facing hers and sitting down. "You were young, beautiful. Headstrong and vibrant. That's what pulled Amil to you. He became so obsessed he pushed Sarah away, not knowing how much that would hurt her. And Sarah being as impulsive as she was, jumped off a bridge into the Gulf. She left a note blaming Drew—Amil. That was too much drama for your parents; they wanted Amil away from you. Away from me."

"Wait. I don't want to know all of this right now. It's too much. I need time to process it all. And you need to tell me the story slowly so I can get an idea what—or who—I'm up against."

"I agree. We'll have more time to talk when we get to the Serrano. Right now, you should try to relax."

"Relax? You must be kidding."

"Well then, try to at least not get any more stressed out. You and I are going to get through this. And I know you. You can deal with any situation, which is probably why you became a lawyer."

He loosened his tie, sat back. "Why did you become a lawyer, Jerri?"

"You know, please don't call me that. I don't know you and I would rather keep this professional."

He smiled and again the dimple deepened. He was handsome, but not with the mannequin allure of models one saw on the runway or on the pages of *GQ*. He was instead a cleaned-up version of a laborer, a very suave one, with a well-developed torso as though he was used to lifting heavy objects and stretching muscles, working his pectorals. She could see the lines of his chest through his lightweight shirt.

She realized she was staring only when he said, "Are you remembering or just curious?"

"Remembering what?"

The smile was gone. "Us."

She swallowed hard. "There was an 'us'?"

He nodded and she saw his features settle into a wistful sadness. "I was the reason you left Amil. You and I had been . . . together . . . for months. Then we argued about something—I don't even remember what now—and you tried to hurt me with Amil. I don't think you meant it to go as far as it did; I don't think you ever meant to hurt him. But leaving him the way you did once you decided you didn't want to stay married to him, that did something to him. You ran back to your parents' house and he followed. There was a fire and your parents were killed. You fell down the stairs trying to find them and hit your head. You were in the hospital for months."

"Amil started the fire?"

He nodded. "At least that's what the police thought since he was found passed out near your home. He had matches on him and an empty gas can was near his hand. Drew, Amil, swore up and down that he didn't do it, but he couldn't explain why he had the gas can. Add in the fact that you left him that night—at the hotel, no less—and it seemed an open-and-shut case as far as the jury was concerned. Because he couldn't afford a decent lawyer, he had to settle for a public defender who wasn't nearly up to par. The prosecutor crucified him and Amil got twenty years for your parents' murder and your attempted murder."

She shook her head in frustration. "I don't remember any of this, I swear I don't. All I remember is going to live with my mother's sister. From that point on is where my memory is clear. Anything before that—even my childhood—is muddled inside my head. Still, you'd think I would remember being married, or at least us. How close were we?" She set the unopened can of soda down on a coaster on the table, not sure if she really wanted the answer.

"I don't think you're ready to know all the details. Just know that we were lovers, and you were very young and determined to get out from beneath your parents' thumb—which is why I wondered why you became an attorney. They had planned that for you, and you really didn't want

that. I thought maybe your aunt had persuaded you to follow their plans."

Jeralyn shook her head. "She never pressed me on anything about a career. She always treated me too delicately,
like she was compensating for my losing my parents. In the
end, she let me do what I wanted—and I ran wild for awhile.
But then I realized I didn't know what I wanted out of my
life and that I was heading nowhere. Maybe what my parents drilled into me surfaced at that point, I can't say really.
Going into law seemed like the thing to do at the time.
Now, I'm not so sure."

"You're not happy with your choice?"

"I don't know if happiness is what I was aiming for. I
think all I wanted was some structure, some purpose . . ."

He shook his head, a wry smile on his lips. "That's not
the Jerri I remember. You wanted to be an artist. You used
to paint beautiful scenes of the coast. You liked to go diving
and you liked to take pictures. You used to rush headlong
into perilous, sometimes idiotic situations, especially if you
thought someone needed your help. You were a busybody
and quite nosy. But those were things I loved about you.
Now that I think about it, it was probably those very traits
that led you to become a defense attorney."

"How much do you know about me . . . now?"

He shook his head. "Not much. After your aunt took
you away, I didn't try to find you. I thought it would be better for you if I stayed out of your life. You didn't remember
me anyway, or anything that happened between us. And
even if you had, I convinced myself that you wouldn't want
to have anything to do with me after what Amil did. The
years passed and then Amil got out of jail . . ."

"Why does he call himself that?"

Adrian gave a small laugh. "I don't know. Probably a
name he picked up from a movie or book somewhere. All I
know is he refuses to answer by his own name, only Amil.

Anyway, once he got out, he didn't bother looking me up. And when I got word that he was out, and that he was looking for you, that's when I did my own investigating. He's let so many things turn him, turn his soul. And now he's driven by revenge. But he's been angry all of his life. He never liked growing up poor—neither one of us did. And maybe he resented you and your parents. After all, your father was CEO of an oil distribution company, your mother a professor. They looked down on him and the idea of you with either one of us. They had their summer cottage in Naples and we were working there at a hotel. None of this would have ever started up if I hadn't seen you, if I had just left you alone. You had just turned seventeen and I was twenty-two. Amil was twenty-three, although we looked so much alike people mistook us for twins. He was already close to Sarah to the point it was just assumed they were going to get married. Then he saw you, us . . . and something in him changed."

"So I became a tug-of-war between you two? And that was supposed to be 'love'?"

He stood and walked to the bar, and poured a glass of something amber. She couldn't see the label.

"You weren't a trophy . . . at least not to me. And we weren't a fling or a thing that was just for the summer. At least not on my part. I thought. . . . Well, it doesn't matter now anyway. Do you know how hard it is to sit with you here and for you not to remember ever loving me? And for me to remember every minute of it? You can't know how I wish I could undo all of the hurt and pain. The least I could hope for was that you find some happiness in your life— and now I see that didn't happen. I thought you would have found someone, be married with kids, and painting like you dreamed of doing."

"Well, if I had a talent for painting, I don't remember it.

And painting definitely wouldn't pay my bills. As for being married—overrated, I'm sure. I know too many divorce lawyers not to have some insight and a big avoidance issue. I guess I'm fine the way I am. No thanks to you or your brother. He's mad at me? He doesn't have the right to be mad. And neither of you have the right to destroy my life again, I don't care what happened in the past."

"After this is over, you can be sure that I'll be out of your life as quickly as I came into it. This isn't a happy reunion for me, either. Do you think I want to have to deal with my brother's obvious loss of reason or even see you again?"

"I'm sorry it's a hardship being in the same room with me. But remember, you came and got me. I was totally unaware of all of this . . ."

"And totally a target. Do you want me to step aside now? Do you really want a face-off with your quite peeved husband?"

"Stop calling him that!"

"That's what he is. And it wasn't me who made that so. You wanted to prove some silly point."

"Okay, okay, maybe some of this is my fault, I don't know. I just know that it's in the past, and it should stay there. That includes whatever was between your brother and me—or you and me. I can't handle all of this coming at me, not now. I have one of my biggest cases and damn if it's going to be screwed up pretty soon."

He seemed to relent a little. He nodded his head to the phone on a nearby desk. "You should call the court office, say you have a family emergency. Which you do."

For some reason, she wanted to resist his directive, even though it made sense. There was something about him that made her want to defy reason even. Maybe because he made her feel unsure about her existence, the life she'd been living. That he knew more about her than she obviously knew about herself was too disconcerting. She wished she could remember holding a brush in her hand, how it would feel to paint a sunset. And to know it was good.

The only thing she held in her hand right now was the phone. She gripped it so hard, the blood stopped flowing to her fingers.

Three

Amil grabbed the passwords from the compromised server, then proceeded through the backdoor of the system, where he began plugging in various passwords until he found the one to open the registration pages of the Grand Hyatt Hotel. He ran down the list of guests and room numbers, looking for a familiar name. He found it halfway down the screen: Martins, Allen. He checked for a second name, but it wasn't there. She would be too easy to find.

And he knew the moment he saw the the alias that his brother was setting up a dodge. He checked for a second name, but it wasn't there. Of course, Adrian had only registered one name, not hers. Because Adrian knew too well that Amil was on his trail. He could have very well used another alias, but had chosen a recognizable one, hoping that Amil would tap in and find it.

Which meant the hotel was a pit stop to somewhere else, another "safe haven." Although how safe Adrian thought he could keep her was going to be severely tested. Because Amil had no intention of letting her get away a second time. He had spent too many years in his cell thinking about her, about how she had deserted him that night. The one night when everything wrong in his life was to have turned around. Instead, his life ended that night—or might as well have. She had left him, and smashed his dreams to dust. And in the days, the hours, the minutes he wasted away behind bars, she had consumed him. Out in the yard (when he wasn't in solitary), he had imagined her face beyond the electric fence that was the perimeter of his world. Her face had been reflected up from the dirty dishwater in the kitchen where he cleaned hundreds of scummy post-meal dishes. He had dreamed about her in the infirmary while recovering from a shiv in the back courtesy of someone whose path he had crossed too many times. In prison, he had had time to think about all of the dreams he had let go. Most of all he thought about what he had done to Sarah.

He had turned from certain love to something illusory, that had never been.

Because Jeralyn had been using him to make his brother jealous.

Adrian wanted him to forget. But Amil would never forget how she had used him and ruined his life.

He pulled out his cell and hit a speed number.

The party answered. "Yeah."

"They're going to move soon. Follow, but hands off. Just report in to me."

"Sure thing."

Amil clipped his phone, and thought about Adrian.

He didn't want his brother to get hurt. That wasn't the goal. But if Adrian attempted to save her, that would be the result.

And then she would have taken someone else from him.

Still his blood pulsed faster when he thought of her. And it wasn't just the anger.

It was the memory and scent of her eager flesh, the feel of soft arms, spicy lips on his. . . . And always the image would morph into the pale, bloodless face of the woman who had washed up on shore, the pulp of her eyes already lost to the sealife. Those vacant eyes that always accused him in his dreams.

"Why did you leave me?" the disembodied voice questioned inside his head. The voice was as familiar as it had been when he first heard it.

"What're you carrying?" she'd asked years ago, that tingly voice suppressed with giggles. He had turned, a pineapple in either hand, to find a red-haired angel with brown eyes, luminous beacons to a halycon soul.

He'd destroyed her. With more than a little help from Jeralyn. Two women he had loved . . . one woman he had chosen. Only to find that she had never chosen him.

He wanted to see the fear in her eyes, wanted her to remember his name. To remember him.

He had reason to know that the amnesia wasn't real. That she knew very well what happened that night her parents died. Because she had been there, standing, looking at him at the bottom of the stairs, unharmed if frightened.

What she didn't remember, she chose not to remember.

But he would make her. Before she died.

He tried not to stare at her but couldn't help it. The dress fit perfectly. Moved against curves she hadn't had when she was seventeen. Her body was a woman's, unfamiliar to him. The girl he had made love to a millennia ago was long gone.

And he denied to himself that he wanted to get to know the woman better. Because he knew that wasn't going to happen. If they got out of this mess, she would go her way and he would go back to his world of meetings, reports, and mergers. The world he would have eagerly shared with his brother, but Amil had rebuffed such a staid life.

Adrian didn't know how his brother financed his lifestyle, but Amil wasn't poor by any definition. And he had every means to finance his vendetta—which meant this could drag out for some time.

She wouldn't leave her life easily. But, in the end, she might have to leave it to save it. And he would have to convince her somehow.

He already detected the stubbornness that had flared that long-ago summer, especially when she thought she was right.

"You got the exact size," she said, examining the dress in the mirror. "Strange, the way you know so much about me. So, what else do you know?"

He didn't answer as he checked his watch. It was almost nine. Time to leave.

He was expecting Amil's men to be looking out for them. But with her hair up and in that dress, she looked different than the woman who'd entered the hotel. He had changed into jeans and a T-shirt along with a black leather jacket. Amil's spies would be looking for a well-tailored suit.

Just in case, he had something else planned. A diversion that would distract searching eyes long enough for Jerri and him to catch a second car and get away.

"We're going out now."

He saw her hesitancy and the fear. "Don't worry. He's not going to harm you. I promise."

"Can you actually promise that? After all, I'm putting a lot of faith in you."

"It isn't the first time," he said softly.

She half turned to look at him. "Maybe one day I'll remember."

"Yeah, maybe one day." Then he took her arm and led her to the door.

She was quiet on the elevator ride down to the garage, too quiet. He could barely hear her breathing.

When the door opened, he saw what he expected to see.

A group of tourists milling around the elevator. Some were walking toward vans, others were waiting at a line of cars.

He'd had someone arrange several tours to meet here at nine. Enough bodies to blend, to confuse anyone looking out for one man and a woman leaving. And just as he had also arranged, a nondescript Volvo pulled up near one of the waiting vans. He kept a tight grip on her arm as he led her to the car. She was no doubt confused. No one expected to see this many people waiting in the private parking dock. This wasn't the usual place for guests to board touring vehicles, but a couple of greased palms had assured this stage of his plan.

The driver, dressed in a casual linen suit, exited the driver's seat, letting Adrian take the wheel as Jerri got in on the passenger side. And as planned, several of the cars were beginning to pull off. These were the plants he had arranged. They were not part of the tour groups, but were there to add to the confusion. The cars were lined up; his car was the third in the queue. The first car moved and the line followed until they were at the exit. Then the several cars took off in various directions.

He headed straight down Stockton, traveled a few blocks before turning west toward Taylor. Just a few blocks, but that was part of the ruse. Amil's men, already confused about whom to follow, would believe he would travel farther to distance himself from the Hyatt. One of the other cars had a man and woman traveling toward the city's boundaries.

He pulled into yet another parking underground. He saw her peer around, her hands tight around her purse. He wondered if she really did have a gun in it—wondered if she knew how to use it.

At least he had his Smith & Wesson M&P. This is what it had come to between him and his brother. Ever since Jerri had entered their lives and stolen both their hearts.

They got out of the car and took the elevator up to the Serrano's lobby. He had already registered, already had the cards to their room. His alias here was a new one; actually he had never stayed here before. Old-style Spanish and Moroccan influences marked the elegant décor of the restored hotel. Only a few people lingered in the lobby, guests checking in. A man in a gray silk three-piece suit sat on a couch off the lobby reading the *Chronicle*. A couple stood with three small children waiting at the elevator bank.

Everything seemed innocent, but he couldn't afford to underestimate any situation, no matter how innocuous. That sense had moved him up in the corporate world and had saved his ass on a number of occasions. Hopefully, it would save Jerri. He just didn't know.

They got off at the next to top floor then walked to the the end of the hall to one of the king executive suites. He wanted luxury for her, the only amenity he could offer for uprooting her life, even if this mess wasn't his doing. In some respects, though, he *was* responsible: For what was happening today as well as what happened those many years ago. He should never have pursued someone so young, someone only starting to understand what she wanted in life. He shouldn't have pressed her for more than she had been willing to give. His pressing had made her rebel and run to his brother Drew. Drew, whose soul was long dead and had been replaced with a specter of a man too willing to hurt and destroy.

"This is beautiful," she said, eyeing the entry parlor. Dark teak woods, red brocade wing chairs, red-and-gold striped silk drapes created an exotic setting. Even he was impressed, though the whole suite was smaller than he was used to.

"So, do you think he followed us?"

"I don't know; I don't think so. There were enough diversions."

"Your doing?" she asked as she walked into the living

room area. The colors carried into here as well, emblazoned by black wall sconces and lamps. A dining cart stood near the window that looked out on Union Square. He'd left arrangements to have the food delivered after nine so that it would still be hot when they arrived. The briny smell of lobster and butter competed with the sizzling charcoal aroma of grilled loin steaks. A side of asparagus risotto rounded off the meal. There was also a large fruit salad of melons, grapes, and pineapple, as well as a bottle of claret. A vase of roses sat in the middle of the dining table set with gold-edged plates and glasses. The slight floral scent brought back memories of the roses from that long-ago summer. Blood red with a tantalizing fragrance, they had been specially bred by an elderly woman who lived along the beach.

Adrian had taken Jerri's virginity among the roses and the smell of the flowers had been strong that night. The smell would mark that memory forever. The roses on the table were just ordinary roses, though. Not as beautiful as the ones remembered.

"You still like lobster?" he asked.

She looked over the offering. "Always. Though I can't tell you how long."

"You once told me it was your favorite food. We even went lobster fishing one evening. Rode out on a kayak, brought along a mesh cage stuffed with bait fish. It took nearly all of the night, but we finally got one. The puniest, skinniest thing you ever saw. You refused to keep it, threw it back in the water. I thought it was because you wanted something bigger. But when I looked at your face, I saw how pained you were about killing a living thing."

A small smile appeared, just for a second. And disappeared just as quickly. "Yeah, I can't even step on bugs. I have a hard time with death, just looking at it. Maybe that's why I can't remember my parents' death."

He pulled back a chair at the table and she sat. He took

the adjoining seat to her left. A momentary look of discomfort flashed on her face, and he realized she didn't want him this close. Too bad. She was going to have to get used to him for however long they had to be sequestered away together.

He reached for one of the medium rare steaks. If she was hungry, she would decide to join him. After a few seconds, she reached for a lobster tail instead and the accompanying lime dipping sauce. He pretended not to watch her as she cracked open the shell and dug out the meat with a familiarity that brought the past forward in his mind.

Her hair was longer, straighter. Before it had been a wild, lustrous cloud of tangled curls, soft to his fingers. It had haloed around her face, emphasizing angel eyes, full lips, smooth coffee skin. Her eyes settled on him and he felt his pulse rev a pace.

"If I seem ungrateful, I don't mean to be. You have to understand how strange this all is."

He nodded. "I wish I could have averted this for you, but my brother isn't someone I can reason with anymore—which is why I've had to take this measure."

"Guess this has disrupted your life as well. Do you live here in San Francisco?"

"No. I'm parked on the east coast in New York. I have a software development company there."

"Oh really. What type of software?" she asked before taking a bite of a juicy bit of lobster tail.

"We customize programs to help companies manage personnel data and also maintain Internet security. The company's growing along with the market. A lot of viruses and trojans out there."

"Yeah. My system got trashed by one of those damn things. Could've used your help a couple of months ago. So, is this what you saw yourself doing when we knew each other? I mean, owning your own company, working corporate?"

The steak was moist, savory. He swallowed before answering. "I wanted a lot of things back then. I think, in a way, I settled for what I could get. Worked my way through internships, then saw an opportunity to get in on a good deal."

"But this wasn't what you wanted, or is it?"

She was reading him. Strange. She had always had the ability, and he would have thought that would have been lost a long time ago. He tasted the claret. Crisp and clean, with just a bit of a sweet aftertaste.

"I wanted to survive. That's all I ever wanted. I came from the streets back in the Bronx. And those streets were hard. I wanted to settle into one place with someone, maybe have a couple of kids. I wanted to forget the rootlessness of bouncing around from foster home to foster home. Maybe if my world had been all daisies and roses, I would have pursued something more esoteric, like my music. I had fantasies of starting a band, playing my guitar, and writing music for a living. Maybe that's why we were pulled to one another. Our fantasies of music and art, and escaping our lives."

"Did Amil want to escape his?"

He remembered his brother, the way he used to be. That hard glint in his eyes. "Amil wanted another life, just like I did. We were working that summer at a hotel restaurant, making chump change but . . . well, there were always the ladies who liked to tip large. Neither one of us had been to college, but we weren't going to let that stop us. We were going to find a business that we both could do together, make a name. My fantasy about being a musician was just that, a fantasy. I couldn't take that chance."

"Take the chance to do what you wanted?"

"Life doesn't allow you those chances, not if you're going to succeed in it. Only a few people are allowed their pipe dreams, but to most of us, those dreams don't get you a damn thing. That's probably why your parents wanted you to pursue something sturdy like law. A good profession with plenty of payback."

"But payback should do more than feed your face and your pockets," she said softly, almost to herself.

"Yeah, well . . . if I didn't have money, I wouldn't be able to protect you now."

"And if your brother didn't have money, he wouldn't be able to come after me like he is. Money can do a lot of harm as well as good."

"True. So what other ways has money harmed you?"

She was quiet and had stopped eating as she contemplated her answer. "I guess I've used it to fill up those places in my life that should have been filled with other things. My job has become so much of a priority in my life, like it's the only thing that defines me now. I don't know. I really wish I could remember painting or something else that fills the soul. It might have led me to other choices."

"You're lonely," he said, then immediately wished he hadn't. It came out an indictment.

"I wouldn't say lonely . . . just alone. I don't mean to sound pitiful. I just wish things might have been different. I wished I had had my family. It's a void that can't be filled."

"Trust me, I know."

"What happened to your family? Are there others or is it just you and Amil?"

"My mother died in a car accident along with our two-year-old sister when Amil was eight and I was seven. It was so long ago, I barely remember. And as for our dad, he checked out sometime before that. So, I guess you can say it's been me and Amil most of our lives. Even when we went to separate homes, we would always find each other."

"I'm sorry—for then—and for now. It has to be hard going against your only family."

"I didn't go against him; he's going against me. Sometimes those closest to you can become your worst enemies. Worst because they know you, know your vulnerabilities. Not to even think about betrayal and loss of trust. Of love, even. The thing is, no matter what my brother does, I'll always have him somewhere inside me. I may not be able to forget what he does—or even forgive—but that won't keep me from remembering that he was there for me through most of these years. Before all of this—when we were just boys—he was a protective older brother who taught me how to be tough under the worst circumstances. If he hadn't taught me that, I wouldn't be here—a survivor. Actually, make that a thriver."

"Why did you say he still loves me? If what you say is true, he probably hates my guts."

"Amil has hated a lot of people in our lives. People who've crossed him before, tormented both of us. But he's never lost it, not like he has with you. That's not hate driving him, even though he thinks it is. It's pain and a remnant of the love he felt. You see, even though Sarah came before you, you were the first: The first time he actually let someone in. Before that, women—maybe even some men—had been just a fuck to him. It's an offensive word, but it fits. There was just me and him and no one else. And then there was you."

She looked down at the lobster on her plate as if she didn't know how it came to be there. "Me? It's strange to think I could have that much power over anybody. My love life hasn't been all that exciting recently. I may inspire lust, but an all-out vendetta? That's definitely someone else."

She paused, looking at him fully for the first time, as though she were only now really seeing him. There was something intimate about the scrutiny and he felt his temperature shoot up a degree or two.

"Did you love me?"

He hadn't expected that question. Had anticipated every question but that one. And he realized he wasn't prepared to answer. Yet he knew he had to. She deserved that at least.

"Yes." It was . . . a matter of fact, so he said it matter-of-factly, without emotion, as though his world hadn't nearly been destroyed, too.

"So, did I love you?" Another unexpected question.

The pain came rumbling up from inside, tearing from the place where he had kept it all these years.

"I thought you did. I hoped you did. I may have been wrong."

"Because of Amil," she said sadly. "I don't even know that side of myself. I'm not a game player and I don't like being around them."

"You were a teenager, and teenagers tend not to think, but act on their impulses. You wanted to hurt me . . ."

"Because you'd hurt me? I was a vengeful little ass, then. I would never do something like that now. I'd appreciate any love that came my way, know how precious and rare it is. I don't even remember being in love ever. Not then, definitely not now. I've actually wondered if I'm capable of the emotion."

"You are. You just need to remember that part of you—or at least, find it again. I know how much you loved your parents, no matter how frustrated they made you. And I remember how you used to look at me with that fire in your eyes, the way you said my name. I thought that it couldn't get any better than that. You made me feel bigger than I was. Amil may have given me the drive to live, but you gave me confidence. It was strange to have learned it from someone so young. So I guess I owe you for getting me as far as I have."

"I'm glad I didn't totally mess up your life. But still, I don't think I like who I used to be."

He didn't mean to touch her. But her sadness was palpable and he reached out a hand instinctively, like he used to do, to touch her hair. It was still soft.

She stiffened, but he noticed she didn't pull back either.

He should have dropped his hand but instead he ran a finger along her brow where a strand of hair touched the skin. She flicked her bottom lip with her tongue, something she did when she was nervous. Something that used to drive him crazy. It was disconcerting to realize that it still unnerved him. He thought he was long over her. Thought he was just here to save her from Amil and then this would be over, one way or another. He was wrong.

He finally pulled back his hand, and he heard an audible breath. She'd been holding it in.

"Do you have . . . someone special? In your life?" Her voice wasn't as steady as before.

"Actually, no. I date—and I've had a couple of steady relationships, but they never seem to last. It wasn't them, it was me. I just can't seem to let myself—" he stopped.

"Trust," she finished his sentence. "We seem to have the same issues." She paused. "Do you think you'll ever be able to love again?"

He didn't have to think about the answer. "I never stopped loving—you."

The surprise on her face made her look so vulnerable, so much younger. It was as though her earlier self had morphed in and was there again, waiting for him.

And he suddenly realized he didn't want to wait any longer. He had another chance, and he wanted to take it.

Four

The kiss took her by surprise. It was a pleasant surprise. Soft, light on her lips.

She wanted to open her mouth to him, to let him in, to go where he wanted to lead her, but she fought the impulse.

He pulled back finally and she found it hard to take in her next breath. The irony was that she should've been used to his kiss, his touch. But it was all new to her.

"I can't do this," she said. "I can't be that girl again. She's gone. I'm someone else now—someone totally different. I don't remember her, you . . . or us."

He sat back, sighed. "I know. That was an idiotic thing to do. And you're right. You're not that girl anymore. But then again, I'm not the bullheaded fool I once was, either. Still, I can't deny that I still have feelings for you. And your being here right now is driving a lot of these emotions to the surface. But that's my problem it seems. Not yours."

Her own emotions were in turmoil. She'd waited a long time for someone to move her this way, but here wasn't the time, the place, and definitely not the circumstances she wanted to discover the possibility.

He turned back to his steak, allowing her to finish her

meal. The food was delicious, but she wasn't tasting it now. She simply finished out of courtesy for his efforts.

After he was done, he stood. He looked down at her, and the vantage was disquieting.

"You probably want to settle in, get comfortable. I have something planned that should throw Amil off, but it may not be enough. So at least for tonight, you're my guest. Your room is through there," he pointed to a room off the living room. "There's a Jacuzzi in your bathroom. Let me know what else you might need."

She stood, also, fighting off the lingering ghost of his kiss that was plaguing her. Telling her she wanted more.

Instead, she said, "I'm going to need a change of underwear. I don't suppose you thought of that."

The slow smile was unexpected. "You used to hate wearing underwear . . ."

She winced. "Okay, don't tell me any more . . ."

"Actually, I did buy underwear. Hopefully I got your size right again and that you like silk and lace."

Up until now, his tone had been measured and had run the gambit from stern to conciliatory, even apologetic. Now, there was a seductive strain that hadn't been there before. The way he had said "silk and lace," as though he imagined her wearing his offerings, caused an involuntary shiver.

"I also bought some other clothes for you, just so you can feel free to change. Obviously, I don't know your tastes now, so you may not like everything."

"Liking isn't important. I just don't want to have to walk around in the same thing . . . or naked."

The slight blush caught her by surprise. But he stepped away, walking toward the room he'd chosen as hers. After a few seconds, she followed. She was tired and needed downtime to digest everything that had happened in these last few hours.

He led her into a moderate-size room showcased by the large king-sized bed. The dark contrasting prints of the drapes and bedcovers almost overwhelmed. Yet, the dim lights in the room soothed what would have been a busy palette of colors.

"Do you want me to run your water?"

He was too close. She stepped back. "I can do that, thanks. So your room is where?"

"On the other side of the suite. But I'm within yelling distance if you need me."

He left the room, and for some reason it seemed smaller without him. She walked into the bathroom and immediately noticed the set of expensive-looking bath soaps and oils that she knew had not come with the room. She looked over the offerings: Almond-scented bath oil and jasmine soap from Sephora. He'd planned her lockdown well. She loved the smell of almond cookies.

She started the water, took the terry-cloth robe off the hook and walked back into the bedroom to take off her clothes. Five minutes later she was steeped in a hot bath that initially stung, but then began to seduce her skin with invigorating heat. She turned on the jets, felt the pulses against her legs and hips. She hadn't thought she would be able to relax even a little bit considering the mess her life had suddenly become, but some of the tension began seeping away as she settled back.

The water was soothing and soon the quiet of the luxurious bathroom took her out of her body and she felt her eyelids dragging down. Strangely she heard her mother's voice calling to her, screaming—"Jerri! Get out! Get out!"

She didn't know what to do. The flames were at the top of the stairs and her parents were trapped on the second floor. The heat traveled down as the black smoke billowed upward to the landing above. She tried to see her mother, but just as quickly as it had taken her to reach the stairs, the second floor blackened into a deadly night, even though the lights had been ablaze moments before.

"Mama! Daddy!" she screamed and screamed until the smoke forced her back down the stairs. She turned at a sound near the open door and saw him standing there, looking at her in fear. The face so familiar and yet different. He took a step toward her and she stepped back and fell on the steps. Just before she passed out, she saw someone else standing in the doorway, her red hair dripping . . .

Someone was shaking her, but she didn't want to open her eyes, didn't want to see the flames, know that they were racing toward her mother and father. Didn't want to imagine them burning, choking, like she was choking . . .

"Jerri! Wake up!"

He was half pulling her from the tub, wrapping the terry-cloth robe around her. She didn't realize she was crying until his finger trailed a tear.

"You were having a nightmare. Oh, God, I'm so sorry, Jerri. I wouldn't have put you through this for anything."

"Why are you here?"

"You were yelling. I heard you all the way across the suite. I thought one of Amil's goons had gotten in, but you were alone, your eyes closed, screaming out to your parents. You were remembering, weren't you?"

In all these years, everything about that night had been blurry at best, with her remembering only instances outside the house after it had gone up in flames. This was the first time that she could remember the moments before the devastation, before her parents' death. Her mother's warning still rang in her head. Her only concern had been making sure that Jeralyn got out of the burning house. The thought was too much for Jeralyn to bear.

Adrian walked her back to the bedroom, sat her on the bed, and let her cry silently. He knelt on the floor beside her until she found her voice again.

"I heard my mother calling me. It was like I was there again, actually hearing her voice. It was so real. The smoke and flames—I couldn't get to them. I didn't remember any of this until just a few minutes ago. Maybe this situation is opening up things inside of me, things I don't want to remember. I can't remember or I'll go crazy."

He rose to sit on the bed next to her, pulled her head against his shoulder, and put his arm around her. She didn't pull away.

"You're not going to go crazy, Jerri. This is actually good, what happened. I know it's painful, but if you refuse to remember, you'll go through the rest of your life with this hole inside of you, wondering what there was that used to fill it. The question is, do you want your life back?"

She wiped another tear and remembered. "I saw Amil— Drew—standing there. But he didn't have anything in his hand. Some of it is starting to come back. There was someone else there beside him, though I couldn't really see her face . . ."

"Her?"

"It was a woman, I'm sure of it. She was so pale with red hair . . ."

She felt Adrian's shoulder stiffen. "Red hair?"

"Yeah, and the strangest thing was she was dripping wet. Why? Do you know who she is?"

He sat there holding her, not saying anything. "It must have been a dream then. The girl you saw would have been Sarah. But she couldn't have been there at the fire. She died a week before your parents were killed and was already buried."

Jeralyn closed her eyes, tried to picture the woman again, but couldn't. "You're right. I'm mixing things up in my head, remembering them wrong. But at least it's something."

His lips grazed her forehead, a whisper of a kiss. It set off something hidden deep inside her memory. He used to do this. Before. Buss her forehead while they sat together watching the sun descend over the water. He would hold her hand while they discussed their future. Why she suddenly knew this now, she didn't understand.

She reached for his fingers with her own, settled them between the grooves of the long, tapered digits. He closed her hand in his. It felt natural somehow.

Surprising herself, she moved her cheek against his jawline. The stubble grazed her skin. Again, this was something familiar. It seemed her mind had forgotten, but her body had held on to its impressions of him and were giving them back to her.

She heard a slight groan, a shaky intake of breath. He was holding himself back because she had told him earlier that she didn't want this. But her body was proving her wrong.

His mouth trailed a line to hers, tasted the rim of her bottom lip. She instinctively knew that he could be gentle, that he could also be rough, if he wanted. If she wanted. And he was waiting for her to tell him.

He still wore the T-shirt and jeans he'd changed into earlier at the Hyatt. His arms were toned and well-developed, indicating time in a gym. The white cotton stretched tautly across his stomach muscles and she had a desire to stroke the flesh beneath. She felt no embarrassment nor the slightest hesitation as she untucked the shirt and settled a hand along his stomach. She felt a tremble go through him as she stroked the warm, downy skin.

"You really want this?" he asked, his eyes darker than they had been. His jawline was strained; she saw a tic working along his brow. He was reaching a point of no return. All she had to do was take him there.

"Yes, for now. But this isn't the start of anything. It's just, I don't know . . ." She couldn't find the words.

"A way to remember—and forget," he said softly. "Okay, then. Let me help you do both."

He slid the robe off her shoulders, slowly pushed it down to her waist. Beads of moisture clung to her arms, her torso, her breasts. He traced his forefinger along the trail of water, his eyes locked with hers. She was held motionless by the vortex of blue that seemed to darken several shades. She didn't move even when his fingertip finally touched the tip of a nipple, setting her nerves on fire. Another part of her, a quickly diminishing voice, told her that this was crazy. Yet her body told her that he was her lover, or had been at least. She was ready to discover—rediscover—feelings and sensations that she had hidden away for most of her adult life. Feelings that had never arisen with anyone else, but in these few hours with him, had flared and were burning inside her.

His fingers closed around the nipple, stroked it lightly. A throbbing shot through her core, sent a message to every extremity. In answer, a growing pool of moisture began creeping down the insides of her upper thighs.

"The first time I touched you, really touched you, we were in a garden of roses. They had this seductive smell—I can't describe it, even now. We were trespassing and it was late. You were worried about what your parents would say. But I wanted to break off a rose for you, so we snuck into the garden. You thanked me with a kiss, and then with another one, and another one. We never made it back to your house—not until the early morning. That was the first time we made love—the first time ever for you. I was worried about hurting you, but you told me you were ready, that it was what you wanted."

"How was I?" she tried to joke, smile her nervousness away, pretending that his finger wasn't making her crazy. She was as nervous as she must have been that night.

He smiled, dropped his hand. She immediately regretted her question.

"Funny. You asked me that back then, too. You were young, inexperienced, uncertain of what you wanted. I'm sure it wasn't all you expected it to be."

"Well, I'm neither young nor inexperienced. And I still don't know what I want. It's a first time and yet it's not. But at least I know there's nothing past this night. Probably back then, being young and stupid, I might have believed we were going to be together forever."

"Yeah, that was the plan."

"I'm sorry things didn't go like you hoped."

"I stopped hoping a long time ago. I learned long ago to reach for certainties, and not the maybes. It's easier that way. That night was special, but I also learned that summer how easily hope can be taken away."

"I feel like I'm never going to stop wanting to apologize. I don't know why I did what I did, but I can't change the past. Maybe if I hadn't done something so stupid, we might have been together still—or maybe not. Who knows? But I do know about uncertainty. And no matter how well you plan out your strategy, something unexpected always comes up. The only thing you can do is rethink your plan."

"The lawyer-speak is really doing something to me," he said, his expression straight, but his eyes sparkling. It made her burst out laughing.

"I'm sorry. The legal parlance comes with the package."

"Well, the package is very alluring." His eyes roamed the curve of her breasts, traveled down the length of her stomach to the crevice peeking from beneath the half-opened robe. When he looked up and caught her eyes again, all the mirth was gone.

"I want to love you, make you feel safe. If only for tonight."

She wanted this, too, but didn't use words. Instead, she reached out a hand to stroke his cheek, to run her fingers along his jaw, feel the five o'clock stubble rasp her palm.

She dipped her finger along his lips, and he caught it in his mouth, ran his tongue along the length. The wet heat sent a shiver through her, a stab of need in her crotch.

He grasped her shoulders and pulled their bodies down onto the bed with her on top. His hands pushed the robe the remaining inches down her hips until it fell to the floor. Immediately, the air began chilling the moisture clinging to her exposed behind, the backs of her legs.

His fingers moved across the firm flesh of her ass, kneading the ample mounds, at the same time pulling her body into his until there was no space between them. She felt him hard and stiff beneath his jeans, felt the very perceptible bulge against her stomach. His mouth found hers, his tongue tasting the inside of her lips, probing her tongue. She sucked it, her desire rising to match his. A vague shadow of the past flitted through her mind. Another time, another kiss . . . exploration with hands, fingers . . . skin meshing together . . . like now.

She broke the kiss and moved back to allow space for her fingers to find their way beneath his shirt. They roamed over the warm muscled flesh of his stomach, moved up to his chest, pushing the material upward with her quest.

"Want me to take it off?" His voice was raspy, almost a whisper.

"I can do it," she said, surprised by her own aggression. She hadn't had sex in almost a year, waiting for the right someone to come along. And now that he had, and knowing that they only had one night, she wasn't about to act coy or shy. She moved his arms to navigate the shirt off, which she tossed unceremoniously off the bed while she took note of the beauty of his upper body. Just as she had imagined it would be. She watched his eyes glaze over as she took the lead, kneading his nipples as he had done hers moments before.

She leaned down to flick a nipple with her tongue, and felt a tremor go through him. He shifted suddenly, pulled her upward until her breasts were flush with his face. He leaned up, caught a nipple and gave her a payback that made her squirm her hips. She wanted to grind, needed to grind into him, wanted him to do the same to her.

She had denied herself this pleasure by one foolish act. This night could have been repeated so many times in the last fifteen years. Would she have already grown tired of him at this point? He shifted her again and buried his face in the mounds of her breasts, his tongue doing indecipherable hieroglyphics on her sensitive flesh. She sighed, her question answered. No way would she ever tire of this. Not the way he was doing it.

She wanted him inside her. Now. But he had other things in mind. He released her breasts and she moaned in frustration of his absence. Another shift and she was no longer on top of him but facedown on the bed, the silk covers satiny against her skin. She had only a second of hesitation, wondering what he would do next. Then she felt his hands on the small of her back, his fingers inching down followed by the unmistakable push of his tongue in their wake. He slithered a trail of saliva along her ass, covering the terrain of her skin with rivers. The sensation was excruciating, causing her to bite her bottom lip to keep from crying out. Her heart was beating too fast against her ribcage, making her feel light-headed; she felt the blood rushing through her whole body. It suffused her already wet vulva, which was now receiving the tongue-licking her ass had just enjoyed.

He sucked at her other lips, teasing the labia with his teeth, trailing his tongue in the crevices, teasing the entry, making her squirm in the agony of denial. He finally gave her what he had tacitly promised. His entry was hot, wet, totally filling the tight canal. His fingers were still doing a nerve-tingling massage on her behind. He kept a slow rhythm to his thrusting, taking time to touch along her walls. His hands stopped their ministration, and he moved eager fingers past her thighs, searching then finding her clitoris.

His finger began circling the orb while his tongue maintained its own action. She couldn't stop the orgasm, nor did she want to. The waves shook her body, made it tremble among the now rumpled silk coverlet.

Minutes passed and he was bringing her to another climax. She balled the covers in her hands, panting for breath, wondering how in a matter of hours, she had gone from her stale, staid life to having a stranger's face buried in her ass. A stranger who had forced his way into her life and changed it forever.

She didn't want this to end.

Five

He never wanted this night to end. But tomorrow would come soon enough and Amil would have to be dealt with. And Jerri would leave his life forever. But for now, he was living the dream he had had every night for fifteen years. And it was sweeter than he'd ever imagined. Sweeter for the fact that it was the last time. And that he'd never thought he'd have this chance again.

Her scent filled his senses as he licked, tasted, drank her. He'd thought it would be like before. He was wrong. This was so very different, so much better. He wanted to take her now, wanted to make it last beyond these hours.

She moaned, the sound muted in his ears by the cushion of her thighs and the river of blood rushing in his ears. His engorged penis strained against the confine of his jeans, needed release in the worst way.

He released her finally. He drew in breaths of air, still smelling her juices. He would remember her smell, the smell of the woman, not the girl, just as he remembered the scent of the roses that long-ago summer. He stroked the back of her thigh, felt her tremble, waiting.

He shifted up on the bed next to her. She turned to greet

him with a kiss. Probably, she could smell herself, taste herself still wet on his lips. But she didn't seem to mind as she pushed in deeper, invading his mouth, seeking out the tongue that had pleasured her.

Without releasing his lips, her hand reached for the zipper to his jeans, jerked it down impatiently. She was on fire for him, which stoked his own flame. He stood abruptly, keeping himself out of her reach as he shed the rest of his clothes and shoes. Naked, he climbed back onto the bed to lay beside her.

"God, you're beautiful," she whispered almost to herself. He felt himself blushing; women had admired his body before, but no one had ever used those words. Or said it so wonderfully.

"I'd hardly describe myself as beautiful; that crown belongs to you. No one could ever beat you on that."

"How did we first meet?"

He smiled as he thought about a summer morning, a car ride to the hotel. When he looked up and saw a beautiful girl standing outside an ice cream shop. He stopped his car and pulled over.

"Outside of an ice cream shop. You had on white shorts, a yellow T-shirt. You were standing with some friends, but I don't even remember what they looked like now. Didn't even notice them then. There was a slight breeze and your hair lifted from your face and I saw this brilliant smile. You turned at that moment and saw me staring at you from my car. And you winked. You were doing it more for your friends, trying to show off. But I wasn't going to let you off that easy. Your face almost froze when I got out of the car."

"Hmmm, I guess I wasn't all that shy."

"You had your moments where you seemed younger than you were. But a lot of times, you showed more wisdom for a girl your age. I think that contradiction made you someone

I could see myself with. Mercurial, impulsive, and capable of so much love."

"So, what drew me to you?" She smiled and rolled over, her rear end a tantalizing invitation. He wanted to bury his face in it, taste it again.

"Oh, I don't know. Might have been my car. It was a Nineteen-ninety silver Camaro. You seemed mightily impressed."

"Okay, I couldn't possibly have been that shallow. Besides, didn't I have a car myself?"

He nodded. Yes, she had had a car: A Toyota. He wondered whether she was starting to remember more.

"I'd think it was your smile," she said, more sober. "And your eyes. Your mouth . . ."

"Hey, are you trying to seduce me?" He smiled. "Because you don't even have to try."

"That easy are you?"

"Hell, I can be a veritable slut when it comes to you."

"Then show me what else you can do."

There was mirth, but something more serious underlying her request. She was searching for something in their sex, in him. This was something more than two bodies coming together. And he didn't want to disappoint her.

He joined her on the bed, settled beside her. He wanted to rediscover those moments when they had come together, touching, kissing. Her innocence had moved him, even as her fervor for his touch had aroused him. Now as he slid a hand from breast to stomach down farther to the warm, wet crevice, he watched that fervor again as he began to caress her, to bathe his hand. She arched her back and he expected her to lay there and to savor the sensation. But she reached out a hand, grazed his penis tentatively, then began to stroke him firmly. The touch of her fingers was bringing him nearer to his climax and he didn't want to come now.

He pushed her hand away, then quickly moved his body to cover hers. She accepted his weight, moved her thighs around his back, enclosing him. He liked this closeness, them cocooned together. He could lay with her this way forever, forget all the busy details of his life, the drama that was all Amil, the deadness of his home when he finished up another day and retired to an empty house which he hadn't wanted to share with anyone since Jerri.

He entered her with one motion, moved into her warm chasm that eagerly sucked him in deeper. The suction of her walls closed him in, embraced him tightly, completely. Even if she didn't love him now, her body enjoyed him and that was another thing he would hold on to long after this was over.

He settled into a rhythm, with slow and long thrusts, moving out halfway, moving in with one motion. He teased her lips, not with full kisses, but butterfly touches, small little licks that promised something more.

The vibrations of her moans against his lips urged him on. He quickened his thrusts, and was rewarded with her thighs tightening around him, her breaths breaking into gasps that alternated with her moans. Her eyes were closed, but he kept his open, staring at her face, memorizing it at this moment. He planned to relive this night in his dreams.

He was so swollen, it was only a matter of seconds before he burst. Sweat broke out on his brow with his efforts to give her pleasure and hold back his own. In the end, the strain was too much and he let go with everything he had, pumping desperately into her, releasing himself. He heard her cry out, the sound of it drowned out by his own sob.

He rolled off her, lay beside her. He fought to recover as he listened to her ragged breaths. As spent as he was, he wanted to make love to her again.

He wanted to hide from all of his problems. Problems that were just hours away.

"So, was it like this between us, before?" she asked breathlessly.

"Hell, no. This was so much better." And then he turned over to show her what he meant.

Six

Amil's head throbbed. He always got these debilitating headaches after one of his rampages. And he had gone off on his men until the early morning, railing at them for fucking up. If he weren't paying them so well, no doubt they would have walked a long time ago. Or killed him.

He grabbed his bottle of aspirin off the bar, upturned it in his mouth, downed several pills, crunching the bitter tablets between his teeth. The nasty taste shook him out of his funk. Soon, the pain would be gone and he could plan his next move.

He'd been at his task for hours, breaking into the systems of most of the major hotels in the city. But he now knew his brother was using an unknown alias. He'd underestimated Adrian. Of course, his brother wouldn't be stupid enough to keep her in an obvious destination—which would be any hotel that he was known to patronize. They could be anywhere; hell, they could have left the city, the state even, by this time.

Yet, somehow he felt they were still here. Still, there were just too many hotels where they could be, if they were even at a hotel. Adrian could be renting a house or an apartment.

He didn't have time to wait them out.

He'd tried calling his brother's cell, but it was shut off. No way to track him down through the signal.

Part of him, the rational part, told himself the whole plan was fruitless. That he should just go on about his life and leave her alone. But at night he would dream about those many hours, minutes, seconds in that hole that had been his life for nearly fifteen years. All for a crime he never committed, a crime she could have cleared him of just by speaking up.

Of course, she had to know he didn't kill her parents.

Maybe she'd set the fire. And somehow knocked him out and planted the evidence to shift the guilt to him. And with his past, he'd been a perfect scapegoat.

Even if she hadn't done it, she had seen him come in the house after the fire started; he hadn't had enough time to set any fire. Besides, he'd never wanted her parents dead. He'd never wanted anyone dead.

Until now.

He rose from the chair, walked to the window that looked out over the bay. The early sun skirted along the water, reflections of silver and blue. Toward the horizon, silhouettes of boats moved in a queue. Far below, traffic was just starting to grow as workers began their commute. Everything was normal for an early San Francisco morning.

He should have had her here now. He'd planned to lure her to the old Avalon home, with its hidden rooms where screams could be muted. And he'd planned to make her scream—in pleasure and pain.

She was technically his wife and he'd never had even one night with her. They were long overdue for a honeymoon. And this time she wouldn't get a chance to run away.

He'd been humiliated when he'd entered their motel suite that he'd scraped money together to book only to find her and her clothes gone. Nothing left but a note: *"I made a mistake. I don't love you."*

More than anything that came afterward, those words tore at his soul all these years. She'd played him for a fool and it had all been for his brother's benefit. She'd deliberately pursued him, made him forget everything and everyone, made him feel she loved him, cared for him. That was something he'd never had before. Something she pretended to give and then took away so easily.

Ironic, that she became a lawyer. Upholder of justice. Bullshit. She was nothing but a liar. And still pretending that she had no recollection of that part of her life, of his.

When he'd spoken to her over the phone, for a few minutes he thought that maybe she really didn't remember. But then again, it had been fifteen years; she'd probably forgotten his voice. Now if it had been Adrian speaking with her . . .

She had had no problem going off with Adrian, supposedly a perfect stranger. Had no trouble holing up with him in a hotel. They had probably fucked the night away if he knew his brother. Adrian had never gotten over his "angel." It was pathetic.

He could be honest with himself and wish that things had been different—that she'd never walked out on him. Even if she hadn't loved him, she might have come to that in time.

He didn't take rejection well. Never had. Very few women had done that to him. And they'd paid a price for it.

No, she wasn't getting away from him. He'd find her again no matter where she went.

His cell phone rang. He opened it, saw the number. And smiled as he answered.

"Adrian, so I'm guessing you had a good night. How was she? Anyway, don't let that give you the impression that you've won anything. You can't hide her forever."

"I don't plan to. I need to talk with you in person." His brother's voice was tight, low. Indicating a raised stress level. Good.

"About what?"

"Don't fuck with me, Drew."

"Don't piss me off, Adrian. You know my name. And why the hell would we meet together? Unless you have something planned against my interest. Now, you wouldn't actually try to harm me now, would you, brother?"

"Only if you force my hand. You're not going to hurt her . . ."

"Oh, really? Are you're so sure about that? You know, I think someone's got his dick whipped. Still a good fuck is she? What's that bible verse, you know, about coveting your brother's wife?"

"Only legally. That's a technicality that's going to be taken care of."

"Well, all of this is—what's that lawyer's term, moot?—anyway. That's something Jerri would know. Yes, the marriage is going to end, but my way. You know, until death do us part? She and I both took those vows and I'm going to make sure she honors her end. Then you and I can go on our merry way and forget this nastiness."

"She didn't set you up, Amil. I swear she doesn't have any memories about that night, about that summer. So why don't you just let this crazy scheme go?"

The anger exploded in his head, exacerbating the ebbing pain, bringing it back full force again. "She's playing you, just like she played both of us back then. Why can't you see that she set us both up? She wanted to get rid of Mommy and Daddy, and that's just what she did. It could've very well been you she planted that stuff on. But I was the one with the record, something I told her about. Must have given her some ideas. Because of her, I lost a large chunk of my life—"

"We both know that's not the real reason you want to

hurt her. It wasn't just because you think she played you. It's because she made you love her. And she didn't return that love. We both know how much that hurts."

"You're talking about yourself, brother . . ."

"And then there's Sarah. Poor Sarah, who you threw over so casually. But Jerri had nothing to do with that. You were the one who dumped Sarah. You rejected her, just like Jerri rejected you. And the guilt has been eating away at you all this time."

Amil closed his eyes and when he did, the phantom of pale skin and wet, dripping hair invaded. He shook it away, opened his eyes to daylight again.

"I don't want to talk about Sarah. She's long gone. As dead as Jerri's going to be."

"Amil! You want revenge, take it out on me! Nothing you do is going to get those years back. But at least I can give you some compensation. The same you would recover in court and a whole lot more. I just took my company through a merger. The books are worth several million now, and that's not even counting the extra ten million of debt collectible by the company. I know you're not hurting in the wallet, but this will go a long way to padding it."

Amil shook his head. "You're willing to give up your whole fortune? For her? And you think I'm the crazy one."

"Her life is worth everything I have. I'm asking you as your brother to just forget about this. Killing is not going to give you the satisfaction you want."

"Don't be so sure."

"Look, just name the place; I'll meet you in an hour, ten o'clock. I have the paperwork already drawn up. We can talk this out man to man, brother to brother. No strings. Just enough money to make you wealthy until the end of your life. However long that may be."

"It's going to be a whole lot longer than yours, especially if you keep standing in my way. Look, keep your money. I don't want it. All the money in the world isn't going to stop me from getting my justice. She's a lawyer; she should understand that concept. And you should understand that she never loved you, either, and this playing Sir Galahad isn't going to get you squat. So she lets you screw her—big fucking deal. That's what she's good at. Believe me I know."

"You never touched her."

"You don't know anything about what happened that night. Only what she's been feeding you. But trust me, she does. She knows everything, and you're stupid to fall for her act—again. She's had time to perfect it over the years, just in case one of us caught up with her someday. Money makes people do crazy things, including kill their parents for the insurance and blame a lackey. But she picked the wrong man. No one fucks me over. No one. And no amount of pussy is going to turn my head."

"Amil!" But Amil shut off his phone, not willing to listen to another word.

Amil walked over to the bureau and opened a drawer, pulled out a Nighthawk Custom. Checked the chamber, holstered it on his belt.

What he wanted done, he was going to have to do himself. He was done waiting on third parties who didn't know their mouths from the cracks in their asses. His brother was still in the city. He was sure of it. Felt it in his bones. And he would track him down soon. And once he found Adrian, he would find her.

He'd made a mistake in playing this game: The invitation, the rose, the attempt to lure her to Avalon. In playing silly games, he'd let too many opportunities get away. She should have been dead by now.

He grabbed his coat, donned it.

But before he left the room, he downed another couple of aspirins with some vodka.

His head felt like it was going to burst.

Seven

"No!"

She felt the bile churning in her stomach. Adrian had said he was going to meet with his brother, but Amil had turned him down. If this was Plan A, there had better be a Plan B. Something other than what he had proposed earlier. They'd even argued about it. But here it was, coming at her again.

"There's no other way, Jerri!"

"I've already lost most of my identity. You want me to what now? Fake my death and have me start over somewhere else? I can't. It's crazy."

"Not as crazy as pretending that there's not a hit out on you." His raised voice reverberated. He was more than angry, his brows raised, the tic working both brow and right jaw. The lover from last night was replaced with someone else. Someone not used to hearing "no" and in that respect, he was probably more like his brother than he wanted to admit.

"My life is here!" she tried again.

"From what I see, it's not much of a life."

She felt as if he had slapped her. She'd been honest with him yesterday, had let him see a bit of her loneliness. And now he was using it against her.

"It's more than what you know."

"What do I know, Jerri?"

"Jeralyn . . ."

"Jerri," he said with emphasis. "You're the one who said you had nothing here."

"I have my job . . ."

"Which you care nothing about."

"Stop it! You don't have any right to say that to me. And don't think that last night gives you that right."

The statement hit where she wanted. His eyes hardened.

"Yeah, we both agreed that last night didn't mean anything. So I'm glad you didn't let yourself get carried away."

She drew in a shaky breath. Because he was wrong. Waking up this morning next to him had changed things.

Watching him sleep, knowing all that he was doing for her, remembering his kisses, his hands, his breath, remembering him, just a bit, more than she had previously. She'd realized how hard it would be to walk away once this was over. If it ever was.

"Do you want to die, Jerri? Because Amil isn't playing. I was wrong. I had hoped he had some residual feelings left for you, something to leverage against his need for revenge. But his anger is the foremost emotion he's feeling now. He thinks you set him up—that you killed your parents."

"That's crazy!"

"Amil's crazy. He's always had a short fuse and has never been one to suffer those he thinks pissed on him. So, you want to take your chances with him? Fine! But look, the only other way this is going to end is with Amil's death—and right now, that's not an option."

"I don't want you to kill your brother. I don't want any of this!"

"Well, this is what you've got. So face up to the reality."

"Do you even think he'd buy it? It's too convenient. He would see through it."

He sighed as though a weight was on his lungs. "Not if it's done right."

Her head was spinning. Everything was just a mess! This morning she had seen the televised news report that the Ballard case was being delayed because of an unexpected request for a continuance by the defense attorney. So now everyone was probably thinking she was holding off a losing case, trying to stretch out the time in hopes of finding more evidence. Any suppositions by the jury at this point were going to work against her client, especially if they were assuming she thought the case was weak.

And Steve Ballard wasn't the only one she was letting down. She had several clients she had meant to get to in the past day. They must all be wondering what had happened to her. Not to mention Ann, who must also be getting worried. But Adrian had advised against calling anyone for right now, his paranoia working overtime. She was a prisoner—without an advocate on her side.

The smell of bacon, eggs, waffles, and coffee hung in the living room. The breakfast was set on a cart, still untouched. Neither one of them had an appetite. She walked over and picked up her neglected cup of coffee, tasted it. Bitter and tepid. She set it back down.

"Where would I go?" she asked sadly. The contemplation of starting over, in a strange place without the comfort of friends even. Her aunt and grandparents were dead and there was no other family she knew of. Maybe a distant cousin. No one anywhere with an obligation of family. No one to comfort her.

Last night had given her a brief illusion that maybe . . . but that wasn't an option. If this ended badly, and she was still alive, this was hardly something to begin a relationship with. To build a relationship on. All of this stemmed from something stupid she had done in the past. She had set brother against brother. And if Amil died, had to die, would Adrian ever forgive her?

He had sat down in one of the chairs facing the window overlooking the city streets. His anger was not as evident now, his face drawn in silent contemplation. As she watched him quietly, she wondered about this man with whom she had made love last night, and not for the first time. She knew so little about someone who had figured so largely in her life. She also wondered about his brother. Was he that crazy? What had attracted her to him? Or had she just used him as he was claiming?

Which led her to wonder about herself. She knew the woman she was now, at least she thought she did: Meticulous to the point of anal, loyal to friends, cautious around strangers. So, was the woman born of the girl she'd been? Was she following subconscious cues from her unremembered past that made her less likely to open up, to reveal much of herself. Renata, one of her friends, had said this about her: That she kept her secrets, leaving those close to her to wonder what she was hiding. All this time, she didn't know what she was hiding. And now, her secrets were finally revealing themselves.

Amil thought she'd killed her family and let him be blamed. There was no way she could have ever done that. What she remembered, the little bits and pieces, showed a loving mother and father. How could anyone think she would turn on them for whatever reason?

Now she was angry. Angry enough to hit something, or somebody. Preferably her "husband."

"I want to see him face-to-face, talk to him, get this out of the way."

At that, Adrian laughed, a bitter sound. "Trust me, no, you don't." His laughter died. "I know it's frustrating, but

don't ever think that you can reason with Amil. He's bent
on hurting you."

"You mean killing me, don't you?"

He didn't answer. Instead, he stood and grabbed his
leather jacket off the back of the chair. He was dressed in
his T-shirt and jeans again.

"I have to take care of something. I don't need to tell you
to stay here. You want anything, just ring room service. I've
got to make some preparations to get you out of the city. It
may take a couple of hours, so please, be patient and don't
do anything stupid."

"Like what?"

"Jerri," he warned.

"Fine. I won't do anything. But I'm going to go crazy up
in here."

He walked up to her and unexpectedly kissed her forehead. "You were always impulsive. I hope that's not still the
case."

"I told you, I'm not that girl. I know when to be cautious."

"Good, then." But he didn't look reassured. He searched
her face as though looking for a clue to what she was thinking. And then he left.

Jerri was about to dig a trail in the carpeting with her
heels as she paced the length of the suite's living room. Not
overly big, the suite now seemed confining. Even the expansive view didn't ease the claustrophobia that was creeping
up on her. She might as well be in a prison, albeit well fur-
nished.

Her nerves were tattered and frayed, her stomach roil-
ing. The silence of the rooms . . . only added to her tension.
It was worse than white noise. Even with the danger she
was in, she was worried about her clients. Ballard was probably cursing her into next week right about now. The

court session had been scheduled for nine-thirty. It was almost ten. She should have been in front of the jury now, giving closing arguments, pleading for Ballard's freedom. Instead, she was hiding from a lunatic about to go crazy on her own damn self. And Ann was probably frantic, even though she had left word with the court administrator that she was out ill. Even so, going off without a word was something she wouldn't do—not unless something was wrong. Ann would instinctively know something was up.

She hated doing this to her secretary. Ann was her confidante on a lot of matters and both of them had been through the grind of starting up the firm, getting clients, as well as losing them. Although she had never cried on the woman's shoulders, those shoulders had been offered to her more than once. Ann was privy to more of her secrets than even some of her friends. Not to even think of the stress Ann was already going through with a sick mother and a five-year-old son she was raising alone.

She walked to the phone before she had time to think over her impulse and question herself. She had promised not to do anything stupid, so she wouldn't tell Ann where she was, only that she was okay and not to worry.

The phone rang only once before Ann picked up.

"Yes?" Ann's voice was tight and unnatural. She sounded nervous.

"It's me, Ann. I wanted to let you know that I'm going to be away from the office for awhile and I don't know when I'll be back. Personal matters I have to attend to. I just didn't want you to worry."

"Yes," Ann said again. There was something in her voice, an edge. "I understand."

Jeralyn's skin pricked. Spider nerves.

"Ann, is everything all right? What's going on?"

The man's voice that came on definitely wasn't Ann's, but was frighteningly familiar.

"Hello, Jerri."

So like Adrian's and not. Her throat constricted as she imagined the situation that was happening on the other end of the phone.

"Who is this?" she asked barely above a whisper.

"You know who this is, so let's not play games. I've been waiting a few hours wondering if you were going to call in. I took a chance and obviously it's paying off."

"Look, don't hurt her, Amil."

"Oh, so you know my name now. The other morning it was like we were total strangers, but we both know that's not the case. Right?"

"Look, I don't remember, I don't care what you believe! And I'm not playing games! What do you want?"

"Well, let's see, what do I want? Well, for one thing, you never got back with me about tomorrow."

"Tomorrow?"

"Yes, the little function I invited you to for this weekend. But then again, why should we wait until the weekend? I'm so eager to see you again, face-to-face. Aren't you just a little bit anxious to get reacquainted? After all, we are married, or did you forget that as well?"

"I did forget, I swear," she said softly, needing to appease him, wanting to hurt him.

"Hmmm, now why don't I believe you? Could it be that you're a proven liar and that you will do anything to get what you want? Yes, I believe that's it."

"How did I lie? You can't believe that I actually set you up? I would never do that."

"*I would never do that*," he mimicked in a falsetto voice. "Okay, let's be straight for once. I'm sitting here holding a very big gun on this little lady here. I think the bullet will blow out both lungs, take out part of her spinal cord, rip through some major arteries and veins. It's bound to be messy. So why don't you spare yourself a large cleaning bill and let's meet up at your office. I trust you haven't forgotten where it is seeing how you have trouble remembering things."

"I'll be there." Her mind was spinning out of control. But there was no way she could sacrifice Ann, not to save her own life.

"Try to make it as soon as possible, sweetie. I hate waiting . . . and I've been waiting a long time for you."

He hung up, leaving her grasping the phone, trembling. She placed it on the cradle and grabbed her purse from the table. On the way to the door, she accidentally stumbled against one of the tables in the room, but she didn't feel the pain. She didn't feel anything but cold, blood-numbing fear as she opened the door and walked out.

The silence was the first thing he noticed as he closed the door to the suite. It was unnatural, empty. He knew after a few steps that she was gone. And the realization chilled him. Still, he raced through the various rooms calling out her name, praying to a God that he hadn't been on speaking terms with in a while.

His mouth ran dry as he called down to the front desk only to hear that no one had noticed a woman of her description leaving. Nor anyone that looked like Amil.

Why had she left after promising him she would stay put? She couldn't be that foolish.

Or had Amil or one of his men somehow gotten in? Maybe dressed as a hotel employee?

There were too many possibilities and too little time. He didn't have the luxury of ruminating over various scenarios.

The only places he could check were her home, her office . . . maybe the courthouse. Her sense of duty might have led her there.

He raked a frustrated hand through his hair, took a deep breath, gathered his thoughts.

Trouble was she could be anywhere.

With a sinking certainty he knew that wherever she was, Amil was there with her.

He walked to the door and slammed out, trying not to picture her dead body, but not succeeding.

Eight

Jeralyn paid the cabdriver, then stood there looking at the door to her office building long after he had pulled away. She half-expected to see a face staring out at her from the plate window that fronted the reception area where Ann usually sat at her desk. Someone with Adrian's face, but without the passion that Adrian had bathed her with. Instead, Amil's face would be full of hatred.

She took a breath and walked to the door, turned the knob. It wasn't locked.

She walked through the empty reception room, her legs numb. Her whole body was numb. Was this how death felt? The short path through the room felt long and lonely. The carpeting absorbed her footsteps as she turned down the hallway.

Her office door was closed. But she knew he was inside waiting.

She turned the knob, opened up the door on a scene that was almost nonsensical. Ann was seated away from the window, her eyes bulging and turned sideways, focused on the gun held near her head. A rose stem was stuck between her lips. A trickle of blood ran down her chin, trailing to her already stained blouse; obviously the stem had thorns.

Jeralyn winced at the thought of the pain and terror Ann was going through. But it would soon be over.

It occurred to her only at that moment that maybe he wouldn't be satisfied with just killing her. That he would still kill Ann if only to keep her from talking.

She had to make sure that didn't happen.

She finally let herself look into the face of the man holding the gun. He was smiling. A horribly cold smile.

He resembled Adrian, but barely. Although around the same height, he was much thinner, his jawline too angular, his lips thinner. The blue of his eyes was more opaque, startling. His dark hair was longer than Adrian's, in need of taming. He wore a black Windbreaker over a black shirt and black leather pants. He should have been sweltering, but he looked composed and cool.

He looked like a vampire wannabe. But vampires were creatures of myth. This was a flesh-and-blood man born without a heart. Or someone who had lost his soul a long time ago, because only a soulless fiend could torture poor Ann the way he had. Ann had now focused her terrified eyes on Jeralyn and Jeralyn fought back her tears.

"Please, don't point that at her. I'm here. I'm who you want to hurt. Not Ann. She's done nothing to you."

"Uhm, I don't know . . ." He gave Ann a disdainful once-over as though considering a pesky insect. "She's got such an irritating nasal twang. It bothered me, so I thought I'd shut her up. I think the rose is a nice touch. I remember how much you liked them. I had some especially sent from Naples for you. Refrigerated to keep them fresh. They're from that beachfront cottage—you know, that special one. I heard you and Adrian talking about it years ago, something about an evening you spent there beneath the rosebush? I thought I'd try to give you a piece of that memory."

"Look, I don't feel like talking about the past. You wanted me here, I'm here. So let Ann go and stop with these fucking games . . ."

"Oh, such language. Saucy! Have you convinced yourself that you're in control of the situation? Hmmm, funny. I'm the one who seems to have the gun, so I think I should be the one making the rules."

"Do you want me to beg? Then I'm begging. Do what you want to me . . ."

"Trust me, I will." There was no mirth in his voice now.

Jeralyn felt a bolt of fear stab through her, sever her core. No matter what she had done in the past, she didn't deserve to die the way he was going to make her.

"What are you going to do to me?" She couldn't help the slight tremble in her voice.

Even the new smile contained no humor. "I'm going to give you some pain, I'm going to let you savor that pain for as long as possible. After that, who knows? I'll write the script as the mood moves me."

All this time, Ann's eyes had widened on Jeralyn, realizing that her boss was talking about her own death. Jeralyn caught the silent message: *"Run!"* Jeralyn shook her head slightly, almost imperceptibly, but Amil noticed anyway.

"Yes, she does seem worried about you. Such undeserved loyalty. I think she should be worried about herself." Again, he turned a look on Ann. Ann didn't look at him, but felt the force of his stare. She shut her eyes, as though ready to die now. Jeralyn had to speak up fast. She steadied her voice, approached the thought as she might have in court.

"Ann has a young son. And an elderly mother. And she won't do anything that would take her away from them, including going to the police. She's not going to cause you any trouble. Besides, you have money to go anywhere out of the reach of the police."

"Yes, I have money. I guess I should thank you for that.

Met some people inside that hole, made some connections. Let's just say methamphethamine is the new gold in town. So my pockets aren't hurting thanks to you. Maybe I'll keep that in mind as I'm working on you."

Working on you. Jeralyn was too aware what that meant. She'd had clients who had *worked* on people. Sometimes death was preferable. Obviously, she wasn't going to get a quick one.

"Well, counselor, if you've finished running your mouth, we can get on about our business. So, I've taken what you've said in consideration about your secretary and here's what I think . . ."

And with lightning speed, he rammed the butt of the gun against Ann's temple. Jeralyn gasped as the limp woman slid from her chair to the floor unconscious. The rose was still in her mouth.

She was immobile with fear as Amil moved toward her, his vengeance like lust in his eyes. They were finally alone.

"You didn't have to do that," she said tearfully. Blood was already pooling beneath Ann's head.

"And have her rushing to call the police as soon as we left? I don't think so. As it is, you should be thanking me that I didn't simply pump a couple of bullets in her." He paused. "So, go ahead . . . thank me."

Jeralyn held her tongue, but quickly realized as he stared her down that he was waiting for just that. He truly was insane, which meant she had to play cautiously.

"Thank you, Amil," she whispered, thinking that he might have killed Ann already anyway. If no one found the woman in time, she could bleed to death. Or suffer irreparable damage. But the welfare of a human being meant nothing to this man.

He took her by the arm, deliberately applying unnecessary pressure to cause her discomfort. She refused to wince, especially when he tracked her expression, looking for a desired reaction. Not getting it, he smirked, knowing there would be plenty of time to get what he wanted from her.

He pocketed his gun. They both knew she wasn't going to run, because if she did, he would just come back and finish Ann off. And she knew he'd do it without a thought.

She wondered how many people he'd killed, besides her parents.

Outside he led her to a black Aston Martin parked a few feet away from her door. She hadn't noticed it before. He and his brother seemed to have a thing for expensive black sports cars. Sibling rivalry. Amil wanted everything his brother had, including her.

Several minutes later they were on the highway heading north. From time to time, she would peek at him from the sides of her eyes, thinking to spy on him. But he would turn his eyes toward her at the same moments, uncannily feeling her. Thankfully, he kept silent. Just hearing his sarcastic voice was enough to make her scream.

In less than forty minutes, he was turning down a side street in the Pacific Heights area, and she knew exactly where he was taking her: Avalon Hall. He was going to play out his sick games in the privacy of the old rambling home, so large that her screams would be insulated inside and no one would find her body for days, if at all.

This had been his plan from the moment he sent that invitation. And the rose.

They pulled past a set of open gates into a driveway that fronted an imposing façade of Old World influence in the form of the neo-gothic columns that stood on either side of the door. The old was juxtaposed with modern-style intrusions, like the enormous windows that were unadorned. The windows were dark.

Before he opened his car door, Amil pulled the gun from his holster. "You get any ideas about running or screaming, I'm going to plug you before you can get two steps away.

Then I'll kill anybody who comes to help or even peeks inside. You may not care about yourself, but you seem to hate the idea of other people getting hurt because of you . . . unless, of course, that other person happens to be me."

She stepped outside the car and waited quietly for him to lead the way. She was numb, already reconciled to her fate. She could only pray that he would have mercy—or get impatient—and put a bullet through her head.

They walked up the driveway, climbed the three white-painted stairs to the elaborate oaken door. He pulled out a key chain, inserted a silver key into the lock. The door groaned as he pushed it open as if the house itself was protesting its imminent misuse.

Jeralyn said a silent prayer as she stepped inside the dark foyer. She needed a miracle.

Nine

The speedometer was clocking nearly ninety; Adrian put more pressure on the gas pedal. He had almost collided with a car at the last red light, which he had run through, but nothing could make him slow down.

He'd circumvented the security guard of her building, had gone up to her floor. Getting no answer when he yelled her name, he'd broken down the door of her condo, expecting to find the worst.

Only marginally relieved to see no body or any other sign of violence, he quickly left knowing she had precious little time if Amil had found her—which Adrian had every reason to believe was the case. How he had found her or how she had put herself in harm's way no longer mattered. He exited the expressway and raced down Irving, almost hitting a woman who had just stepped off the curb. He didn't have time for guilt or anything else.

He parked in front of the townhouse where her office was located, jumped out without locking the car door. The door to her office was unlocked and he strode in, calling out her name. Silence.

He rushed past the reception area, toward the rear, looking through open doors. The disappointment was palpable. No one was here.

The last door down the hall was half ajar and he stepped in. His heart froze and a pain shot through his chest. He saw the white slacks and shoes first—but that wasn't part of the wardrobe he'd bought her. When he stepped around the desk, he understood why. It wasn't Jerri. The woman had lost a lot of blood by the looks of the stain on the carpet. The corner of her blond hair was red and sticky. His brother had definitely been here.

He stooped down, put a finger to her pulse. It was there, but barely. She would be dead soon.

He reached for the phone on the desk and dialed 9-1-1 and gave the situation and address to the dispatcher. When he put the phone back on the cradle, he spied a cream-colored square off to the edge of the desk sitting atop a pile of manila folders. The handwriting made him pause.

It was Amil's writing on the envelope. Adrian picked it up, pulled out the invitation inside: "You are invited to a private gathering at Avalon Hall on Saturday, July 21, at 8:00 P.M. Formal dress required."

What were the odds? Very good if he knew his brother.

Amil liked setting elaborate ruses. He knew the place, knew that it had hundreds of rooms, any number in which he could have set up a veritable torture chamber for her.

He paused, guiltily looked down at the unconscious woman. An ambulance was on its way. He hoped they got here in time, but he couldn't stay to wait. Another life was pending.

He raced out of the building in time to see a young thug opening the door to the Jaguar. In a couple of steps, he was on the redheaded teen, pulling him out of the car and promptly laying him out flat in the street. He got in the car and didn't look in the rearview mirror to see if the screeching car he heard had hit the kid or not.

Hopefully, he didn't have blood on his hands.

But most of all, he hoped he could get to Jeralyn in time.

The unfurnished room was barely lit. And it was unusually cold despite the heat of the day.

She sat in the chair, the only piece of furniture in the room. On their way to the room, they had passed a bevy of darkened rooms, the silhouettes of heavy furniture discernable. She'd wondered how he had gotten access to the mansion and who he had to hurt to get the keys?

Now, he stood away from her, looking out the window next to a large, dark fireplace. Strangely, she had expected something more ornate and rich, but the sparcity made the room seem plain.

Amil hadn't spoken to her in several minutes, which only exacerbated her nervousness. The expectation of pain was as excrutiating as whatever he had planned. But then again, probably not. She just wished he would get it over with.

Another five minutes passed before he spoke. When he did, the voice was solemn, sad, and without its earlier sarcasm. It also had more of a Bronx accent.

"I used to dream about you every night when I was locked up. Sometimes I pictured us like this, a large house, with you to myself to do with whatever I wanted. Other times, I saw you staring at me, looking at me with those eyes, questioning, silently asking me what I'd done. And I'd get so angry, I'd wake up and have to get up to pace to get my pulse to stop racing. You saw me that night, saw that I had come in after you, long after the fire started. I'd chased you from the hotel? How in the fuck would I have had time to do what I was accused of?"

She took a chance, even though he might retaliate, but

she had to ask: "If you followed me directly from the hotel, when would I have had time to set the fire, Amil? You say you know me. Did I ever say I hated my parents, that I wanted to get rid of them? Was there anything about me that said I could do something so heinous?"

Now the questions were out there, but she really didn't expect any answers because they both already knew she didn't kill her family. And she believed that he hadn't, either. It was in his voice, in the sadness of his profile. He may have become a killer since then, but he didn't kill that night.

He stepped away from the window, walked toward her until he was standing over her. The gun was still in his hand. Such a large gun. One of its bullets could probably rip her apart. And then this would all be over.

"I hoped when you finally came to in the hospital that you would clear me, tell the police what happened. But that's not what you told them—you said you didn't remember anything, not a damn thing about that night, about us, about even your supposed true love, Adrian. But I knew you were lying, so I figured that you must have had something to do with the fire, because why else would you lie?"

"But I wasn't lying . . ."

"Shut up! Just shut your fucking mouth!" His hand was raised to strike, but after a moment he lowered his arm. She could see him visibly fight for control. He obviously hadn't planned this charade any farther than just getting her here. He'd said he was writing the script as they went along. Part of the script seemed to be exorcising his anger, getting at the truth.

If she had to die today, she wanted to know the truth, also. Wanted to know why her parents had died, why she lost so much of her life that night. She didn't care how angry her questions made him.

"I didn't remember . . . not then. But things are fighting

to come back to me. Now, since you and Adrian have come back into my life, I remember Sarah . . ."

"Don't you dare mention her name! Sarah was the only one who truly loved me, and I gave her up because you swung your pretty little ass my way . . ."

"I'm so sorry." She meant it. Such a stupid mistake.

"You think I want to hear your apologies. It's too late . . . for me, for Sarah, even for you."

"I know it now. That's probably why I dreamed about her, about you . . . my guilt about what happened to both of you. I never meant . . . at least I don't think I could have been so cruel."

"But you were," he said quietly. "You couldn't bear me touching you. Couldn't bear being in that bedroom with me. The thought of me disgusted you."

"No, I don't think so." The haze was clearing, just a little. She reached out and touched a memory.

"I wasn't disgusted by you, Drew."

"Don't call me that . . ." The tone wasn't as strong as the words. He just seemed tired now.

"I think I was just frightened about what I had done. It was never about you, or how I felt. I think I did believe I could love you . . ." She remembered the room, decorated in tropical colors, like paradise. It was her wedding night and she should have been happy, but she wasn't, because she only realized then the mistake she'd made trying to make Adrian jealous, playing such a cruel game on Andrew— Drew—who had kissed her so sweetly . . .

"You kissed me and I remember that I wanted to make love with you, but I knew it would be a lie because I didn't love you . . . not the way I loved Adrian."

"So at least you've stopped playing your games. You remembered all along—admit it."

She shook her head. "No. I didn't. But I don't think my

memory loss was physical . . . I think until now I just didn't want to remember. Don't you understand the pain I was in? Can't you remember losing your mother? I heard them screaming, yelling . . . who would want to remember that?"

She didn't care about the tears flowing or about the man standing with the gun in his hand. His hatred couldn't reach her now, couldn't overwhelm the sadness and grief that she hadn't allowed herself to feel. Now it came rushing at her, the intensity just as devastating as it had been that night she tried to run up the stairs and couldn't get past the wall of smoke and flames.

"I deserve to die, but not because I framed you. Because I only thought of myself and I ruined lives because of it. You think you want to hurt me now, go ahead. I don't care. I just don't want to remember anymore. I don't want to re-member . . ." This last ended on a soft moan.

The heartless monster was gone as he reached over a fin-ger and traced a tear, much like Adrian had done the other night. They were alike in many ways she was discovering.

"If you didn't set the fire and I didn't, then who did? And who planted the gas can in my hand because I didn't have it when—I don't even remember how I came to be uncon-scious. One minute I was standing there and we were look-ing at one another, and the next, the police are standing over me, guns drawn."

"Why were you so certain that I had done it?"

"Because the can of gas came from your garage. The po-lice were able to trace your father's fingerprints on it. The only other prints on there were mine, though. I didn't think your father was crazy enough to start the fire, but then again, what do I know? I've spent the last fifteen years going over that night again and again, and I still don't know."

"It was easier to think I did it because I was the one who

had been lying to you up until that moment. So why wouldn't you think I was lying about the memory loss. It must have seemed so convenient to you."

His nod was hardly perceptible. He stepped away from her, looking toward the window.

Somewhere in the house, water was running as though someone had turned on a faucet.

Amil's hand tightened on his gun and he walked silently to the door, opened it a bit and listened. Now the sound of running water was unmistakable.

Someone else was in the house.

"Get up!" he ordered, holding the gun on her. She got up, but stood there. "So my brother has found us, huh?"

He waved the gun at her, signaling her to move toward him. She tried not to hope, to believe instead that she was going to be rescued. In the end, it could be faulty plumbing that was acting up. Because why would Adrian go upstairs and turn on the water?

He pulled her by her arm as he led her to the foyer where the grand staircase led up to the second landing. He practically dragged her up the stairs.

"Adrian!" he called out when they reached the landing. "C'mon out and rescue your lady love! She's here waiting for you!"

Only silence answered him—which made him angrier. What détente they had reached back in that empty room was null. His anger was back, aimed at her, at Adrian. At a situation no longer under his control.

She followed him as he strode toward the sound of the water. There was a door at the end of the hall; the only closed door in an aisle of open rooms. They reached the closed door which he kicked open, hoping to surprise his brother. Instead they were looking in on an empty bathroom. The tub faucet was on and water was filling into the tub.

"Who turned this on?" he asked, his voice brutal with its suspicion. But how would she know?

"He's here, isn't he?" He was paranoid. Angry. Ready to explode.

He reached to turn off the water, but the knob wouldn't turn.

"Okay, what the fuck is going on?" She thought she heard an edge of fear in his voice now. "Why does this keep happening?"

"What keeps happening?"

"Shut up! Everywhere I go, the water runs, turns on by itself. Dammit, I'm tired of this shit. Even in prison, it did this."

She would have thought he was imagining things, except she was looking at the water that had turned on by itself, that was running, and couldn't be turned off.

And her imagination was flaring up because she thought she was seeing a hint of red hair floating in the water.

"Oh, God, no! Sarah, please!"

Sarah? The woman who'd drowned herself? Who'd appeared to Jeralyn during her bath in a dream. A woman who'd been standing next to Amil in her dreams, dripping wet, her red hair plastered to her head.

Adrian had assumed it was a dream, not a memory. But he'd been wrong.

Sarah had been there that night. The certainty crystallized as the form in the tub became more distinct.

She was lovely. Pale. And quite dead.

She opened her eyes, her body still floating just beneath the surface. And she was looking at Amil. Drew. Andrew.

"No, this isn't happening—not again. You aren't real. You never were."

The spectral Sarah didn't like hearing that she didn't exist. From the man she had sacrificed her life for.

She turned those pale green eyes on Jeralyn. Sad eyes. As Jeralyn backed away, she wondered how eyes could be so sad and yet accuse her?

The ghost might as well have pointed at Jeralyn, spoken her name, and told her that Jeralyn was the reason she had died.

She turned to run just as Amil began shooting into the tub, trying to kill his dead lover. She tripped down the first steps, regained her balance, and continued down the path to freedom, away from a madman, away from illusions that were coming to life . . . again.

She reached the door just as it opened and she screamed to see Amil coming at her again. How had he gotten down here before her?

Determined to fight her way out of the house, she aimed at his face with her closed fist, felt the contact. Heard her name called by a different voice.

"Jerri! Stop it!"

The voice exploded through her craziness, her fear.

Adrian. He was here. But how?

"C'mon, let's get you out of here."

Amil's scream halted them. It was horrible, full of panic and fear—of terror.

"Stay here!" Adrian demanded and she might have, but for the fact that she knew instinctively that she was no longer in danger.

"He's in the bathroom," she said weakly. "At the end of the hall."

He took the stairs two at a time, racing toward his brother. The screams had stopped. She followed slowly, a deadweight settling on her. Maybe Sarah was still here, as she'd been at her parents' summer home.

She'd been there even before Jeralyn and Drew had arrived. She'd been an angry ghost. But no more.

Even before she stepped into the bathroom, she knew Amil was dead.

The thought should have made her feel relieved. But as she came up beside Adrian, looking down at Amil floating just beneath the surface, his eyes open, all she could feel was sadness and guilt. She would feel these two emotions for a long time.

The pain ebbed a little when Adrian took her in his arms, but it didn't shut out the man who eventually died because of her.

Ten

Gasps and cries erupted as the verdict was read. Jeralyn wasn't as stunned as some, but was a little surprised. The verdict could have gone either way. Steve Ballard shook his fists in victory, then reached over to pull her into an impromptu bear hug. She stiffened, patted his back for show.

The judge's gavel came down and the courtroom quieted down. "Okay, a little order here. Mr. Ballard, you are free to go. The bailiff will escort you out."

Jeralyn quietly gathered up her folders, put them in her briefcase, then followed her client out. She felt a pair of eyes on her and turned to look into Deborah Trenton's face. The pain and guilt were edged with condemnation. Yes, she'd had an affair with her brother-in-law, but did that make him less of a murderer?

Only the jury had decided he wasn't. Or at least, that there wasn't enough proof.

She turned away and continued out of the courtroom. Ballard was waiting near the door, his face beaming. Reporters were a pack herd, waiting down the hall to pounce. But there was something Jeralyn had to ask him.

Softly, where only her client could hear, she asked: "Did you do it?" She'd never asked before.

He feigned ignorance. "Did I do what?"

She took a breath, asked again, a little firmer. "Did you kill your wife?"

He tried an expression of indignation, but he couldn't make it last more than a second. The indignation was quickly replaced with a smirk. "You wanna know now, after everything is over? What do you think? Bitch was going to divorce me, get all my money. That's what she threatened. Told me she was going to get my house, my car, hell even Stanley, my dog. I couldn't let her do that."

She felt as though her face had frozen into its mask of neutrality.

"Strange, I always figured you knew. Well, I would've lost that bet, huh?"

He shrugged, then walked away with his hands in his pocket, a smile on his face, leaving her standing motionless in the court hallway. She could hear the reporters flaring up with questions as their quarry bounded toward them.

She gripped the handle of her case, trying to steady her breath. Yes, she'd known. Somewhere deep inside, she knew that her client was a murderer, sketchy timeline be damned. Somehow, he had pulled it off and now another killer was free to walk the streets and hurt someone else. But she'd done what she was paid to do, what the law requires: Zealously defend her client.

She felt the acid in her stomach burning through the lining. She couldn't do this anymore. Not one more day.

She walked in the opposite direction of the reporters to another elevator bank. On the ride down, she felt the burden and tension ease out of her body. By the time she reached the lower floor, she'd already made another decision.

* * *

"But, are you sure?" Ann asked, leaning forward in the hospital bed. Her head was still bandaged but the doctors had told her that they would be removing them in another week or so. Her face was ashen, but otherwise she was recovering and that was an answer to many prayers. When Jeralyn had first walked into this room over a week ago, she'd moaned to see her secretary lying unconscious, the monitor blips the only sign that the woman was alive. Ann's mother had questioned her: "How could this happen?" but Jeralyn hadn't been able to answer.

Now, she sat down in the unoccupied chair, alone with a woman who'd nearly died because of her. She tried not to add that to the accumulation of guilt, but she couldn't assuage the truth. She noted a large floral arrangement sitting on the table near the window: Deep red roses interspersed with white babies' breath.

"I need to step away from this now. Maybe, I'll come back to it, but right now, I have to find out some things about me. I've been running, even though I hadn't realized it. I'm getting more bits and pieces from the past and I need to know more."

Ann settled back against the pillow, sighed. "I guess you have to do it. It's your life, your past. You have a right to it."

"And Ann, don't worry about the hospital bills. I'm putting the condo on the market; whatever I get, I'm putting toward the bills. And of course, I'm going to give you such a glowing letter of recommendation that they'll be clamoring to hire you."

"Don't worry about me, Jeralyn. I'm a survivor."

"Yeah, but sometimes surviving isn't enough. Sometimes you need to thrive. Someone reminded me of that recently."

"I'm going to miss you."

"Well, there's this invention called the telephone, so I'll be a few numbers away. And of course, once I'm settled, you've got to come to visit."

Ann shifted to get more comfortable. She was putting on a brave face. This wasn't something she'd expected to hear, but she understood it was what Jeralyn had to do. Both of them had come too close to death to just worry about bills and paychecks. They'd entered a place few would understand. But they understood between each other.

"I hear Naples is pretty. I really hope you find what you're looking for."

Jeralyn stood and bent to plant a kiss on Ann's forehead. The act made her remember, but that was in the past. He was in her past now.

"I hope so, too." And then she left, wondering for the hundredth time what the hell she was doing.

She was sealing up another box when the doorbell rang. She let out a sigh of frustration as she stood and looked around. Her once gorgeously decorated unit was now filled wall-to-wall with moving boxes and packing cases. The temporary place she had found in Florida was too small for her furniture, so most of her stuff had gone into storage.

She turned toward the door and nearly tripped over one of the boxes. She stifled a curse.

"Coming!"

When she peeked out her peephole, she stepped back as if the door had become untouchable.

"Jerri, open up." She hadn't heard his voice in nearly three weeks, enough time for her to start to force him out of her mind, to close up her heart again.

Her hesitation was ridiculous, she told herself. He was here to settle matters. And she had to stop reacting with emotions. She was still a lawyer, dammit. She should be able to handle situations.

But that admonition didn't stop her heart from leaping when she opened the door. When he had taken her to the hospital to be checked over, she'd told him she would be fine, that he didn't need to stay. He'd stayed anyway, and later had driven her home. At the condo, he'd kissed her forehead and then left.

That was the last she had heard from him in these three weeks. She'd tried to understand, after all she was the one who said they should go their separate ways once all of the craziness was over. And he had done just that.

Now he was standing here in her hallway, a day's growth on his face, his eyes tired. He had lost some weight as well.

And still she wanted him. Was holding on to decency to keep from rushing him.

"Adrian . . . hi." The words sounded like they came from a tongue-tied twelve year old. "What're you doing here?"

Despite the tiredness, he still looked cool and attractive, his dark hair newly trimmed, his mouth full despite being drawn into a tight line. She self-consciously realized she was dressed in an old blue shirt and tattered jeans.

He was hurting. He'd had to bury a brother.

"I called your office. I thought that would be a neutral place to talk, but there wasn't any answer. Then at the hospital, Ann told me you were leaving."

"Ann? I hadn't realized you were visiting her."

"I've been keeping track on her progress. I felt bad leaving her unconscious in your office. She's doing well."

"I'm sorry. I should at least invite you in," she said with a nervous laugh, moving back to let him enter.

She closed the door, kept her back against it for support. He was a few feet away, but still within reach.

"The flowers . . . in Ann's room—they were from you?"

He nodded, looking uncomfortable at the acknowledgment. "She told me you were selling your condo."

"Yeah. I'm leaving town for awhile. Time for a break."

"I'm sorry Amil upset your life. I mean, me and Amil, that is . . ."

She shook her head. "No, you don't have anything to be

sorry about. Actually, despite everything, it actually has helped me face my past. Now I need to immerse myself in it, find out the past so I can see my future clearly."

"By the way, you don't have to worry about Ann's bills. Or for that matter, what she's going to do about her job situation. I've talked with a friend, a lawyer here in San Francisco who has a firm and a need for some extra hands and a brain. I told him he'd be getting a valuable employee. I figured since she worked for you, she must be good."

Jeralyn smiled. "She's very good. I'm glad, really glad."

He was distracted. Kept looking over at the boxes. "I'm sorry I left so abruptly, but given the circumstances—and what Amil had done to you—I thought it was best. Besides, I had to take care of the business of claiming my brother's body. Of course, there were questions from the police."

"Yeah, I had my question session, too. The police seemed to accept my version, although they were very curious how a grown man drowns in a tub. Too many unanswered questions. Eventually, it'll go cold case and be forgotten."

"Yeah, forgotten."

"I hated that it ended this way. Hated that you had to be hurt, again."

"Jerri, I'm not the one who got hurt in all this. Yes, he was my brother, and yes I loved him, but the man he was, who he'd become—"

"Because of me—"

"No! Because of him. The choices he made, the things he did—all him. So, once and for all, stop blaming yourself for everything. Yes, you did something stupid a long time ago. But you shouldn't have had to pay for it, not like this. Losing your parents, your memory, then being stalked by a crazed husband . . ."

"Thankfully, the police didn't know that part, otherwise I might be behind bars now."

He pinned her with his eyes. Beautiful blue, mesmerizing. She couldn't move.

"So, now it's all over and you're starting your life over. Trying to find the past."

"I have to. You were the one who said that I would always have this void if I didn't face the past."

"Let me help find it then."

"What?"

"I'm taking a sabbatical from the business. Maybe a few weeks, months, however long it takes . . ."

"Takes to what?"

"To find something I lost a long time ago: A chance for happiness."

"I don't understand . . ." And she tried to pretend that she didn't, because the truth of it was too much for her.

"I want to see if there's a chance for us. I know I promised I would just walk away, and I did try. Believe me I tried. But I can't anymore. I'm tired of being alone. Aren't you?"

She stood silently, waiting, afraid to answer, afraid to reveal how very tired she was of the solitude. Of the rootlessness. She wanted to find the girl she'd lost so long ago.

He took her answer from the silence and walked toward her. Her back was pressed against the door as he leaned in to cover her lips with his own. The kiss was desperate, caught her unexpelled breath.

His hands moved over her shoulders down her arms, detoured to her waist. He pushed in farther, melded their bodies. He was growing hard against her stomach and she remembered him pounding inside her, remembered the heat of the intrusion, the friction against her walls. She throbbed in anticipation, releasing a stream of moisture that was all for him.

He pulled her into a clinch, whispered against her ear, "I thought I'd gotten over you. But I never did."

No one had brought her to this point and no one else ever would.

The last time had been sweet and passionate. Now, there was a tinge of sadness, of desperation.

She needed him to remember the past; he needed her to forget the present. Still clinched, they slid to the floor, the hardwood uncomfortable beneath her back, but she was past caring. She hadn't known it was possible to want someone so much. She could see herself loving him all too soon.

There was no foreplay this time. They were past that. For right now, both of them sought a connection that would sustain them until they could reconnect on a deeper level. He was there ahead of her and she was quickly in pursuit.

He brutally tugged her jeans and panties down around her ankles, then without ceremony pushed his penis inside her. His hands roamed across the canvas of her breasts beneath the shirt and her bra as he moved slowly in and out of her, his lips, his breath trailing her neck. She moved her hips to meet his, letting his hunger devour her. She was past the point of saturation, but his fast thrusts were causing nerve-tingling friction. Her hands held his ass even as she clenched him inside her.

He rested his lips against her lips, and began whispering, "Remember me, remember us . . ."

"I do," she moaned back. She did: Envisioned the younger Adrian, his eyes behind shades, walking toward her, ice cream dripping down her hands . . .

"What do you remember?" he asked breathlessly, his thrusts relentless, telling her body to remember . . .

"The roses, I remember roses—and the smell—oh, God, they smell so good . . ."

He caught her lips between his, nibbled them. He used to nibble her, nibbled her that first night. He had taken her firm young breasts in his hands . . .

His hands moved beneath the shirt and pushed it up,

pushed up the bra. His head lowered and he captured a nipple in his mouth . . .

She heard the waves breaking on the beach, the rush of the water nearly drowning out his words . . .

"I love you . . ."

And she heard those words now.

One day, she knew she would be able to say them with her whole soul. But for right now, it was enough that she knew she belonged in his arms, that being with him was the most natural thing in the world.

And that they were continuing a story that began a long time ago. . . .

Yes, she smelled the roses. . . .

Please turn the page for an exciting
preview of Lucy Monroe's
SATISFACTION GUARANTEED
Also available right now from Brava.

Beth was shaking with nerves by the time that Ethan buzzed her condo that night.

She'd told herself over and over again that this was not a real date. It was an opportunity to solidify their cover. Right. And the fact that they would be sitting across an intimate table for two should not be sending her libido into overdrive. She'd read somewhere that women were at the sexual peak in their thirties. Well, she was only twenty-nine and she'd been peaking for Ethan for almost two years.

Which meant it wasn't some kind of hormonal joke her body was playing on her. She wanted the man. So much that she'd stopped calling herself depraved and learned to deal with the urges. Only now, she was faced with more temptation than she'd ever had where he was concerned. She didn't know if she could deal with *that*.

Darn him anyway for being the one man she was sure would not only not balk at her sexual fantasies, but who would know what to do with them.

She bit her lip as she took a final look in her full length mirror. She had not morphed into a cover model for *Vogue* in the last ten seconds, more was the pity. Because while she was sure Ethan would get her sexual fantasies, she was equally certain he would have no interest in sharing them. She was not his type.

At five-foot-six, she was at least three inches too short, a cup size too small in the curves department and several lovers shy of the experience a man like him was no doubt used to.

None of that had stopped her from trying on six different outfits, doing her makeup three times, and trying her hair four different ways before settling for a sloppy topknot with tendrils framing her face that went well with the simple black dress she'd settled on. It left a good portion of her legs and back bare . . . all in the effort to look as sexy as she could for him. For this non-date. Sheesh.

She needed to get a life.

The problem was that she didn't want a life . . . she wanted *him*. Every sexy, tantalizing, irresistible inch of his six-foot-three frame.

The buzzer sounded again and she jumped, grimacing. Showtime.

She rushed to release the entrance lock for downstairs. Ethan was knocking on the door less than a minute later.

She opened it, keeping the kittens back with one wary foot. "Hi."

"Hi, Sunshine. Is there a reason you're blocking the door?"

"The kittens." She scooted back, keeping the cats away from the opening as she widened it to let him in. "Come on in and I'll get my jacket."

Ethan moved swiftly, grabbing Beethoven as the black and white kitten tried to make a break for the hall and shutting the door immediately upon stepping inside her apartment.

"Thanks. They want to go exploring, but with my luck they'd end up at the manager's apartment. She's allergic to feline fur and was very dubious about letting me get the cats."

Ethan grinned. "I can imagine." He whistled as he looked around. "Nice place. Exotic."

That's what she'd been going for. She'd decorated with Byzantine colors and rich textures like silks and velvets as well as faux fur throws on her sofa and chaise lounge. It fit her, but usually surprised people that did not know her well. Even some who did.

Ethan didn't looked surprised, only intrigued.

She grabbed her vintage velvet dress coat from the back of the chair where she'd left it in preparation. "I'm ready to go, if you are."

"Dinner's not for another hour." He took the coat and laid it back over the chair.

Then he shrugged off his own leather jacket and put it on top of hers. And she let him. Without a protest. Weird. This man brought out more than one unexpected reaction in her. Even odder . . . she then just stood there staring at him and trying really hard to remember . . . *this was not a real date.*

But his dark sweater clung to his muscular chest in a mouth watering way. He looked so hot . . . in every way.

He cocked his brow at her and her stomach dipped. "Um . . . if not dinner yet, then what?"

"I thought we could have a drink and talk a while before we go." He looked around her living room again. "I want a chance to soak in who you are away from the office so I can relate to that person in front of Preston."

It sounded reasonable, but Ethan Crane was the last person she wanted to invite into her life on a more personal basis.

Here's a sensual sneak peek at
THE OBJECT OF LOVE
by Sharon Cullars.
Available now from Brava.

After a second, Lacey sighed. "That's not a promise you can make, Sean. You live long enough, you're going to say something . . . do something . . . that's going to hurt someone. That's a given. It's called living."

Instead of an answer, his finger came up, traced along her jaw. Her body stiffened. "Living is more than pain or hurt. It's pleasure, too."

His mouth stopped her protest. The sudden heat and liquid of the kiss caused an involuntary moan. She had to hold on to his shoulders to keep from totally melting into him. Through his coat, sweater, she felt the hard tendons of his muscles.

Sean's lips consumed hers. She had no time to catch her breath or to think as every atom of her body responded to his need. He pulled her to him, tightened his arms around her waist, not allowing her any escape. She felt the hard swelling of his penis against her stomach, ached to take all of him inside her. Her panties were soaking with her own need, her walls spasming with anticipation.

She tried to find the common sense she had only a few moments ago, but any trace of it was pushed out of her head as his tongue pushed farther into her mouth, and she found herself sucking it eagerly. It'd been so long since she had been kissed completely. For the first time in days, she was totally here, her body and mind together and not operating separately like a zombie's. His mouth pulled away and she immediately missed it, but then it traced along her jaw, down the crevice of her neck. The feel of his desperate breath against her flesh almost made her come.

Her hands found the top button of his coat, nearly ripped it out of its catchhole. He stepped back to finish her task, his hands impatiently working the rest of the buttons until he could finally rid himself of the woolen barrier. He threw it unceremoniously to the ground.

"Do you want me to go on?" he asked breathlessly.

She didn't know whether he was asking about his clothes or permission to continue what they had started. Either way, her answer was yes. With her consent, he pulled off his sweater, began unzipping his jeans. As he shed each piece, she realized the madness of the situation. They were outside with the temperature just a little above forty. And here he was, undressing. And now he stood totally naked, waiting for her. Her eyes were drawn to his tumescence. The shaft was thick, the head purplish, moisture already beading.

Suddenly, she felt self-conscious, which left her immobile. He closed in, touched his lips to hers again, softly at first, then with a growing insistence. He took one of her hands, moved his lips to her ear.

"Touch me, Lacey," he whispered. The need in his voice, the way he said her name, was raw and naked. As naked as the skin beneath her exploring fingers—the smooth flesh of his chest over hard and firm muscles; his stomach, lean, just a trace of soft down around his navel; traveling farther downward, the thicker texture of pubic hair, springy between her fingers. Finally, her fingers enclosed the rubbery texture of his shaft, tightened eagerly. His eyes had been closed as he savored her touch, but they popped open as she began moving her hand up and down his penis, setting a rhythm. He moaned as her lips retraced the path her fingers had already taken.

During her marriage, Darryl had often encouraged her to explore him with her mouth and she had halfheartedly complied, more to avoid an argument than from any true desire. Now, she wondered at her eagerness, her craving to taste Sean. She lowered to her knees, felt his hand caress her face as she took him in her mouth. She worked her tongue along the grooves, heard his intake of breath. His scent was heady, the taste of his moisture so different from her husband's. She found herself wanting more of it, and began working her mouth and tongue, drawing him in farther.

"Oh, Lacey . . . oh God!" she heard him cry out. Her hands moved to his ass—firm, compact—and squeezed the young flesh hard until she elicited another moan, a half-strangled cry. His hand guided the back of her head as she worked him, as she sucked liquid from him, drew life from him.

Without warning, Sean shoved her away, and she blinked up at him, confused.

"I want to be inside you." It was a demand, not a request. Without ceremony, he joined her on the ground as his hands tugged her sweater over her head. The inferno in his eyes frightened and excited her.

He gave a frustrated groan as his fingers tried to work the front hooks of her bra without success. The sound of his frustration settled her nerves, made her feel in control. She leaned over to him, put her lip to his ear.

"Sssshhh, let me do it." She pushed his fingers away, unhooked the bra, and freed her breasts. Her already firm nipples became even more erect as the cold air hit them. Self-conscious, she worried that he would be turned off by the slight sagging, would begin noticing her other flaws. She wanted to remain beautiful in his eyes, didn't want to see them fog over with the reality of the aging woman before him. But instead of disgust, his eyes shone with fascination as he reached out a hand to circle a nipple, then bent to enclose it with his mouth. He licked it as avidly as she had worked him minutes before.

She moaned as his tongue played along the button, back and forth, stopping in half circles, completing full arcs along the screaming flesh. If he didn't stop, she was in danger of coming, and she desperately didn't want to come now. She wanted to draw out this moment as long as possible. Because she knew that this would be the first and last time she would make love with him. That after today, she wouldn't allow him near her. But today, she would take everything he had to offer: pleasure, comfort, moments free of pain. She knew that in subsequent lonely nights, she would touch herself, think of him, remember the ways he had touched her, how wonderful he had made her feel.

She pushed his face away, forcing his mouth to release her. "Finish undressing me." Now she was the one demanding.

He smiled, laid her on her back as he unbuttoned and unzipped her jeans. He tugged them down to her knees, pulled them down farther, cursed as they caught on her sneakers, which he quickly discarded, then pulled the jeans all the way off. She liked the way he caressed her with his eyes, as though he were staring at a treasure hard won. He bent to nuzzle her stomach with his nose as he slowly pulled down her panties. The touch was feathery, accented with a whiff of breath that sent tremors through her. His mouth followed the panties' descent, traveling downward until his head rested between her thighs. He flung the panties on the mound of discarded clothing as his tongue found her clit, fastened onto it. He had already brought her too far, too fast, and she cried out helplessly, spasming after just a few flicks of his tongue, leaving her whole body trembling. She moaned in frustration; she hadn't wanted to come so soon.

Sean burrowed his face deeper into her chasm, his hands holding her thighs steady as he licked and tongue-fucked her. Another wave slowly began building, radiating from her core to her extremities—thighs, legs, even her fingertips. She had never orgasmed more than once, had never come close. Only now did she realize that she could . . . that she would. The surge hit hard as he brought her to climax again. Tears streamed down the sides of her face, disappeared into the grass. Crying had become a normal state for her these days.

She felt a cool rush of air as his head moved from her thighs. He easily shifted over her length, her scent on his face, his breath. He positioned his lean frame on top of her, blocking out the cold, giving her his heat.

"Sshh, sshh, don't cry. It's OK." He kissed her softly, gently. Then, "Do you want me to stop?"

Every doubt had been kissed, licked, and stroked away. All she wanted right now was to feel him deep inside her.

"Fuck me, Sean," she ordered quietly. Her choice of words left no ambiguity. There was no wavering, no hesitancy.

He immediately complied by plunging into her as deep as he could go. The sudden invasion forced her to draw in a sharp intake of breath.

"Tell me . . ." he started, but the rest of his words were lost in a tortured sigh as he began a slow thrust.

"What?" she breathed, enraptured by the sex, by the sensation of him inside her finally.

He tried again, his voice strangled. "Tell me what you want . . . fast . . . slow . . . hard . . . soft . . ."

"God, yes," she gasped and he did his best to oblige her, alternating his pace, his thrusts. She barely caught her breath as his varied rhythms shook her, pushed her body into the cold ground. A limb with a prickly thorn had attached itself to one of her thighs, and as Sean thrust repeatedly into her, the thorn became imbedded deeper into her flesh, another invasion. Instead of diminishing the pleasure, the pain seemed to heighten it, every sensation merging with one another. Lips, hands, penis worked her to a final frenzy. Sean caught her half-scream with his mouth, sucked it away from her. Fucked the hell out of her, fucked away the pain, the sadness. Kept fucking her until he released deep inside her with a sob. He fell limp, his penis still lodged in her. She throbbed around his pole, pulling the last moisture from him.

She might have lain there all afternoon, well into the evening. Would have willingly stayed on the cold grass with him inside her, both of them clenched together as he breathlessly peppered kisses along her face and neck.

And please sample
PASSION FOR THE GAME
by Sylvia Day,
coming next month from Brava.

"Do not be fooled by her outward appearance. Yes, she is short of stature and tiny, but she is an asp waiting to strike."

Christopher St. John settled more firmly in his seat, his eyes riveted to the crimson-clad woman who sat across the theater expanse. He disregarded the agent of the Crown who shared the box with him. Having spent his entire life living among the dregs of society, he knew affinity when he saw it.

Wearing a dress that gave the impression of warmth and bearing the Spanish coloring of hot-blooded sirens, Lady Winter was nevertheless as icy as her title. And his *assignment* was to warm her up, ingratiate himself into her life, and then learn enough about her to see her hanged in his place.

A distasteful business, that. But a fair trade in his estimation. He was a pirate and thief by trade, she a bloodthirsty and greedy vixen.

"She has at least a dozen men working for her," Sedgewick said. "Some watch the wharfs, others roam the countryside. Her interest in the agency is obvious and deadly. With your reputation for mayhem, you two are very much alike. We cannot see how she could resist any offer of assistance on your part."

Christopher sighed, the prospect of sharing his bed with the beautiful Wintry Widow was vastly unappealing. He knew her kind, too concerned over their appearance to enjoy an abandoned tumble. Her livelihood was contingent upon her ability to attract wealthy suitors. She would not wish to become sweaty or tax herself overmuch. It could ruin her hair.

Yawning, he asked, "May I depart now, my lord?"

Lord Sedgewick shook his head. "You must begin immediately, or you will forfeit this opportunity."

It took great effort on his part to bite back his retort. The agency would learn soon enough that he danced to no one's tune but his own. "Leave the details to me. You wish me to pursue both personal and professional relations with Lady Winter, and I shall."

Christopher stood and casually adjusted his coat. "However, she is a woman who seeks the secure financial prospects of marriage, which makes it impossible for a bachelor such as myself to woo her first and then progress from the bed outward. We will instead have to start with business and seal our association with sex. It is how these things are done."

"You are a frightening individual," Sedgewick said dryly.

Christopher glanced over his shoulder as he pushed the black curtain aside. "It would be wise of you to remember that."

The sensation of being studied with predatory intent caused the hair at Maria's nape to rise. Turning her head, she studied every box across from her, but saw nothing untoward. Still, her instincts were what kept her alive and she trusted them implicitly.

Someone's interest was more than mere curiosity.

The low tone of men's voices in the gallery behind her

drew her attention away from the fruitless visual search. Most would hear nothing over the rabble in the pit below and the carrying notes of the singer, but she was a hunter, her senses fine-tuned.

"The Wintry Widow's box."

"Ah . . ." a man murmured knowingly. "Worth the risk for a few hours in the fancy piece. She is incomparable, a goddess among women."

Maria snorted. A curse, that.

Suddenly eager to be productive in some manner, Maria rose to her feet. She pushed the curtain aside, and stepped out to the gallery. The two footmen who stood on either side to keep the ambitiously amorous away snapped to attention. "My carriage," she said to one. He hurried away.

Then she was bumped none-too-gently from behind and as she stumbled, was caught close to a hard body.

"I beg your pardon," murmured a deliciously raspy voice so close to her ear she felt the vibration of it.

The sound stilled her, caught her breath and held it. She stood unmoving, her senses flaring to awareness far more acute than usual. One after another impressions bombarded her—a hard chest at her back, a firm arm wrapped beneath her breasts, a hand at her waist, and the rich sent of bergamot mixed with virile male. He did not release her, instead his grip upon her person tightened.

"Unhand me," she said, her voice low and filled with command.

"When I am ready to, I will."

His ungloved hand lifted to cup her throat, his touch heating the rubies that circled her neck until they burned. Callused fingertips touched her pulse, stroking it, making it race. He moved with utter confidence, no hesitation, as if he had the right to fondle her whenever and wherever he chose, even in this public venue. Yet he was undeniably gentle. Despite the possession of his hold, she could writhe free if she chose, but a sudden weakness in her limbs prevented her from moving.

Her gaze moved to her remaining footman, ordering him silently to do something to assist her. The servant's wide eyes were trained above her head, his throat working convulsively as he swallowed hard. Then he looked away.

She sighed. Apparently, she would have to save herself. Again.

Annoyed, her next action was goaded as much by instinct as by forethought. She moved her hand, setting it over his wrist, allowing him to feel the sharp point of the blade she hid in a custom-made ring. The man froze. And then laughed. "I do so love a good surprise."

"I cannot say the same."

"Frightened?" he queried.

"Of blood on my gown? Yes," she retorted dryly. "It is one of my favorites."

"Ah, but then it would more aptly match the blood on your hands . . ." He paused, his tongue tracing the shell of her ear, making her shiver even as her skin flushed, ". . . and mine."

"Who are you?"

"I am what you need."

Maria inhaled deeply, pressing her corset-flattened bosom against an unyielding forearm. Questions sifted through her mind faster than she could collect them. "I have everything I require."

As he released her, her captor allowed his fingers to drift across the bare flesh above her bodice. Her skin tingled, gooseflesh spreading in his wake. "If you find you are mistaken," he rasped, "come find me."